Praise for the works of Gerri Hill

Timber Falls

Another great crime story by Hill with a lovely romance as well. These are the things I love.

-Sam D., NetGalley

This is my first Gerri Hill book and I really enjoyed it. For me it was the perfect romance... sweet, and it moved at a nice pace for me. Hill can write a wonderful mystery/romance story! Her characters are well written and developed. The writing was great and kept me intrigued throughout the entire novel. The story was phenomenal and honestly, I already have her backlist books saved. The mystery was a favorite of mine. I was hooked and didn't want it to end so soon.

Rubie C., NetGalley

The Great Charade

One of the big loves I had for this book, among other things, was it is so full of rich dialogue. I am a sucker for running dialogue that fills a story, it gets me to relate to the characters even more because you just have their voices and direct interaction running in your mind's eye throughout the story and Ms. Hill does this brilliantly. There isn't much angst in regard to the MCs, just a heartwarming holiday story, which can be read anytime of the year, of Nic just trying to make it through the holiday (again no spoilers, but me wiping away a few tears) and Abby slowly falling for Nic.

-Carol C., NetGalley

The Great Charade really is a heartwarming, romantic holiday book that I'm really glad I was able to read this season. If you're looking for a great novel to read this holiday, this may be the one you are looking for.

-Betty H., *NetGalley*

Red Tide at Heron Bay

One of the best things I love about Ms. Hill's writing is she takes the time to describe the environment and surroundings within the story, not so much as to stall the storyline but more to enhance the feeling of really being there with the characters... Ms. Hill does a wonderful job of blending mystery with a love story (reminds me of *Devil's Rock* and *Hell's Highway*) and she did it justice again in this book.

-Carol C., *NetGalley*

Love the Hawaiian shirts and the person wearing them. This romantic intrigue had my attention from the beginning. Detective Harley Shepherd, upbeat yet sad as she deals with the loss of someone close to her. Lauren Voss, resort manager, shying away from relationships as she continues to deal with a relationship that went off the rails. Both women "ran" to Heron Bay to heal. Little did they know that tragedy would be waiting for them right around the corner. I enjoyed the flirting and teasing. Some of the comments had me chuckling and laughing out loud.

-Kennedy O., NetGalley

The Stars at Night

The Stars at Night is a beautiful mountain romance that will transport you to a paradise. It's a story of self-discovery, family, and rural living. This romance was a budding romance that snuck-up and on two unsuspecting women who found themselves falling in love under the stars and while gazing at birds. It's a feel-good slow-burn romance that will make your heart melt.

-*Les Rêveur*

Hill is such a strong writer. She's able to move the plot along through the characters' dialogue and actions like a true boss. It's a masterclass in showing, not telling. The story unfolds at a languid pace which mirrors life in a small, mountain town, and her descriptions of the environment bring the world of the book alive.

-*The Lesbian Review*

Gillette Park

This book was just what I was hoping for and wickedly entertaining. The premise of this book is really well done. Parts are hard to read of course. This book is about a serial killer who targets mostly young teenagers. The book isn't very graphic, but it still breaks your heart in places. But there is also a sweet romance that helps to give the book a sense of hope. Mix that with some strong women, the creepiness of the paranormal factors, and the book balances out really well. There is a lot of potential with these characters and I'd love to see their stories continue. If you are a Hill fan, grab this.

-Lex Kent's Reviews, *goodreads*

Hill is a master writer, and this one is done in a way that I think will appeal to many readers. Don't just discount this one because it has a paranormal theme to it! I think that the majority of readers who love mystery novels with a romantic side twist will love this story.

-Bethany K., *goodreads*

After the Summer Rain

…is a heartwarming, slow-burn romance that features two awesome women who are learning what it really means to live and love fully. They're also learning to let go of their turbulent pasts so that it doesn't ruin their future happiness. Gerri Hill has never failed to give me endearing characters who are struggling with heartbreaking issues, and beautiful descriptions of the landscapes that surround them.

-The Lesbian Review

Gerri Hill is simply one of the best romance writers in the genre. This is an archetypal Hill, slightly unusual characters in a slightly unusual setting. The slow-burn romance, however, is a classic, trying not to fall in love, but unable to fight the pull.

-Lesbian Reading Room

After the Summer Rain is a wonderfully heartfelt romance that avoids all the angsty drama-filled tropes you often find in romances.

-C-Spot Reviews

Moonlight Avenue

Moonlight Avenue by Gerri Hill is a riveting, literary tapestry of mystery, suspense, thriller and romance. It is also a story about forgiveness, moving on with your life and opening your heart to love despite how daunting it may seem at first.

-The Lesbian Review

…is an excellent mystery novel, sheer class. Gerri Hill's writing is flawless, her story compelling and much more than a notch above others writing in this genre.

-Kitty Kat's Book Review Blog

The Locket

This became a real page-turner as the tension racked up. I couldn't put it down. Hill has a knack for combining strong characters, vulnerable and complex, with a situation that allows them to grow, while keeping us on our toes as the mystery unfolds. Definitely one of my favorite Gerri Hill thrillers, highly recommended.

-Lesbian Reading Room

The Neighbor

It's funny...Normally in the books I read I get why the characters would fall in love. Now on paper (excuse the pun), Cassidy and Laura should not work...but let me tell you, that's the reason they do. I actually loved this book so hard. ...Yes it's a slow burn but so beautifully written and worth the wait in every way.

-Les Rêveur

This is classic Gerri Hill at her very best, top of the pile of so many excellent books she has written, I genuinely loved this story and these two women. The growing friendship and hidden attraction between them is skillfully written and totally engaging...This was a joy to read.

-Lesbian Reading Room

I have always found Hill's writing to be intriguing and stimulating. Whether she's writing a mystery or a sweet romance, she allows the reader to discover something about themselves along with her characters. This story has all the fun antics you would expect for a quality, low-stress, romantic comedy. Hill is wonderful in giving us characters that are intriguing and delightful that you never want to put the book down until the end.

-The Lesbian Review

HUNTER'S REVENGE

GERRI HILL

Other Bella Books by Gerri Hill

About the Author

Gerri Hill has over forty-two published works, including the 2021 GCLS winner for *Gillette Park*, the 2020 GCLS winner *After the Summer Rain*, the 2017 GCLS winner *Paradox Valley*, 2014 GCLS winner *The Midnight Moon*, 2011, 2012 and 2013 winners *Devil's Rock*, *Hell's Highway* and *Snow Falls*, and the 2009 GCLS winner *Partners*, the last book in the popular Hunter Series, as well as the 2013 Lambda finalist *At Seventeen*. Gerri lives in south-central Texas, only a few hours from the Gulf Coast, a place that has inspired many of her books. With her partner, Diane, they share their life with two Australian shepherds—Rylee and Mason—and a couple of furry felines. For more, visit her website at gerrihill.com.

Bella Books, Inc.
P.O. Box 10543
Tallahassee, FL 32302

Printed in the United States of America on acid-free paper.

First Edition - 2023

Editor: Medora MacDougall
Cover Designer: Kayla Mancuso

ISBN: 978-1-64247-447-3

PUBLISHER'S NOTE

HUNTER'S REVENGE

GERRI HILL

BELLA
BOOKS
2023

CHAPTER ONE

"Hunter, O'Connor...about time you two get here. The ME beat you to the scene. Again."

"We were downtown," Casey supplied. "Eight o'clock traffic kinda hinders a quick buzz through the city, you know."

Casey looked at Tori and gave a subtle wink. They'd been sitting in a line at a drive thru, waiting on breakfast.

Tori paused at the front door, turning around to survey the street. It was an older neighborhood with equally older homes, all showing their age. For the most part, the yards were well kept and tidy with large shade trees blocking out the April sun. This yard, in particular, seemed to have been meticulously maintained. The lawn, with its bright green grass of spring, looked—and smelled—freshly mowed.

"Hunter?"

Tori turned, nodding at Casey, who was following the officer inside. There were several others there, talking among themselves. Conversation ceased when they walked in. She stopped and looked around, meeting curious eyes. They all seemed to be looking at her, not Casey. She shrugged it off and went into the kitchen, finding Rita Spencer bent over the body.

"Time of death seven-forty-eight," Rita said without looking up.

"Wow. You're getting damn good at that, Spencer," Casey drawled. "Right down to the very minute. Next thing you know, you'll be adding seconds to your reports."

Rita looked up then. "The neighbor heard the shots. Found him. Seven-forty-eight this morning." She arched an eyebrow. "What happened to your hair?"

Casey's hand automatically went to the hair in question. "Chopped it off. Trying to look like Hunter here."

"I see. Quit coloring it blond then."

"Mousey blond is my natural color, thank you very much."

Tori sighed. "The body?"

"Single shot to the head," Rita said.

"Where's Mac and his team?" Casey asked.

"They were finishing up at another scene. Must be a full moon—the crazies are out."

"What's with the trash?" Tori asked, pointing at the white plastic bag that had spilled out onto the kitchen floor. An egg carton, a can advertising seasoned black beans, and some soiled paper towels were sprawled across the floor.

"It's trash day," Officer Garza supplied. "Looks like he was taking it out when he was hit." He pointed to the window, which was shattered. "Neighbor heard two shots. One shot to break the glass, another for the hit, I guess."

Tori nodded. "You talk to the neighbor? The one who found him?"

"Rogers did. Mr. Alton. Steve Alton is his name."

Casey nudged her. "Come on, Hunter. Let's chat with him. See what he saw."

Rita rolled the body over then and Tori found herself staring at it. The man was late sixties, maybe early seventies. His hair appeared thick—an attractive shade of gray. The bullet hole to his temple had done little damage. At least on the outside. As she stared, she felt an odd sense of déjà vu come over her. Casey nudged her again.

"You know him, Hunter?"

Tori blinked several times, then shook her head. "No, I don't think so."

"You're white as a ghost," Casey said quietly.

"Detectives…you want to take a look at the pictures we found first?" Officer Garza asked. "The neighbor was pretty shook up. Maybe give him time to settle down before you talk to him."

Tori arched an eyebrow, but it was Casey who spoke.

"Yeah, we kinda like to talk to the witnesses as soon as possible, make sure they don't forget something, you know."

It wasn't Casey he looked at, though. It was her. "I think you're going to want to see these pictures. They cover a whole wall."

She glanced at Casey, who shrugged.

"I guess it's okay with me. Okay with you, Hunter? I don't suppose the neighbor is going anywhere. We're parked in his driveway. He's kinda blocked in."

Before she followed Garza and Casey out, she asked Rita, "What's this guy's name?"

"Charles Griffin. According to his driver's license, he was seventy-one."

She nodded. It didn't ring a bell, yet there was something so familiar about him. She stared at the body a moment longer before leaving. Back into the living room, she raised her eyebrows questioningly. The officers pointed down the hallway. She found Casey staring at, yes, a wall of pictures. Photos. Some black and white. Some color.

"Jesus Christ, Hunter. What the hell do you make of this?"

Tori moved closer, her brow furrowed. Her gaze darted from picture to picture before it finally registered.

They were all of her.

CHAPTER TWO

"Yeah, yeah. We got it, Garza. We're fine. Just give us a minute." Casey nearly pushed Garza out of the room before closing the door. Tori was still standing there, speechless. "You okay?"

Tori moved then, walking down to the other end of the wall. These photos were obviously dated—some were black and white, most were in color. Casey noted that Tori's hand was trembling when she pointed at one that was beginning to fade.

"That's...that's me when I was fourteen or fifteen maybe. That's my aunt's old car." She moved to another one and tapped it. "When I graduated high school."

"Hell, Hunter, look at this one. It's you and me out on your boat. It's when I bleached my hair that one time. What? Four or five years ago?"

"Here's one of me and Sam having pizza at the park."

Casey went closer to her. "Here's the four of us having dinner."

"Mexican food."

Casey grinned. "Margaritas. More specifically, the Rios 'Ritas."

Tori moved to the more recent photos. She touched one of them. "This was a couple of weeks ago."

It was a photo of Tori walking into the station, phone held to her ear, a smile on her face. Talking to Sam, no doubt.

"How do you know a couple of weeks?"

"It's when I went to the deli for sandwiches for everyone." She tapped it again. "The bag."

"What the hell does this all mean? He have some vendetta against you or something?"

"A vendetta?" She pointed down the wall. "Since I was a kid?"

"He's obviously been spying on you."

Tori went back down to the early photos. She stared at them for the longest time, then slowly turned to her. "Not since I was a kid, no. Since my family was killed." She pointed to the very first one on the wall. "This one. I spent some time in a... in a hospital, you know. This is when I got out. My Aunt Carol picked me up. I moved to Houston with her. I wasn't even thirteen yet."

"Who the hell was this guy, Hunter?" She waved at the wall. "He's freakin' dead, and he's got all these pictures of you."

Tori shook her head. "I have no idea."

Casey ran a hand through her hair. They were called to a crime scene. A homicide. Nothing new there. But all this?

"You know Mac's got to process this room," she said. "Gonna take all the photos to the lab, I'd guess."

"I know." Tori took a deep breath. "Come on, O'Connor. Let's go interview the neighbor."

"That's it? There's goddamn pictures of you plastered all over this dead guy's wall and you want to act like it's just another case?"

"I want to find out who the hell this dead guy was." Tori glanced back at the pictures. "Malone will want to pull us from this case."

"No doubt." Then she smiled. "We're not going to let him, are we?"

"No, we're certainly not."

CHAPTER THREE

"I'm Detective O'Connor. This is Detective Hunter," Casey said in introduction. "Can you tell us what happened?"

"I can't believe it, really." Steve Alton twisted his hands together nervously. "I mean, Charlie never puts his garbage out the night before. None of us do. The raccoons get into it and make a mess of things. But he's an early riser. He always has his garbage out before me."

"But this morning he didn't?" Casey prompted.

"No. So I thought I should check on him, you know. I mean, he's over seventy and all and he hasn't been in the best of health lately. I don't know what was going on, but he'd had a lot of doctor's appointments. He—"

"So you went to check on him?" Tori asked impatiently.

"Well, yeah. I go out my back door at the kitchen there." He pointed. "It's closer. I'd just stepped outside when I heard the shots. It was two quick pops, you know. Kinda loud. At first, I wasn't even sure what it was, but then it registered that I'd heard glass breaking—the window, you know. Then I heard running and when I got around the side of the house, I saw this guy jump into a car, and it took off real fast. Squealing the tires even."

"Was the car parked or was someone waiting for him?"

"There was another guy driving. It pulled up out front there just as this guy ran to the street."

"Did you get a look at the car? The plates?"

"Like I told that other officer, it all happened so fast. It was a light-colored car—grayish in color or maybe silver—and it had four doors. That's about all I could say about it."

"What about the guy?" Casey asked.

"It wasn't like in the movies. He wasn't dressed all in black or anything. He had on jeans and a blue T-shirt."

"White guy? Black? Hispanic? Could you tell how old?"

"White guy. I never saw his face, but I saw his arms when he was running. White guy. Kinda thin, I guess. I have no idea his age. Like I said, I never saw his face."

Tori stood up, moving away from the table. She stared out the kitchen window, noting the freshly mowed lawn in the back. "Tell me about Charles Griffin."

"Charlie? Oh, he was such a good guy. Best neighbor I could ever hope for."

Tori turned back around. "You were friends?"

"Friendly enough to share a meal now and then, yeah. More so now since my wife died."

"Does he have a wife?" Casey asked.

"No, no. Never been married."

Tori walked over to the table again, resting her hands on the back of a chair. "How long has he lived here?"

"Oh, he's been here a long time. Thirty or thirty-five years, I'd guess. He was the nicest guy. He'd do anything for you."

"And I don't suppose you knew of anyone who had a beef with him? Someone he had a fight with recently or something. An argument?" Casey asked.

"Charlie? No, no. Everyone loved Charlie. And since he's been retired, he kinda looks after the neighborhood. He doesn't go out much anymore. Grocery store is about it. Well, and the doctor recently."

Tori and Casey looked at each other and Casey nodded. "Well, Mr. Alton, we've taken up enough of your time." Casey handed him her card. "If there's anything else you think of, please give me a call."

"Yes, of course." He glanced at the card. "Detective O'Connor. Do you think the rest of us are in danger? Should we be worried there's a killer out there?"

"It appears that Mr. Griffin was targeted," Casey said. "But it wouldn't hurt to make sure all your doors are locked."

Tori nodded at him, but before they made it out of the door, he called back to her.

"Detective Hunter? Are you *Tori* Hunter?"

She raised her eyebrows. "I am."

"Can I...can I talk to you for a second then?" He slid his gaze to Casey. "In private."

She and Casey again exchanged glances, and Casey shrugged. "Sure. I'll go see if Mac got started."

Tori stood there, waiting. Mr. Alton looked nervous.

"I don't know what to make of this, really," he said. "I mean, what are the chances you'd come here to me directly?"

She frowned. "Forgive me for being blunt, but what the hell are you talking about?"

He moved to the end of the kitchen and pulled open a drawer. From inside, he took out a thick letter-sized envelope. "Charlie gave this to me just last week. He said if anything happened to him, I was to give this to Detective Tori Hunter."

"Had he been threatened?"

"Not that he said. I took it to mean his health. Like I said, he'd had lots of doctor's appointments lately."

He handed her the envelope. Her name was neatly printed on the front. She looked up at him. "You open this?"

"Oh, no, ma'am. It's sealed and everything." He paused. "Did you know Charlie?"

Did she? She shook her head. "No." She folded the envelope in half and shoved it into her back pocket. "Thanks. If we have more questions, I hope you won't mind if we come back."

"Of course not. Like I said, Charlie was well-liked. It's going to be a shock to everyone when they hear. I still can't believe it." His gaze slid out the door. "Wonder what's going to happen to his place," he murmured almost wistfully.

"It'll have crime scene tape up for a little while, I imagine." She opened the door, pausing. "Did he ever mention my name?"

Mr. Alton slowly shook his head. "Not that I recall."

When she went back over to Charles Griffin's house, Casey was on her way out to find her. "Tori, come check this out. Mac found a safe. And guess what? There's a gun inside."

"And this excites you?"

"Yeah, it does. It's wrapped up in this old cloth and Mac says it looks like it hasn't been touched in decades." Then Casey pulled her closer, her voice quiet. "What did he want?"

"He gave me an envelope," Tori said, her voice equally as quiet. "Said Charlie had told him to give it to me if anything happened to him."

"*What*? Well, what was in it?"

"I haven't opened it."

Casey pulled her to the side. "You think it's evidence? I mean, maybe he knew he was going to get whacked. Maybe he fingered his killer."

Tori stared at her. "My goddamn pictures are all over his wall. And now I've got an envelope in my pocket that he left me. I don't think it has anything to do with his murder."

"So you're not going to log it in as evidence?" Casey nearly whispered.

"I'm not. At least not until I open it."

CHAPTER FOUR

Malone motioned for them to sit, and Casey plopped down into a chair first. Tori sighed, then sat down too. Malone rubbed his bald head, then gave an equally loud sigh.

"You know this guy, Hunter?"

"No, sir."

"Yet a hundred or more pictures of you adorned his wall?"

"There were some of me, too," Casey said. "And Sam."

"I'm aware of those, O'Connor. However, Tori was in those as well." He shuffled some papers on his desk—for show, Tori knew. He was stalling, trying to find the words to tell them they were off the case.

"Lieutenant—"

"I know what you're going to say, Hunter, but—"

"And I know what you're going to say," she countered. "Just because this guy had a penchant for taking my picture doesn't mean we can't work the case."

"A penchant? Good god, Hunter, it goes back to when you were a kid."

She wanted to correct him—it went back to when her family was killed—but she didn't. "The more reason we should be on this case."

"The more reason you should be *off* the case."

Casey stood. "Lieutenant, if I may…the fact that he had a couple of pictures of Hunter here doesn't mean that has anything to do with his murder. I mean—"

"A couple, O'Connor? They told me they stopped counting at a hundred."

"Yeah. But still, we—"

"Save your breath. I'm pulling you two. Tucker and Sikes can take it."

"They can assist if you want, but you're not pulling me off this case," Tori said firmly and a bit louder than she intended.

"Goddamn it, Hunter, why is it always so difficult with you? I'm the lieutenant, you're the detective. Do you *know* what that means?"

She leaned closer. "Stan, after all these years, don't you know me by now?"

He stared at her, holding her gaze. "Why do you think he had pictures of you?"

"I have no idea."

"Take a guess, Hunter."

She glanced at Casey, then back at him. "The first one was when I was leaving the hospital. My aunt was taking me to Houston."

He nodded. "And?"

She swallowed. "And maybe it has something to do with my family."

"And you still think you should be on this case?"

"All the more reason, Stan."

He rubbed his head again. "Shit," he murmured. "I should save my breath, I guess." He sighed. "All right. You stay on it. Use Tucker and Sikes if you need." He pointed his finger at her. "But you keep me in the goddamn loop on everything, Hunter. You understand? If you want me to have your back on this, I need to know everything. If—when—the captain finds out, he'll want to know why the hell I let you lead this."

"It's not a conflict of interest," she insisted.

"The hell it's not. And I mean it, Hunter. I want to know every damn thing that's going on."

"Oh, yes sir, of course," Casey said quickly. "I'll make sure of it."

"Thanks, Lieutenant," Tori said.

He waved them out. "Get to work."

Casey led her over to their desks, glancing back at Malone's office. "Christ, Hunter, you didn't tell him about the envelope. He just said we had to keep him—"

"We don't even know if it's related."

Casey rolled her eyes. "Yeah, right. Have you at least peeked at it?"

"No. I haven't had a chance."

"Well, let's do it now. The suspense is killing me."

"No. I don't want to do it here. Too many eyes."

"Let's go in the ladies' room."

Tori glanced around the squad room. Tucker and Sikes—Leslie and John—were nowhere around. Maybe now would be a good time. She motioned to their empty desks.

"Where are they?"

"Les said they got a murder-suicide that went awry. The murder part worked out great. Not so much the suicide. He ran. Apparently, he couldn't go through with it, but he forgot to take the suicide note with him." Casey shook her head. "Dumbass."

"So you think we should bring them in on this one?"

"Hell, I don't know. It's your call, Hunter. We got shit on the killing. Older neighborhood, no security cameras anywhere near there. You talked to the same people I did. A couple said they might have heard tires squealing, but they weren't sure. No one saw anything. Hell, no one heard the shots except Steve Alton."

Tori sat down. "Lots of retired folks living here. It was early. Maybe they were all in bed still."

Casey sat too. "You really think this has something to do with your family? That's been what? Thirty-something years ago?"

She nodded. "I haven't thought of them in a while, you know. Before Sam, there wasn't a day that went by that they didn't cross my mind. Now?"

"You're just living your life, Tori. There's no guilt in that."

"I have the file. Copies of everything. When I made detective, Malone gave me the okay. There wasn't much to it. I was twelve and in shock. I didn't make a good witness. It was two years before I could even talk about it." She closed her eyes. "I could always see his face. Always." She opened them again. "It's...it's like it's in the shadows now." She looked at Casey, holding her gaze. "But I think it was him. My gut tells me it was him."

"Him? Charles Griffin?"

Tori nodded.

"Holy shit!" Casey whispered. "You gotta tell Malone."

"Oh, hell no, O'Connor. He'll pull us for sure."

"You heard what he said, Hunter. You've got to tell him."

"I'll decide after I open the envelope."

"Then let's open the damn thing and see what he has to say."

Tori paused, meeting her gaze. "I'm afraid to open it," she said honestly. "I think I want to do it when I'm at home."

Casey nodded. "With Sam, yeah. I understand that."

Tori smiled at her. "Well, I was kinda hoping you'd be there too. You're my partner."

"Oh. Okay then. Sure, Hunter." She pulled her chair out. "Sure."

"Good." She sat down too. "So, let's start at the beginning. Who was Charles Griffin?"

"Well, according to all the neighbors we talked to, he was the nicest guy you'd ever want to meet."

"Where did he work? What did he do? Where is he from?"

Casey flipped through her notes. "Okay, the lady across the street said he'd been retired for a while. Used to work at a hardware store." Casey looked up. "She couldn't remember the name."

"We'll need to poke into his financials," Tori said as she opened her own small notebook. "It was an older home and according to Steve Alton, he'd lived there over thirty years, so I guess the house was paid for. He drove an older model car. Nothing in the house indicated he lived extravagantly. Everything was neat, tidy."

Casey leaned closer, keeping her voice quiet. "You know, if we opened the envelope and saw what was inside, it might save us a lot of legwork."

"How about we do background first? Does he have a record? Did he hang out with unscrupulous people?"

"He was seventy-one, Hunter."

"And? He can't have thugs for friends?"

Casey was tapping on her keyboard, shaking her head. "He's not in the system. Got a handful of Charles Griffins but none with his date of birth. All younger." Casey looked up. "So no record, Hunter. Probably no thugs for friends, either."

Tori leaned back in her chair. "We've got a seventy-one-year-old man, seemingly a saint, according to his neighbors. He gets assassinated in his own kitchen, and there are no witnesses, and we have no motive."

"Assassinated? Maybe it wasn't a hit. Maybe someone was trying to break in."

"Come on, O'Connor. He was shot from outside, through the window, while he was taking out his trash. If you're planning on breaking in and you see someone in the kitchen, you run. You don't shoot them and then run. It was a hit."

"So how do we find out why?"

Tori sighed. "We open the envelope."

CHAPTER FIVE

Casey went out to Tori and Sam's back patio and automatically pulled two chairs into the sun where the rays still hit. It was after five and the air would be getting cooler soon, but as was their habit, they'd sit out for a bit before Sam got home.

The house that Tori and Sam had bought at the country club lasted only three years. Casey smiled, remembering how much fun she and Tori had had buzzing around in a golf cart, pretending to play. Mostly, they'd drink beer and make fun of the upper crust, as Tori liked to call them. They didn't fit in, though, and Sam had agreed. Sam had then found this house and Tori jumped at it. It was only six blocks from her and Leslie's house. However, with Sam still at CIU and Leslie teaming with Sikes, their schedules didn't always mesh, and it was hard to get together.

But summer was coming, and they usually managed to find at least one weekend a month where the four of them could spend some uninterrupted time on Tori's boat. Those were the best days, in her opinion. Even though she and Tori were partners and were together all the time, their relationship took on a different tone then. Then, they were simply best friends enjoying a fishing date and a couple of days on the water. Leslie and Sam were just as close, and the four of them had formed a tight-knit family. None of them had any real family around. She hadn't spoken to her brother in more years than she could remember. Tori didn't have anyone but her uncle left. An uncle she didn't speak to. Sam's family—still in Denver—had practically disowned her. And Leslie? Her mother was on husband number five and living on the West Coast and her father was in Indiana somewhere with his new family. She spoke to them maybe once a year. It was just the four of them and they were as close as any blood family could be. She couldn't have asked for more out of her life.

"You daydreaming, O'Connor?"

She spun around, smiling at Tori. "Just thinking about our lives, that's all. Being thankful."

Tori handed her a beer. "Yeah. We got it pretty good, don't we?"

"I'll say."

They sat down, side-by-side, their legs stretched out toward the waning sunlight. They drank a swallow of beer and sighed in unison.

"I'm ready for summer," Tori said.

"Yeah, and then I get to listen to you bitch about the heat for the next five months." She glanced at her. "You tell Sam about the pictures?"

"No. She had an interview this afternoon. I haven't talked to her."

"What kind of interview?"

"With the DA's office. You know she's not happy at CIU."

"DA's office? As a detective?"

Tori nodded. "Lead detective. She'd have a team under her."

"Well, that's great, right? Why didn't you tell me?"

"Because she only decided yesterday to go on the interview. Sarah Baker's the one who's been pushing for her. She's the Chief Administrator. She and Sam met a couple of years ago."

"Yeah, she used to be one of the Assistant DAs. She has a good reputation."

"Yeah, Sam likes her. She's just not sure she wants to cut ties with Dallas PD."

Casey nodded. "Afraid if she hates it, she won't be able to get back in?"

"Right. But she's not happy where she is. I told her to go for it. It would be normal hours, for one thing."

"That's good. Is it a done deal? Is the interview just a formality?"

"Not sure about that. I think there're eight people—all attorneys—that'll be in on it. But I think Sarah makes the final decision."

Casey touched her beer bottle to Tori's. "That's great news. I hope it works out."

Tori smiled at her. "Why are we sitting here making idle chitchat?"

"Because you won't open the damn envelope."

Tori shifted in her seat and pulled it out of her back pocket. "You think I should read it before Sam gets home?"

"I'm going to say yes, only because I'm curious as hell what it says."

Tori set her bottle down beside her chair. "It's been burning a hole in my pocket all day long." She turned it over, staring at the front. "Okay. Let's open it."

Casey saw Tori's hand trembling as she carefully broke the seal. Inside were three letter-sized pieces of paper, folded together.

"Maybe you should read it."

Casey's eyebrows shot up. "Me? Really? You want me to read it?"

Tori handed it to her. "Yes. Read it out loud."

Casey scratched her forehead for a second, then put her bottle down too. "Okay."

She took a deep breath, then stared at the words. The handwriting was neat, eloquent almost. "'My name is Charles Griffin.'" Casey read the next few words silently, then glanced at Tori. "Well, he gets right to the point."

"Just read it, O'Connor."

Casey swallowed. "'I killed your family. I'm not writing this letter to ask for forgiveness. I don't deserve or expect that. But if you are reading this, then I am no longer alive. It's a race as to whether they get me first or the cancer does.'" Casey looked over at Tori. "Guess that explains the doctor's visits."

Tori's eyes were closed, and she said nothing. Casey continued.

"'I'm sure you've seen the pictures by now. I've been keeping tabs on you over the years, feeling responsible for how your life got turned upside down. You made out good, it seems. Finally found some happiness in this horrid life. For my story, I'll start at the beginning. I was pulled over for speeding and arrested with possession of a controlled substance and the unlawful possession of a firearm. I know what you're thinking. What fool doesn't obey the speed limit when they've got drugs in the car?'" Casey looked at Tori again. "So he's got a sense of humor."

Tori opened her eyes. "I don't."

"Sorry." Casey waved the papers at her. "But wait. There was no record that he'd ever been arrested. Nothing."

"Just read it, O'Connor," she said again.

"'They took the drugs and pocketed them. Right in front of me, they shoved them in their pockets. Then they put my gun in the trunk of their patrol car. I was cuffed, shoved in the back seat, and hauled in. I was held for two days. I wasn't allowed a phone call or an attorney.'"

"That's not possible," Tori murmured.

"'Then I got pulled out of jail and taken outside. The cop gave me this large manila envelope. Told me my attorney had left it for me. Of course, I didn't have an attorney. Then he handed me the keys to my car and just walked away. My car was parked on the curb, and I got the hell out of there as fast as I could. When I finally opened the envelope, there were several pictures of my parents and my older sister and her family. There was a note. It said that they would be killed unless I did something for them. Then there were instructions to go to another location.'" Casey put the papers down. "Do we believe this?"

"It was thirty-three years ago. Maybe. We know surveillance wasn't what it is now. Electronic files were in their infancy. Probably easy to hide someone in a jail cell for a couple of days."

Casey cleared her throat. "Okay. Let's go on. 'I went to a storage facility. Small units. It was inside a locked gate. Unit 13. I remember looking at it thinking Lucky 13. It was empty inside except for two things. A gun and a manila envelope. It looked just like the one the cop had given me. Inside was a picture of this guy. Your father. The note said I was to kill him and his family, leaving one alive as a witness. They gave me the address and told me what night to do it. They told me how to do it. Told me to laugh while I was doing it.'" She glanced at Tori, noting that her fists were clenched.

"Go on," Tori said in a near whisper.

"'I chose you as the witness. After it was over with, I went home, not knowing what to do. I was nearly crazy, out of my mind by then. I'll admit, I thought about putting the gun to my own head and pulling the trigger, but I was too weak. Inside my house was another envelope, like the others. There was a wad of cash in there with another note. It said if I kept quiet, then my family wouldn't be hurt. Up to that point in my life, I hadn't exactly been a model citizen and I'd done some dishonest things and hung with the wrong crowd. And yes, I'd killed before. Not intentionally. As they say, it was a drug deal gone bad and I escaped with my life. But this? No, this wasn't me. I was a grown-ass man but scared and afraid for my family's lives. So I did it. But a day didn't go by that I didn't think about what I'd done.'"

Casey paused, seeing a lone tear escape the corner of Tori's eye and trickle slowly down her cheek. "Tori?"

"I'm okay. Keep reading."

Casey looked down at the paper, reading a bit more silently before continuing. "'I'm writing this now because I was contacted four days ago. It was a distorted computer voice on the phone. They said they had a target for me. An elderly man, they said. I hung up on them. I can't go through all that again. I'm going to rot in hell as it is, deservedly so, but I won't kill again. The calls kept coming. I told them I would go to the police if they continued. Since then I've seen a strange car on the street. An older model four-door Chevy Impala. Silver in color. Saw it two days in a row. When I spied it today, they took off. Two men inside. I know it's connected to the phone calls. That's why I'm writing this. I fear my time has come, probably rightfully so.'"

She read a few more lines silently. "He's kinda rambling now. Going back over—"

"Read it."

"Okay. 'I had no business living such a long life, considering what I did to your family. And now if you're reading this, I'm no longer here anyway, most likely to spend eternity in hell for what I've done. My only consolation is that my family was able to live out their lives in peace. My parents died of natural causes and my only sister, Norma, passed on just last month. I'm sorry to even write that, considering yours didn't have that opportunity, because of me. I wish I could say something other than I'm truly sorry for what I've done, but know that I am. A day did not pass that I didn't think of your family and the sin I committed. I wish I could tell you why it happened and who was responsible, but I simply don't know. What I do know is that the police were involved somehow. Like I said, I was allowed no phone call. Normal procedures weren't followed. I know the cops were behind it. Dirty cops.'"

She paused again. "You believe that? That it was cops?"

"I don't know. What else?"

Casey glanced down at the letter. "There's not much more. He's convinced he's going to hell, that's for sure."

"Finish it."

"'Yes, I'm going to rot in hell where I belong, but I did change. I tried to become a better person. I got my shit together. I got a job. I never took a wife, though. I was afraid to have a family, afraid to have kids. So I lived alone. I lived in fear that they would contact me and want me to kill again. I lived with that fear every day of my life. And now they have come again. So I'll end this letter. It's my confession to you, Detective Tori Hunter. I know you hate me and rightfully so. I wish I could say I'm writing this to bring you some peace somehow—some closure—but what I really hope is that you can find out who directed me to kill. And then I hope you finish off that son of a bitch.'"

Casey folded the three pages together again. "That's it. His signature at the end."

Tori nodded but continued to stare out into the backyard. The sun was below the trees, and shadows were creeping closer to them. She felt the chill in the air.

When the back door opened, she and Tori were both startled, she nearly jumping off the chair. It was Sam. Her blond hair was kept a little shorter these days but was still long enough to tuck behind her ears. She did that now and smiled affectionately at her.

"Casey. What a nice surprise," Sam said when she came closer. She bent to kiss her cheek. "Where's Les?" Sam then eyed Tori. "Or are you two working?"

"Later. She's coming later," Casey said. "We thought we'd order a pizza or something."

Sam arched an eyebrow and turned to Tori. "What's wrong?"

"Nothing. How was the interview?"

Sam bent down and kissed Tori on the mouth. "We can talk about that later."

"I already told O'Connor."

"I think it's great, Sam," Casey said. "You'll be good at it."

Sam smiled. "I should have known Tori couldn't keep a secret from you." She put her hands on her hips. "Now, will one of you tell me what the hell is going on? I know you both too well. Spill it."

Tori looked over at her and nodded. Casey handed Sam the papers. "We got this today. Caught a case. This guy's dead. He had a bunch of pictures of Tori."

"Pictures? Why?"

"That letter will pretty much explain it." Casey stood, wanting to give them some privacy. "I think I'm going to raid your liquor cabinet. I could use a shot of something."

"Bring me one, would you?" Tori asked. "A double."

Casey nodded, watching as Sam took her seat. She read the first few lines, then jerked her head up, staring at Tori.

Tori simply nodded. "Yeah."

CHAPTER SIX

Tori watched as Sam read through the letter, her hand squeezed tightly in Sam's. The occasional "oh my god" was uttered but not much else. When she finished, Sam simply moved closer, falling to her knees in front of her chair and pulling her into an embrace. Tori sank against her—eyes closed. She had so many emotions running through her, she didn't know where to begin to try and sort through them all.

"Honey, are you okay?"

Sam's voice was soft, quiet. Tori pulled away, seeing the misting of tears in Sam's eyes. She met them, those green eyes that could look into her very soul. Sam had always been able to do that, even way back at the beginning when they'd first met.

"I'm a little numb, I think. Not really sure how I'm supposed to feel."

"What do you mean?"

"It's just kinda surreal, you know, that this falls into my lap like it did. I never thought I'd find out who did it. Never thought there'd be closure."

Sam looked at her gently. "Do you feel like you'll have closure now?"

She shook her head slowly. "No. If it was a hit all along—like I always thought it was—then knowing who pulled the trigger doesn't solve anything."

"So you think it's all true then?"

"True that he killed them?" Tori shrugged. "I see no reason to doubt it. I mean, the guy was gunned down this morning. Probably by the guys in that silver Chevy he was describing."

Sam leaned back on her heels, still squatting in front of her. "Tell me about the case."

"Not much to it. Neighbor heard the shots, saw some guy running away. He jumped into a car, and they sped off."

"And where was this letter?"

"The neighbor had it. He said Charlie—Charles—had given it to him last week. As the letter said, he thought they would be after him. Whoever *they* are."

"What does Malone think?"

Tori gave a quick smile. "He doesn't know about the letter."

"Oh, Tori, you've got to tell him."

"He'll pull me from the case."

Sam stood up then. "Do you really think you should be on it? I mean, if this guy killed your family, it's way too personal for you. You have no business being the lead on this."

Tori stood up too, going to the edge of the patio and running a hand over her hair. "If what he says is true, I have more questions now than I had before."

"But this letter makes it sound like the department was involved."

"If he was really arrested and spent two days in jail and there's no record of it, then, yeah, someone on the inside was involved." She saw Casey at the door and motioned her to come out. "But we're talking over thirty years ago. Gonna be hard to prove. Damn near impossible."

Casey was carrying two tumblers and a glass of wine. "Thought you might want this," she said to Sam.

"Thank you. Can you believe this?"

Casey shook her head. "Not really, no. But I guess it's real enough. I think we're going to have to be very delicate with this one, especially if cops were involved. But how the hell do we go back that far?"

"I think you need to tell Malone about the letter," Sam said.

"That's Tori's call, not mine."

Sam turned back to her, again holding her eyes. "You can't keep this from him, Tori. You know you can't."

Yeah, she knew that, didn't she? Malone had always been there for her. Always. Hell, before Sam came into her life, she'd practically lived at the station. Instead of admonishing her for that, he'd had a cot brought into the downstairs locker room. When she'd gone through partners in fleeting succession, he'd been there too, taking her side, not theirs. He'd turned a blind eye to her and Sam's affair back in the early days, and he'd welcomed Casey to the team at her request. And when she'd soured on working at the FBI after five years and wanted back in, he'd pulled some strings and brought her back to the team. He'd always been there, and he'd always had her back. Just like he said he'd have her back now.

"You're right. I'll tell him in the morning."

She could see the relieved look in both Sam's and Casey's eyes. Casey handed her the glass of whiskey with a grin.

"Good, Hunter. I think if we present this the right way, he won't pull us from the case."

Tori took a sip, savoring the smoothness of it. "He'll try. It's the only sensible thing to do. As Sam just said, I don't really have any business being on this one."

"But we'll talk him out of it."

"Don't we always?"

Sam laughed. "You two are quite a pair. I'm surprised Stan hasn't separated you by now."

"We're good together," Casey said. "The other alternative is to pair me with Sikes and Tori with Les. And no offense, Hunter, but my wife would request a transfer after a week with you. You're too damn bossy. You're just lucky I'm so good-natured that I let you get away with it."

"Right," she said dryly.

"It's the truth and you know it." Casey looked at her watch. "Les should be here pretty soon. I think I'll order pizza now. The usual?"

"Yes, please," Sam said. As soon as Casey went inside, Sam moved to her, lightly touching her arm. "You're okay?"

"About the news? Or the fact that I'll be trying to solve the murder of the man who killed my family?"

"Both, I guess."

"That was like another lifetime ago. These years with you, I sometimes forget about them. Forget about that night."

"But?"

"But I guess that letter brought it all back. And if we're to believe everything he said, he was but a pawn in it all. Were there dirty cops back then?" Tori met Sam's gaze. "I guess I'm about to find out."

* * *

Later, after pizza and after Casey and Leslie had gone home, Sam found Tori staring out the patio door. She watched her for a moment, wondering what was going through her mind. She'd pretended like nothing was out of the ordinary, but she'd been too talkative, too jovial, as if afraid there would be a lull in the conversation. A lull that would allow her to think. Like now.

"You want to talk?"

Tori turned then and gave her a half-smile. "Maybe you're right. Maybe Malone is right. Maybe I don't need to be on this case."

She moved closer, sliding her arms around Tori and pulling her into a tight hug. "And I think maybe I was wrong. And I think Stan is wrong." She stepped back, meeting Tori's gaze. "I think you are the only person who will move heaven and earth to solve this case. I have no doubt about that."

"But what if it's been too long? What if I can't?"

"Is that what you're afraid of? That you won't find the truth?"

"If it's dirty cops from thirty years ago? How do you prove that?"

"You show the letter to Stan, you talk it out with him. He'll stand by you, you know that."

"It could get ugly."

Sam smiled. "I've never known you to worry about stepping on toes before. I doubt you'll start now. That's what makes you so good. That's what makes you the best."

Tori pulled her closer, kissing her gently on the mouth. "Thanks, Sam." Then she smiled. "You think I'm the best?"

Sam laughed lightly. "You know you are." She took her hand. "Come on. Let's go to bed. I'll let you show me how good you can be."

CHAPTER SEVEN

Before she could ask to see him, Malone motioned them inside. Casey sat down in her usual chair against the wall and Tori took the chair nearest the door. Malone appeared nervous as he shuffled some papers on his desk. Tori looked at Casey with raised eyebrows. Casey gave a slight "I don't know" shrug.

"The lab called me," Malone finally said. "Got ballistics back on the gun that was found at Charles Griffin's place."

"Why did they call you instead of us?" Tori asked.

Malone folded his hands together. "Mac called me. Got something to tell you, Tori. It's gonna be a shock."

Tori leaned back and crossed her legs, resting her ankle on her knee. "Was it a match to my family's murder?"

Malone jerked his head up. "I told Mac not to tell you. I wanted to be—"

"The lab didn't call. I haven't talked to Mac." She pulled the folded envelope out of her back pocket. "He confessed. Among other things." She handed the envelope over to Stan. "His neighbor gave this to me yesterday. We kinda had a group reading of it last night."

Malone stared at the front for a second, then put his glasses on before opening it. He read the first few lines, then looked up. Tori nodded. She and Casey sat quietly as he read through the letter, his brows furrowing from time to time. When he finished, he pulled his glasses off and tossed them down.

"That probably explains why my father's case went cold," Tori said. "They weren't really trying to find his killer."

"You can't take his statement of dirty cops to heart, Hunter. It makes no damn sense. Why would cops put a hit out on your father?"

"Something he was working on. A case. Maybe he was getting too close."

Malone leaned on his desk with his elbows. "I'm not even going to waste my time and tell you to back down, Hunter. But this goes against all protocols. If this guy killed your family, you have no goddamn business working his case. Hell, just the fact that he had all those pictures of you—"

"Who better than me? For thirty-three years I've wondered who killed them and why. Charles Griffin may have pulled the trigger, but he wasn't who ordered it. And we're still no closer to knowing the why of it."

Malone rubbed his eyes with a thumb and forefinger. "O'Connor? What are your thoughts on the matter?"

"You mean as to whether Tori can work this case? I agree with her. Who better?"

"You think there were dirty cops?"

"Come on, Lieutenant. There have always been dirty cops. You hear about patrol officers writing bogus tickets all the time. And that's just scratching the surface."

"And those are dealt with," he insisted.

Casey smirked. "Come on. They're only dealt with if someone rats them out, which is rare. Nobody wants to be a snitch. But this is something completely different. Murder? They must have been mixed up in something pretty big to put a hit out on another cop."

"So they got Griffin to commit murder for them, take out Tori's family," he said, glancing quickly at her. "And all these years, they leave him alone. But now, out of the blue, they contact him again." Malone shook his head. "Makes no sense. If they were willing to go so far as to kill him, why not take care of this so-called target themselves? Why involve Charles Griffin again?"

"Maybe they couldn't get close to their target," Casey said. "Maybe it was someone they knew."

"Maybe they weren't really planning to kill Charles," Tori said. "Maybe when he threatened to go to the police, they panicked."

Malone spread his hands out. "And who are *they*?"

Tori met his gaze. "If we're to believe this letter, then *they* are connected to the police somehow. Or they were back then."

Malone leaned back with a sigh. "How do you plan to proceed?"

"Finding out who had a hit on my father will tell us who killed Charles Griffin. I'd like to see what my father was working on when he was killed."

"His old case files? They went over that, Hunter. That's standard procedure."

"Who went over it? How thoroughly?" She leaned closer. "It's a cold case and it went cold rapidly. I was the only witness, and I was pretty useless at the time. Even when I was finally able to give a statement, it wasn't like it helped."

"So you want to look at his old files? From thirty-something years ago? Or you want to pull the case file on your family's murder?"

"I already have copies of that. There's not much to it. And his old case files that he'd been working on—they'd been reassigned. I never got to look at them. Don't know if it would have done any good. I didn't know what I was looking for. Still don't but I'd like to take a look at them just the same."

He stared at her for the longest time. "You're taking this all pretty calmly, Tori. There was a time when—"

"When I slept with the file? When I would go back over everything five, six, seven times?"

"Or more."

She nodded. "My life has changed a lot since then. Sam, you know. I'm not alone any longer. I've got a—" She glanced over at Casey. "I've got a new family now. And so yeah, I guess I do feel a little detached from it all. That's not to say I didn't shed some long overdue tears last night." She met his gaze. "I did. But when O'Connor read me the letter, it wasn't a shock. I think I already knew. The pictures. The familiarity."

He frowned. "Familiarity?"

"When I saw him, I had this gut feeling that I knew him from somewhere."

Malone gave her nod. "Okay, Hunter. I'll request your father's old files. What else? What kind of background do you need on Griffin?"

"There's not much background, Lieutenant," Casey said. "No record. He's not in the system. He's retired so there're no coworkers to question. Neighbors said he didn't get out much, other than the grocery store. Didn't get visitors. Yet he was gunned down."

"If he hadn't left me that letter, we'd be hard-pressed to make a case," Tori added.

"We're going to pull feeds from traffic cameras, try to get a make on the silver Chevy he described. We might get lucky," Casey continued. "Other than that, we got nothing."

"What about the gun?" Tori asked. "Who will get assigned to reopen my family's case?"

"Well, you know damn good and well it won't be you," Malone said. "Letting you work Charles Griffin's murder is the closest you'll get to it. I'll give it to Sikes and Tucker. It's only a formality anyway. They'll log the ballistics report. Circumstantial evidence, though. With Griffin dead, there's no way to prove he killed them. Not with what we've got."

"What about the letter?" Casey asked. "Or the pictures on his wall?"

Malone picked up the letter again, glancing at it. Then he folded it back up and put it into the envelope, nodding slowly. "The gun and the pictures on the wall, yeah, that might be enough." He nodded "I guess we could try to close the case.

It's not like there'd be a trial and a defense attorney screaming circumstantial evidence."

"We'd still have to get the DA's office involved."

"For your family's case, right. And we don't want to. Not yet." He handed the letter back to her. "For now, let's don't look at this letter as evidence. It's information only. It stays between us."

She nodded. "I agree."

"That means that there's still no closure on the cold case," he warned.

"There won't be any closure until I find out who ordered the hit. Charles Griffin pulled the trigger, that's all. Who was behind it?"

Malone stared at her again. "Are you sure you're okay, Tori? You're taking this pretty matter-of-factly, don't you think?"

"Meaning?"

"Meaning I know you say you feel detached from it, but I would have thought that after all these years, you'd be a little more emotional about it."

She arched an eyebrow. "Hysterical and throwing things? Demanding answers?"

Malone smiled at her. "Something like that. Are you overcompensating? Trying to make me believe you're not taking this personally?"

Tori gave a slight shrug. "As I told Sam last night, I'm not really sure how I'm supposed to feel. Anger? Yes, but at who? Charles Griffin? He did what he did to protect his own family. I think if we find out who killed Charles, we find out who killed my family. That's my focus."

Malone nodded. "Okay, Hunter, we'll go with it. I'll have Sikes and Tucker pull your family's file and your father's old case files. I'm going to try to keep this as lowkey as possible. For anyone outside of our little team here, I want it made clear that Tucker and Sikes are taking the lead. You and O'Connor do what you can with Charles Griffin, but I agree with you. We won't solve that murder until we get to the why of your family's murder."

Casey stood up. "Okay. Then we'll start with traffic cams and see if we can find the silver Chevy."

"Good. Who knows? You might get lucky, and it'll lead right to them."

"Sure, Lieutenant," Casey drawled. "That's just how our luck runs."

CHAPTER EIGHT

Of course, no, they had no such luck with traffic cams. Casey spotted the silver car three times coming up to a light and each time, the car had turned a block before the camera could pick up the license plate. She pointed at the screen now.

"Look here, Hunter. The bastard took a right again." She tapped the screen. "See? They turn."

Tori nodded. "Like they knew where the traffic cam was."

"Doesn't mean they're a cop, though. It's public record where the traffic cams are, toll road cameras, what have you."

Tori leaned back in her chair, twirling a pen between her fingers. "Professionals would know to be cognizant of traffic cams."

"Professional what? Killers?"

"Well, they did kill Charles Griffin."

She leaned back too, watching Tori. "I tend to agree with Malone. If they're willing to take out Charles Griffin, why weren't they willing to off this target of theirs without involving him?"

"Maybe like you said, they couldn't get close."

She sat up, scooting her chair nearer to Tori. "Okay, let's say, for the sake of argument, that cops are involved. Then and now. If they wanted your father killed, for whatever reason, they couldn't do it themselves. Too risky. So they hire someone."

"Not so much hire," Tori contradicted. "Forced."

"Right. And now, say they—cops again—want someone else killed. Maybe, like your father, it's another cop. The cycle repeats itself. They can't kill him, so they try to get Griffin to do it again."

Tori shook her head. "For one thing, the cops back then would all be retired now. Who would know the connection to Charles Griffin?"

Casey frowned. "Oh. I didn't think of that."

Tori leaned forward now too. "Maybe we're looking at this all wrong. If you're a cop from back then and you put a hit out on another cop, do you trust that your hitman—Charles Griffin in this case—will keep his mouth shut forever?"

"He had the fear of something happening to his family."

"Yeah. And his sister died last month. No more family to hold over his head. No more fear for him in that regard."

"So they're afraid he'll now talk?"

"Maybe. Of course he said in the letter that they wanted him to make a hit."

Casey nodded. "Yeah, Hunter, I see where you're going here. They didn't *really* have someone they wanted him to kill. They wanted to get him out there and—"

"Eliminate him."

"And when that didn't work, when he threatened to go to the police, they felt they had to take him out." She nodded again. "So the guys in the Chevy weren't cops—it was a real hit."

Tori sighed. "Can't prove a damn thing, though."

"But it makes sense, Hunter. Because asking a seventy-something-year-old man to make a hit is risky in itself. Especially someone who had his gun wrapped in a dusty, dark safe for thirty-plus years."

"That would mean they had been keeping tabs on him. Or at least on his family, knew the sister died, decided to make their move." Tori shook her head. "We're reaching here, O'Connor. Big time."

"Yeah, we are." She leaned back with a sigh. "Shouldn't they be back by now?" she asked, referring to Les and Sikes. They'd gone to the dungeon, an old tomb of a building where all the old paper files were now housed. Everyone called it the "dungeon" because it was dark and a bit creepy—all of the windows had been sealed and it was simply rows upon rows upon rows of dusty boxes that hadn't seen the light of day in ten, twenty, thirty, or more years. She hated going down there, especially to pull old files. They invariably weren't filed correctly, and you ended up doing a lengthy search to find the right file box.

"How long have they been gone?"

"A couple of hours."

A ding at the elevator sounded seconds before the door opened. Sikes came out pushing a noisy, squeaky rolling cart. Leslie was right behind him. She motioned with her head to the conference room, and Casey turned to Tori with raised eyebrows.

"Do we let them sort through it first, or should we join them?"

"It's technically their case," Tori said diplomatically.

"Who are you kidding, Hunter?"

Tori smiled and stood. "Right. Who am I kidding? Come on."

CHAPTER NINE

Tori walked into the room, then stopped, her eyes on the boxes—an off-white color that was now more faded yellow than white. She imagined she could see the dust floating about as Sikes opened one. She assumed they hadn't been looked at since she'd gotten Malone to get copies of her family's file. How many years ago now was that?

John paused, glancing over at her. "You want to take a look first?"

She shook her head. "I think Malone assigned you and Tucker to my family's case, right? Not me."

He tilted his head, a thoughtful expression on his handsome face. Tori couldn't help but glance at the long-healed scar on his neck, courtesy of John Doe. "Sure, Hunter, that's what he said." He tapped the side of the box he'd opened. "I don't even know what the hell we're looking for."

She moved farther into the room, going to stand beside him. She took only a quick peek inside the box. "I already have copies of all that. There's not much to it. The case was already long cold by the time I was able to give an account of that night.

They took my statement almost as a formality, nothing else." She went to the other four boxes. Her father's old case files. She spun one around toward her, noting her father's name had been struck through. She arched an eyebrow.

"He had four active cases going on," Leslie said. "Two were left with his partner." She glanced at her notes. "William Vasher."

Tori nodded. "Yeah, I remember him."

"The other two were reassigned to new detectives. We brought all four."

"All four are closed. No loose ends," Sikes added.

Casey opened one of the other boxes and sifted through the papers. "This one was a homeless guy beaten to death under the Turtle Creek Bridge." She looked up. "Where the hell is that?"

"Turtle Creek goes through that recreation park over by Maple," Sikes said.

Casey nodded. "They arrested three teenagers. One ratted out the other two." She tossed that back into the box. "Don't think that's going to help us."

Tori pulled out the file from her box, reading through the notes. She recognized her father's handwriting. "This one was a fight at a bar." She read on. "Guy has his throat cut with a broken beer bottle. The assailant ran—Buster Kowalski." She looked at the date. "They located him two months later in Oklahoma." She closed the file. "That was after my father had been killed."

Sikes was reading through one of the other boxes. "Not much here. Open and shut case. Your father caught this one just two days before…" He looked over at Tori. "Before he was killed. Attempted robbery of a jewelry store. The owner shot the guy, who fled. Detective Vasher wrapped it up a week later. The guy died at his mother's house." He, too, tossed the file back into the evidence box. "What is it we're looking for? Malone was vague, at best."

Tori looked at Casey. Casey gave a subtle nod. Leslie already knew the details of the letter. Sikes was the only one in the dark. Tori went to the door and closed it. John looked at her questioningly.

"Charles Griffin killed my family."

"Well, he had the *gun* that killed your family," John said. "And a hundred pictures of you. Even if he was alive, that wouldn't be enough to convict him. Circumstantial. Someone could have given him the gun."

"He confessed. He left me a letter."

"When did he leave you a letter?"

"He left it with his neighbor," Casey said. "He knew someone was watching him. He felt threatened."

"It might be easier to let him read the letter," Leslie suggested.

Tori pulled it from her back pocket, the envelope looking almost ragged now after the many times she'd opened and closed it. "It goes without saying, Sikes, but this stays between us. Malone knows. Sam knows. That's it. That's our circle."

He nodded. "Okay."

She took the three pieces of paper from the envelope and handed it to him. As Casey had said, Charles got right to the point in the first sentence.

"Holy shit," John murmured as he read.

Tori went to her family's box, absently shuffling through the papers in there. She picked up one of the folders, looking at some of the scribbled notes made by the detectives all those years ago.

"Dirty cops? For real?"

Casey answered. "That's what he claims."

Tori stared at a small notepad, not really seeing the words. There was something familiar about it. She picked it up, her brows drawn together in a frown. There'd been a desk. It was in the corner of the living room. She had a vision of her father sitting there, pen in hand, writing on a pad just like this one. After homework, they would gather in the living room to watch TV for an hour or so before bedtime. Her mother would sit in one of the recliners and so did her dad sometimes. But she could see him clearly at the desk, his concentration on something other than his family. He was obviously—

"Tori?"

She looked up, letting the notepad fall back into the box. "Huh?"

"You okay?" Casey asked quietly.

She sighed. "Yeah. Just thinking." She turned to John. "Well? What do you think?"

"I don't know what to think. Sure, there are dirty cops. Always has been. But dirty enough to kill? To order a hit on another cop?" He shook his head. "That's hard to believe."

"Right. And it was over thirty years ago. Difficult to prove."

"But you're going to try?"

She gave a quick nod. "I am."

"Then what's your assumption?"

"My assumption is that my father was working on something, perhaps getting too close, making people nervous."

"People or cops?" John asked.

"Cops."

"If he was investigating cops, then it had to be at the request of someone higher up," Casey said. "Internal Affairs? Was CIU in existence back then? It wouldn't have been something he'd do on his own."

Tori ran a hand over her hair. "That's had me puzzled too. If he'd been ordered to investigate someone and then he ended up dead, wouldn't that have sent up a red flag?"

"Can Malone find that out?" Leslie asked.

"Any captain or lieutenant from thirty years ago is long retired," she said. "We just need a starting point." She pointed to the boxes. "I had thought there might be something here."

John handed her the letter. "I take it Malone hasn't gone to the captain with any of this?"

"No."

He shook his head. "I'm shocked that he's willing to go this alone. I mean, I know it's your family and all, but suggesting that cops had a hand in their murders…and more than thirty years ago? I don't see how we're going to find out anything, Tori."

She arched an eyebrow at him. "Are you suggesting that he's only doing this because he knows it won't go anywhere?"

He shrugged. "Where the hell can it go? There's nowhere to even start."

She glanced at Casey, then back to John. "How about you and Les just deal with the gun that was found. Get that all sorted out. I'm not supposed to be involved in that anyway." She glanced at Casey. "O'Connor and I will deal with Charles Griffin. That's our case."

Perhaps her tone was a bit more abrupt than she'd intended because John's expression softened.

"Tori, I didn't mean anything by that. I just—"

"I know. It's a long shot. I think we all know that. But it's my family. I've got to try. I owe them that much."

John stared at her for a moment before nodding. "Okay, Hunter. We'll help in any way, you know that."

She nodded briefly, then turned and left. Before she closed the door, she heard the quiet voices inside, knowing that Casey was trying to make John understand how important this was to her.

And it was, wasn't it? For a time there, solving her family's murder had been the most important thing in her life. But as the years crawled by, she knew in her heart that she never would. It was but a dream. A long shot.

When Sam came into her life, she had softened around the edges. So much so that that awful night faded and dimmed, becoming hazy as the years passed. She used to could see everything clearly—them at their dinner table, tied to chairs. The man shooting them, one by one. The man—Charles Griffin?—standing before her, meeting her eyes. Were his blue? Brown? She didn't know anymore. Had she ever? Then he turned, walking out of their house the way he'd come in, leaving her there alone. All alone.

She stood still, staring at the opposite wall, trying to see—*find*—his face. Trying to see *their* faces. Everything was blurry. As she'd told Casey…in the shadows.

In the shadows. Out of sight, out of mind. Forgotten, almost.

Not any longer, no. Not now. Charles Griffin had brought it out into the light. She felt her fists clench, feeling that old burning ache. This was as close as she would ever be. She had no intention of letting it slip away. If she had to go into the bowels of hell to find these guys, she would.

She wanted them to pay.

She wanted revenge.

CHAPTER TEN

"Do you think she's okay?"

Casey looked up, finding Lieutenant Malone standing by her desk. "Hunter? Yeah, I mean, I think so."

"Where'd she go?"

"Said she had something to check out."

"Without you?"

Casey sighed then. "Yeah, well, that does pose a problem. I don't think she's going off the deep end or anything, though."

Malone surprised her by pulling a chair closer and sitting down. "You think this might be a mistake, O'Connor? Letting her run this case?"

Casey shook her head. "No, sir. She's being very calm about it all. On the surface, you'd think it was just another case."

"I spoke with Sikes. He said there was nothing in the old case files. All closed. Nice and tidy, I believe were his words."

"Yeah. After Hunter left, we went through them anyway. Your run-of-the-mill cases, all of them." She put down the pen she'd been twisting in her fingers. "Sikes said something to Tori. Something that made her question your intentions."

He frowned. "What do you mean?"

She chewed on her lip, thinking she should just keep her mouth shut. But no. "Are you only letting it go this far to appease Tori? I mean, the likelihood of us finding anything is slim to none. Hell, we don't even know where to start or who to interview."

He didn't seem surprised by her question. "Maybe. To be honest, I felt like she needed some sort of closure. That confession letter notwithstanding, the chances of her finding something to point to dirty cops is basically zero. I thought pulling the old files, letting her look through them might put an end to it. Might give her that closure." He leaned back. "If there had been something, I'd have had no choice but to pull her. There's no way she could work this case."

"I don't agree. Maybe before Sam, then, yeah, she'd probably have been an emotional wreck. But now? She's put that behind her." She thought about it for a moment, remembering the fire in Tori's eyes. "Maybe she does need some resolution. Maybe she's kept that part hidden from us." She met his gaze. "Hidden from herself maybe."

"Since the old case files didn't point anywhere, then there's nowhere for her to go. Thirty-three years ago?" He shook his head. "She's not going to dig up anything. I'm going to let her try, O'Connor, because she deserves that. I'll give her a few days, the rest of the week. Then we'll have to shut it down."

"What about Charles Griffin?" she asked.

"What about him? You got any leads?"

"No. Traffic cams came up empty. We could spot the car into the first frame, but they always turned. Couldn't get a good read on their plate. Mac has the feed. All he could get was a fuzzy first letter. Could be an 'E' or could be an 'H' or, hell, something else."

"Okay. You dig into his financials yet?"

Casey pointed at her monitor. "Poking around now. Nothing out of the ordinary. He gets a monthly pension—rather small. Then Social Security. Lived a pretty simple life it looks like."

"Relatives?"

"Yeah, his sister had a couple of kids—niece and nephew. They've both been notified. Neither live locally. Other than that, I don't know."

Malone tapped her desk a couple of times with his knuckles, then stood. "Okay, get back to it, O'Connor." He turned to go, then stopped. "You talk to Sam?"

She raised her eyebrows. "You mean today?"

"She would know best about how Tori is handling this. Maybe give her a call."

Casey nodded. "Okay. Sure."

"Let me know."

She nodded again, wondering at his concern for Tori.

* * *

Tori sat cross-legged on the living room floor, four large, plastic storage totes that she'd wrestled down from the attic sitting beside her. She didn't know what was in them. Not really. She remembered sitting numbly on the sofa, watching as Aunt Carol went through their home, sorting through the different pieces of their lives, deciding what to keep and what could go. She'd been little help. Actually, she'd been no help at all, and eventually Aunt Carol had simply shoved as much as she could into boxes without even looking at it. It was the very next day that her aunt had taken her for counseling. A counseling session that had lasted months, not days.

She closed her eyes for a moment. No, not months. Nearly two years total. Two years of being in and out of the hospital. First, here in Dallas, then later in Houston. She'd felt safer in than out, she knew. Out meant staying with her Uncle James, her dad's brother. She'd felt like a stranger, and they'd treated her as one.

She supposed she couldn't blame them. Her dad and Uncle James had never been close, even though they'd both been cops. Her cousins barely tolerated her being there. Aunt Carol had come to her rescue though, taking her away to Houston to live with her and Louise. There she'd found a home. Aunt Carol had all of her things and the stuff she'd boxed up from the house. Tori had never been able to go through it all; knowing that it was there was enough.

She'd moved the boxes with her when she left Houston to return to Dallas. She'd moved them from her old, shabby apartment to Sam's place. And she'd moved them from their first house at the country club to here. Each time she'd done nothing more than glance inside, if even that.

She pulled one of the boxes toward her now and popped off the lid. She shuffled through it, finding carefully wrapped knickknacks and some picture frames. She took the tissue paper off one of the frames, feeling a catch in her heart as she stared at the family portrait. She'd been maybe ten years old, Emily but eight. Scott would have been thirteen and Toby fourteen. Everyone was smiling—on the verge of laughing. Her father had told some corny joke, she remembered. They were a happy family. Always had been. She tried to remember the last time she'd looked at the photo. Aunt Carol had a similar one hanging on the wall in the hallway. Tori rarely had glanced at it. It had still been too painful.

She put the photo down when she felt tears well in her eyes. She didn't have time for that. Not now. She closed the lid and pulled over another box. This one was full of papers and envelopes, old stacks of mail, even some bills. There were several manila folders at the bottom, and she pulled them out. MORTGAGE was scribbled across one. TAXES on another. DOCTOR on yet another. She was about to put them aside, but she opened them, flipping through bank statements and mortgage receipts. A small notepad caught her eyes, and she pulled it out from under a property tax statement. It was a notepad with a spiral binder at the top, one that she remembered her father using. She flipped it open, seeing his handwriting, still familiar to her after all these years. The words there had nothing whatsoever to do with taxes.

She moved more tax papers aside, finding other loose pages of notes made on a half-size notepad. One had a list of names. Last names—Sawyer. Bexley. Hamilton. Cunningham. Casper.

Douglas. Dewberry. Jaworski. Jenson. Below those were four more. All were circled. McMillan. Staley. Harken. And Hunter. She frowned. Hunter? Her uncle?

She scooted back against the couch, leaning there as she studied the pages of notes. Some of it—four pages—she couldn't decipher, as if her father had been writing in code. It was gibberish. She set those aside, then flipped through the small notepad, page by page. It was mostly questions, as if he had been jotting down thoughts so he wouldn't forget.

When do their shifts overlap? What's the common denominator? Has Brewster checked bank records? How high up does it go? Are all four lieutenants involved? What about the sergeants?

Who was Brewster, she wondered?

One page had only two words written. The two words had been circled over and over, as if he'd been lost in thought as his pen wound round and round the words.

Blue Dragons.

She stared at the words for the longest time. Were they significant? She flipped another page, finding Blue Dragons again at the top. Below that were more questions.

Have they really started up again? Who are they? How many? Who is in command?

"What the hell does all this mean?" she murmured quietly to herself.

She got up, still holding the notes. She absently went into the kitchen and took a water bottle from the fridge, then went out to the patio. She sat down, her mind reeling. Why did he have notes from a case hidden in a folder marked as tax records? Why did he have notes from a case at home in the first place? She opened the water bottle, taking a long swallow, again picturing him at the desk, hunched over his notepad with pen in hand. What was he working on? Was it a secret? Undercover? Would his old partner, William Vasher, have known?

No. If he kept all of this at home, then he hadn't wanted anyone to know, not even his partner. But why? Who was he investigating?

Blue Dragons.

She stared out into the backyard. Cops. He was investigating cops.

But if that was the case, who initiated it? Internal Affairs? Surely someone higher up would have known. And then her father was murdered. Surely *someone* had to question it. Yet in all of her snooping around, she'd never gotten even a hint that her father had been working on something undercover.

She put the notepad in her lap and looked through the loose pages. Those four that she couldn't read, she put down too. There were five other pages.

Followed Jenson last night (Tuesday). He met with Bexley. Brief. Less than two minutes. I followed Bexley then. He went to a bar (Breaker's at the edge of Deep Ellum) and stayed inside until ten minutes before midnight, then he came out with another guy. I didn't recognize him. I did not follow. Stayed around to see who he met. Not surprised to see Staley come out shortly after Bexley.

She went back to the list of names. Staley was one of the four that were circled.

I told Brewster that I was concerned about Hamilton and Jaworski. I've worked with them for several years. They've changed. More guarded. Secretive. He seems to think I should concentrate on the officers I've identified and not the detectives. I'm still going to keep up with them.

She nodded. Hamilton and Jaworski. Homicide detectives. They'd worked her family's case way back when.

Sawyer and Casper met up after shift change. A local pub in Uptown (Rudy's). I'd been following Casper. He waited in his car until Sawyer got there. Nothing odd there except that Lieutenant Staley showed up a short time later. Sawyer and Casper work a beat in Little Mexico. How do they know Staley? Coincidence that he was there or was it a meetup? (I don't believe in coincidences.)

"Neither do I," she murmured. She glanced again at the list of names. Staley was circled. A lieutenant. Her uncle had been a lieutenant back then too. His name was circled. Did she assume that the other two were also lieutenants? Were those the four lieutenants her dad mentioned?

Hamilton and Jaworski. Something's not right. My gut says they are both high up the chain. Their relationship with McMillan is different than other detectives, including myself. Brewster is pulling financials on McMillan and Staley. That will tell us something. But who is the leader? Who calls the shots?

She stared at the words and shook her head. None of it made sense to her. Who was Brewster? Was he the one giving her father directions? She put the notes down, staring out into the trees. Who would have known what was going on?

Again, that was over thirty years ago. By the time she'd made detective and started looking into it, there was hardly anyone still around who had known her father. William Vasher had retired the year before she'd made detective. She remembered speaking with him once, while she'd still been on patrol. He was friendly, cordial, and spoke fondly of her father. Maybe she would look him up now, see if he remembered anything. See if he knew anything about the Blue Dragons.

CHAPTER ELEVEN

Sam stood in the living room, eyebrows raised at the sight of Tori's old boxes on the floor. She moved closer, bending down to pluck a picture out of one. It was a school picture of Tori, she guessed. She smiled at the young girl who looked back at her. Tori's hair was touching her shoulders and her dark eyes were bright and alive. She put the photo back, seeing another. A family portrait. She picked it up, staring at the faces of Tori's siblings. She'd not seen a picture of them before. Whereas Tori's hair was dark brown, her sister's hair was light brown, nearly blond. One of Tori's brothers—she knew their names had been Toby and Scott, but she didn't know which was which—looked like he could be her twin. Their hair, their eyes, their smiles were identical. She put that down too, then turned, finding Tori out on the patio. She wondered what had prompted her to get the boxes out. As far as she knew, Tori had never once gone through them.

Had Malone been right to worry? Was Tori in an unfamiliar emotional state? When Casey had called, she'd done so at

Malone's bidding. Casey didn't seem to think anything was wrong, other than Tori had disappeared with a hurried "I gotta check something out."

Sam saw that Tori had a beer bottle shoved between her thighs and she was reading through some papers that she held. When she opened the patio door, the slight shift of Tori's head indicated she'd heard her. She walked behind Tori, resting her hands on her shoulders.

"You're home early."

Tori only shrugged a little. "I could say the same about you."

Sam moved in front of her, meeting her gaze. "Yes, you could. They're worried about you."

Tori arched an eyebrow. "They?"

"Stan. Casey." Then she smiled. "Well, mostly Stan. He made Casey call me."

"So you came home to check on me?"

"Not really, no. I didn't know you'd be here already." She pulled a chair out beside Tori. "You need to talk?"

"I'm fine."

"Are you?"

Tori sighed. "I guess you saw the boxes."

"I did."

"I was looking for something." Tori held up the papers in her hands. "Found this." She put her hands back down without showing them to her. "There was a family picture of us."

Tori looked at her then, and Sam saw a hint of tears in Tori's eyes. She said nothing, waiting for Tori to continue.

"I...I had forgotten what they looked like. All these years, they just kinda faded away. Like they were just hanging around at the edge of my memory."

"I thought you said your aunt had pictures of them, that she displayed them."

Tori nodded. "Yeah." Then she smiled. "That doesn't mean I looked at them."

"Ah. I see."

Tori wiped at the corner of one eye. "They'd be old farts like me now."

Sam laughed. "So now that we're over forty, we're old farts? Speak for yourself."

Tori smiled too, then it slowly faded from her face. "Why do you think I forgot about them?"

"Did you forget? Or did you just tuck them away someplace safe? Out of sight, out of mind?"

Tori nodded. "That phrase came to me earlier. Their faces, their memories, everything was blurry. Nothing was clear anymore."

"That didn't mean you'd forgotten about them, honey."

"No. I hadn't forgotten. I just didn't remember. Two different things, I guess."

"And now?" she asked gently.

Tori smiled again, an almost youthful smile. "I saw that picture and it all came back to me. I remembered how happy we'd been, you know. I think I told you once, how great my childhood had been. Coming home from school and Mom would have baked cookies or a cake or something. And dinner was usually a big affair. We were always together."

Sam noted the still lingering smile on Tori's face. She returned it but kept quiet, waiting while Tori gathered her thoughts.

"I have good memories of my childhood, Sam. I do. But it was almost like I shouldn't. You know? My childhood was cut short, just like theirs was. But I went on eventually. They didn't. So I didn't want to think about how good it had once been."

She reached over and took Tori's hand, squeezing it lightly. "I understand."

Tori squeezed her fingers back. "It's been so many years. Part of me wants to leave it all buried. Leave the past closed."

"Do you?"

"Part of me, yeah." Tori nodded. "But the other part, no, I want to find the bastard who ordered the hit." She turned to Sam. "And then I want to kill him."

Sam's breath caught at her words. Tori's fingers squeezed tighter, but she said no more. Sam, too, stayed quiet, wondering if Tori meant those words or if it was simply her emotions talking.

"You probably shouldn't say that to Malone," she finally said.

Tori dropped her hand. "Probably not." She turned in her seat. "Found some stuff. Some notes. You ever heard of the Blue Dragons?"

Sam shook her head. "No. What is it?"

"Don't know, really. Based on all his notes and my imagination running rampant, I'll guess it's some sort of a fraternity or something."

"Fraternity?"

"Cops." Tori stood. "Let's go inside. I'll show you. I may be way off base."

Sam nodded, noting that the tears had left Tori's eyes. She was all business now, back in detective mode. Yes, she did worry that maybe this case would be too much for Tori, too personal. It would certainly bring old wounds to the surface.

But Tori was strong. She could handle it. And Sam would be there every step of the way.

CHAPTER TWELVE

Tori was hesitant to bring what she'd found to Malone's attention, but she'd promised Sam she would. She wanted to run it by Casey first, though. When she got to the squad room, Casey was already at her desk. Tori nodded a greeting, then motioned with her head toward the small nook that served as a breakroom. Casey stood, glancing toward Malone's door before following her.

"He was already asking about you," Casey said quietly as Tori poured coffee into a cup. "I don't know why he's so worried about you. It's like he expects you to snap and go off the deep end at any minute." She moved closer to her, her voice even quieter now. "There's something else I should tell you."

Tori arched an eyebrow, waiting.

"Something Malone said yesterday after you left." Casey looked behind her again. "He doesn't think you're going to find anything. In fact, he's certain of it. But he thinks you need closure, so he's going to let you work this for a few days—the rest of the week, then close it up."

Tori frowned sharply. "Charles Griffin or my family?"

"The link to your family. But hell, Hunter, we got shit on Charles Griffin. That's going nowhere too."

"So by letting me work this case, it's just for show?"

Casey nodded. "He said if you did happen to find something—something that pointed to dirty cops—then he'd have to pull you from the case, but he doesn't expect anything to turn up. Not after this many years."

"So much for having my back," she muttered. "I don't know if this pisses me off, or if I should be grateful that he cares enough to give me this time."

"Think about it, Tori. The link to your father? If the captain got wind of this, it would be Malone's ass." Casey shrugged. "Besides, there was nothing in the files. There's nowhere to go with this. Dead end."

Tori put the coffee down without drinking any. "I found something. At home. Some of my father's old notes."

Casey's brows drew together. "At home? What are you talking about?"

"I had this vision—this memory—of my dad sitting at this desk we had in the family room. He had this notepad out and he was writing on it. I remembered my Aunt Carol boxing up all the papers from the desk because she didn't know what to keep and what to throw out. Anyway, I've had these boxes of stuff all these years. Never really went through it other than to move it into new boxes one time."

"And you found something?"

Tori looked up, hearing others moving about. "Where's Les? Sikes?"

"Caught a case. Shooting at an apartment complex. Two dead."

Tori nodded. "Let's get out of here. I don't feel comfortable talking here."

"Okay, sure. What should I tell Malone?"

"Tell him we're going to the lab. Tell him I want to look at the pictures that were on the wall."

"Do you?"

"Sure. Why not?"

* * *

"Why did he have pictures of you?" Mac asked.

Tori shrugged. "Who the hell knows. Just want to look through them, see if anything jumps out at me."

"Sure. I kept them in the same order they were in on his wall." He slid a box over to her. "Try not to mess it up."

"I'll make sure she doesn't screw it up for you, Mac," Casey said. "Thanks."

"Okay. Let me know if you need anything else." He paused. "The gun matched...well, you know, your family. Do you think he was the shooter? I mean, why else would he have had pictures of you?"

"Circumstantial evidence, but it's assumed he was the shooter," Tori said.

"And Malone's still got you on this case?"

"It's a case going nowhere, but O'Connor's got the lead on it." She smiled quickly, knowing it didn't reach her eyes. "I just wanted to see the pictures. Personal reasons."

Mac gave a shrug. "No problem, Hunter."

When he walked out, Casey closed the door behind him. "Case going nowhere?"

"Yeah, you said yourself we got shit. Maybe we should close it. We're probably wasting our time."

"You're driving me fucking crazy, Hunter. You know that? Now what the hell did you find?"

The evidence room was secure, she knew. The door was closed. It was just Casey. Her partner. Her friend. Yet, she was hesitant to tell her where her thoughts were going. Hesitant to drag her into it. Because if Malone got wind of what she was thinking, he'd probably suspend her.

"It might be better if you don't know."

"What the hell kind of shit is that?"

She went to the box, absently flipping through the photos. She felt an indifference toward them. It was one thing posing for a picture, having memories of the scene. Completely different to find yourself in anonymous photos where you went about your daily life. Why did Charles Griffin take them? Was he so riddled with guilt that he followed her around for thirty years?

"I've got a buddy at the FBI," she finally said. "Well, buddy might be too strong a word, but I know someone." She turned to Casey. "I'm going to get him to hack into our personnel files here."

Casey stared at her. "For what reason?"

"I have some names. I want to find out where they were stationed, who their commander was, and when they retired."

"You can find that out yourself, Tori. You don't need to hack into our goddamn system."

"I don't want anyone to know. If I go through proper channels to pull personnel files, then someone will know. And I'd have to justify why I wanted the files." She shook her head. "Malone would never go for it. Not with me working the case."

Casey sighed. "Tell me what the hell you found, Tori."

Tori sighed too. The two people she knew she could trust with anything were Sam and Casey. They were the two people she loved the most in the world. But right now, she didn't think she could even tell Sam what she was planning.

"Look, I found some notes. A list of names. Cops. They've got to be. My father was investigating something. Undercover. Whether he was ordered to do it, I don't know. I'm assuming, but he could have been doing it on his own. Maybe that's why he kept everything at home." No, she thought. There was the Brewster her father had mentioned. He wasn't alone in it. "Regardless, I think that's what got him killed."

"But how's this going to help, Tori? You don't even know what he was working on."

Yes, she did know. The Blue Dragons. That was what he was working on. She just didn't know what the hell it was or who initiated the investigation.

"I'm going to contact the people on this list and interview them."

"And ask them what? Did they kill your family?"

"I've got to do this alone, O'Connor. Malone wanted to drop me from the case to begin with. As it should be. I have no business working a case that might be tied to my family's murder. That's just standard procedure." She paused. "I'll probably take a few days off."

Casey shook her head. "Oh, so you're going to go be some rogue cop now? Come on, Hunter. You're not thinking this through."

"I've got this information that I don't know what the hell to do with. I can't go to Malone with it. What the hell else am I supposed to do?"

Casey pointed her finger at her. "You're going to fuck up and lose your shield, Hunter. You can't go all cowboy on me."

"That's exactly why I don't want you involved, O'Connor." She tapped her chest. "This is my problem. My family. And I want some goddamn answers. I don't want closure," she said loudly. "I want to know who the fuck killed my family. And why."

"So you don't want closure. You want answers?" Casey met her gaze. "You want justice?"

"Justice? No, I don't want justice. I want revenge. I want some goddamn fucking revenge."

CHAPTER THIRTEEN

Sam looked up at the knock on her door, surprised to find Casey there. She smiled back at her. "What a nice surprise. Or is something wrong?"

Casey shrugged. "I don't know if anything is wrong or not. Thought maybe we could talk and decide."

"I'm guessing this is about Tori?"

"Yeah, it's about Tori." Casey glanced behind her, hearing voices down the hallway. "Can you get away for lunch?"

Sam eyed the report she was trying to finish, then pushed it away. She would be giving her notice tomorrow. She didn't imagine it would matter if she was late on the report or not. She stood with a smile. "I start my new job in three weeks. I don't guess it'll be a big deal if I slip away early."

"That's great, Sam. Congratulations."

She linked arms with Casey as they walked out. "Thanks. It's scary, I'll admit, but I'm looking forward to it. I've never been a boss before."

"You'll do fine, Sam. Everybody loves you."

"Thanks, Casey, but I know you're biased."

"Yeah, I am."

Once outside the building, Sam stopped. "Want to walk to the deli and sit on the patio? Or someplace else?"

"No, that's fine. Les would be happy I'm getting something other than my usual greasy burger."

Casey ordered a tuna on wheat bread, and she got a garden salad with grilled chicken. They split an order of fries and took their lunch out to the patio, grabbing a table that was in a far corner.

"Does Tori know you're here?"

Casey smiled and shook her head. "She'd probably kill me."

Sam stabbed a piece of chicken with her fork, then paused before eating. "Did she tell you what she found? Or more importantly, did she tell Malone?"

"She told me a little bit, but nothing specific. And she's not going to tell Malone. In fact, that's what's got me worried. She was going to talk to him. She was going to ask him to pull her from the case."

"*What?* Why on earth?"

"Because she's going to go rogue or something, I just know it."

"Rogue?" Sam shoved her salad away. "What happened? The last she and I talked she was going to tell Malone what she found. So what happened?"

"Yeah, well that's probably my fault." Casey shoved a fry into her mouth. "Malone and I had a talk yesterday after Tori left. He basically said he's just letting Tori work this for show, said he'd give her a few days, then shut it down."

"But why? Is he afraid she'll find something?"

"Quite the opposite. Because based on what we have so far, there's nothing to find. Especially without bringing Griffin's confession letter to light. Which, really, is that even admissible? And there was nothing in the old case files, there's nothing new to add, we have shit on Charles Griffin. And I mean shit. Absolutely nothing."

"I see his point. I mean, where would you begin to investigate cops from thirty or more years ago. But Tori found some names. You could start there."

"My thinking is that if she turns that over to Malone, he'll hand it off to someone else—hell, maybe even CIU—and she'll be out of it. If I'm thinking that, Tori is thinking that."

"Honestly, Casey, based on what she found, I don't think there's enough to even begin an investigation. She found some names. She found some notepads with questions. She found some notes that he'd made when he did a stakeout, when he followed a couple of these guys around. There's not much more than that." She picked up her fork again. "Well, there is more, but it's, like, written in code."

"In code?"

"Yes. Some sort of shorthand. It's not legible. It's like the letters are all scrambled."

Casey took a bite of her sandwich, talking around a mouthful. "Do you know what she's got planned?"

"No. I have no idea."

"She's going to get an FBI friend of hers to hack our system and pull personnel files on the list of names she's got."

Sam's eyes widened. "What the hell is she thinking?"

"She's not thinking rationally, that's what. Like I said, I think she plans to go rogue." Then she grinned. "Don't you love that? *Rogue.* It sounds so badass. Perfect for Hunter."

"So that's why she wants Malone to officially take her off the case? So she can go out on her own?"

"She said she may ask him to give her a few days off."

"Oh my god. I can't believe she hasn't talked to me about this. She—"

"She knows what you'd say, Sam. The same thing I said. She'll be lucky not to get suspended and damn lucky not to lose her shield."

"Should we tell Malone about it?"

Casey shook her head. "No way. She's my partner, my best friend. There's no way I'd go behind her back like that."

"Even if it's for her own good?"

"You were right, Sam. She pretended that this wasn't personal for her, she pretended that it didn't affect her, but it did. She's not out for justice. She told me that."

"Then what?"

"I'll tell it to you like she told it to me. 'I want some goddamn fucking revenge.'"

Sam stared at Casey, not really surprised by it all. She should have known, though. Shouldn't she? As passionate as Tori was about everything, she should have known that she was hiding this from her. She had seemed indifferent to the news that Charles Griffin killed her family. She said she wanted to work the case, said it wasn't too much for her. Tori had convinced her of that. Convinced Malone too.

"She doesn't trust anyone else with this," Sam said with certainty. "You're right. Malone would hand the information over to CIU, who might or might not take it seriously. She would be totally out of the loop."

"Sure. But Sam, get someone to hack the system? Then what? She said she wanted to interview these guys. Again, then what? Say she finds something. What's she going to do with it? Tell Malone? After he's through yelling at her for going out on her own, he'll *still* have to turn it over to CIU."

Sam met her gaze. "I'm afraid to say this, but I think if she finds out who was behind it all…she'll kill them. She said as much to me last night."

"I know," Casey said quietly. "And we can't let that happen."

"What are you suggesting?"

"That I follow her. You know, like a bodyguard or something."

She reached across the table and took Casey's hand. "Would you do that? Would you keep her out of trouble for me?"

"It's all we can do. Because I doubt seriously that we can talk her out of this. Whatever *this* is."

Sam had to agree with her. Whatever mission—journey—Tori was on, she felt like she needed to do it alone. And Sam would have to let her. To a degree.

"Okay. Yes. Be her shadow." Sam held her gaze. "But whatever you find out, I want to know everything. Don't keep anything from me."

"No way. It's just me and you. I'm not even going to tell Les. I don't want her to slip and say something to Sikes."

Sam patted her hand. "She'll be pissed to have been kept in the dark. I know I would."

"And are you pissed now that Tori has gone off without telling you?"

"Yes. And when this is all over with, I'll be sure to let her know. In the meantime, we've got to let her do what she's going to do."

CHAPTER FOURTEEN

Tori knocked on the doorframe of Malone's office. He glanced up, then motioned her in. "What's up, Hunter? You got something?"

"No sir. In fact, less than nothing."

"Yeah, that's what O'Connor said."

She should have rehearsed this. She should have gone over it all in her mind before walking in here. But she felt anxious. She felt like she needed to be out there, like she needed to get the ball rolling.

"I don't know how much more there is to work, but I think maybe you were right all along. I don't need to be involved in this."

He tossed his glasses down on his desk and ran a hand over his slick head. "Something happen?"

"No, no. I just...well, it's more personal than I wanted it to be. Pulling the file, seeing all those pictures...it brought it all out again. I'd rather you hand it off to Tucker and Sikes. Or let O'Connor run it alone. Like you said, I don't have any business being on this case."

As he stared at her, she struggled to hold his gaze, fearing he could read between the lines. Fearing he'd see the truth in her eyes. He finally nodded.

"You got that right, Hunter. I shouldn't have let you talk me into you staying on. But like everyone says, there's not much to work on." He leaned forward, tapping his fingers on his desk. "Truth is, Tori, I was going to have to pull you anyway. The captain called me. He heard about the ballistics match with the gun. He wanted to know how you were taking it and he said he hoped like hell I wasn't letting you anywhere near this case."

Tori nodded. "Yeah. Everyone was right. Last night, it hit me and...and I had a little breakdown," she said, hoping he believed her. "In fact, I might want to take a couple of days, if that's okay."

"Take some days off? Sure. I thought you were handling this all too well. I guess you put on a good front, huh?"

She gave a small smile. "Yeah. It caught up with me."

He stared at her for the longest time. "What is it you're not telling me?"

"What do you mean?"

"Oh, hell, Hunter. I've known you too long. What's going on?"

"Nothing, Stan. I just need to get away."

"Look, I know you. You want to see if there were dirty cops involved. There's no way to go back that far and sift through it, Tori. You have to know that. Over thirty years ago? Every last one of them is retired. Some are probably even buried six feet under. There's no way to dig up something like that."

"Yes, sir."

He narrowed his eyes at her. "That's it?"

She stood. "Like you said, over thirty years ago. I thought I was over it. But being involved in all this," she said, waving her hand out toward the squad room, "made me relive that night all over again. I just need to put it to bed, Stan. It's over and done with. The sooner I accept that, the sooner I can leave it in the past. And me working Charles Griffin's case, me thinking that maybe I might stumble upon whoever ordered my family's killing...well, it's too much. The captain is right to keep me out of it."

He nodded. "Okay, Tori. Yes, this is what we should have done to begin with." He waved her away. "Take a few days if you need. O'Connor can handle it alone."

"Thanks, Stan."

When she turned to leave, he called her back. "Tori...you sure you're okay?"

She gave him a quick smile. "Actually, I feel relieved to be able to walk away from it. So yeah, I'm okay."

She left then, ending their conversation. She knew he didn't completely believe her. As he'd said, they'd known each other too long. But this was the only way. She stopped at her desk, pausing long enough to scribble a note to Casey.

Taking a few days off. I'll be in touch.

She left the note beside Casey's keyboard, then, without looking back, hurried out. Once outside, she took a deep breath, realizing that yes, she really did feel relieved. Not for the reasons she'd told Malone though. No, she felt relieved because now she could get to work.

And she would do it her way. No rules.

CHAPTER FIFTEEN

"I need a favor."

Simon eyed her suspiciously. "The last time you asked for a favor, I got suspended two weeks."

"Yeah. And I bought you that expensive bottle of scotch and took you out for steaks."

"Two *weeks*, Hunter."

Tori moved closer to his desk. She hadn't seen Simon since she'd left the FBI. He probably celebrated the day. "It's important. I need some help."

"You said that the last time too." Then he held his hand up. "Wait a minute. You don't even work here anymore."

She smiled. "Have you missed me?"

"No."

No, she didn't suppose anyone had. She hadn't made friends with anyone when she worked here at the FBI. In fact, once inside the building, she hadn't run into a single person she even recognized other than Amber when she'd signed in. She leaned a hip against his desk. "It's really important, Simon."

"You don't have anyone at Dallas PD who can do this for you?"

She met his gaze. "It's kinda off the record."

"You want me to hack into something?" he asked quietly as he shoved his black-framed glasses more firmly on his nose. "Are you out of your mind? The last time—"

"Off the record. Not here. At home. In your free time." She moved closer still. "Come on, Simon. I know you love that shit. You probably hack into stuff all the time for fun."

He looked behind her as they heard voices from the next cubicle. "I haven't had lunch yet."

"Lunch? You want me to take you to lunch?"

"No, Hunter. I want you to get out of here."

She stood up straighter. "Look, I really, really need you to do this for me."

He motioned with his hand. "Not here. There's that food truck a couple of blocks down by that little park. Meet me there."

She nodded. "The barbecue guy?"

"Yeah. Fifteen minutes." He turned his back to her. "And don't talk to anyone on your way out."

She nodded. "Thanks, Simon. I'll owe you."

"I haven't agreed to anything yet."

She retraced her steps down the hallway, ducking into the stairs when a group of four approached the elevators. She nearly jogged down the three flights, then went over to the desk, handing the receptionist her visitor's pass.

"Thanks, Amber."

"You weren't up there long. Couldn't find McKenzie?"

"No. I'll try another time."

"Sure, Hunter. See you around."

She nodded, her smile fading as soon as she left the building. She glanced at her watch, then headed down the street to wait on Simon. True to his word, fifteen minutes later—on the dot— he came walking up. His black-framed glasses had been replaced with sunglasses and he was wearing a ballcap—navy blue with a white D on the front. His long dark hair stuck out four or five inches in the back. He looked nothing like the nerdy computer geek she knew him to be.

She pushed off the tree when he walked past, falling into step beside him. "You come here often?"

"A few times a month. I usually bring my lunch and eat at my desk."

The lunch crowd was mostly gone with only one person in line in front of them. She looked over the menu, glad to see that her old favorite was still there.

"I'll take a chopped beef sandwich with pickles and onions," Simon said when it was his turn. "Easy on the sauce."

"Yeah, I'll have two brisket tacos with spicy slaw," she said. "I'll take his extra sauce."

They stepped to the side to wait, neither speaking. A mere four minutes later, their order was up. They walked over to the park, finding an empty picnic table. She unwrapped one of the tacos and took a bite, nearly moaning at the taste. When she'd worked for the FBI, this was a once-a-week stop for her.

Simon, too, took a bite of his sandwich before speaking. "Gonna keep me in suspense, Hunter?"

She wiped her mouth with a napkin, dabbing at the sauce there. "I need you to hack into the Dallas PD's personnel files."

He paused in mid-chew. "No. Absolutely not."

"Information only. I don't want to manipulate data or anything like that."

"What kind of information?"

"I have some names. All retired. I'm assuming, anyway. I want their records from years back. From, say, 1987 to 1991."

"What kind of information are you looking for?"

"Where they worked, what shift, who their commander was, that sort of thing. Can you do it?"

"Can I? Of course. *Will I do it* is the question, Hunter."

She put her taco down. "Simon, it's a murder investigation. A cold case. I need your help."

"Why the hell do you need me to hack into your own department's files? Why don't you just go to them?"

She didn't know Simon well enough to trust him. Not really. But she supposed she would have to. "When I was twelve years old, a man broke into our home at dinnertime and killed my father." She swallowed. "And the rest of my family. My father was a cop. A detective. The killings were never solved. Now I've got recent evidence that points to dirty cops being involved. So I've got some names."

Simon stared at her for a moment, then took another bite of his sandwich. "Does your commander know you're doing this?"

"No."

"Okay, Hunter. What guarantee do I have that when he finds out—because you know he will—that my name will be kept out of it?"

"Because no one knows I've contacted you, for one. Besides, I have their names. I could just interview them based on that. But I want to know what the chain of command was back then, who they reported to. I want to know who their lieutenant was, who their captain was and so on. I want to see if there was a pattern. If their paths crossed."

He took his sunglasses off and put them on the table and rubbed his eyes.

Tori stared at him. "What? You're worried you'll get caught?"

Simon smiled. "Get caught? Caught snooping around in their files?" He shook his head. "I can be in and out of their system in a matter of seconds. Old files like that? No, they'll never know I was in there. That's not the problem."

"I promise your name will be kept out of it."

"You promise, Hunter? That's all I get?"

"That's all I got."

He stared at her for a long time, then put his sunglasses back on. "I never knew that. About your family, I mean."

"Yeah. It's not something I talk about."

He picked up his sandwich. "Okay. This is what we'll do. I'll set up an email account to make it look like you're talking to real hackers." He smirked. "You know, the ones who charge you big bucks for this sort of thing."

"I'm good for another bottle of scotch."

"Make it two. Anyway, all communication will be through email. My name will be…" He paused. "Boris. Yeah, Boris. So when your captain or lieutenant finds out or whoever else, all they'll have is this email communication."

"And they won't trace it to you?"

"I'll probably place Boris in Russia or someplace like that. We'll even make it look like you paid me in bitcoin." He took his sunglasses off again. "Oh, we can make it look like you found me on the Dark Web. That could fun. We could—"

"How about we just do it the normal way, huh?"

"Not as much fun, but okay." He looked around them as if making sure no one was watching. "Where are the names?"

She leaned back, pulling the list out of her front jeans pocket. She, too, looked around, then slid the paper across the table. He folded it in his hand, then shoved it into his own pocket.

She took another bite of her taco, finally feeling like maybe she was getting somewhere.

"Your cell number still the same? I can find it in your old file."

"Yeah."

"Personal email?"

"It's a gmail account. THunter1015. Capital T, capital H. Hunter, ten fifteen."

He nodded. "Okay. You'll get something from Boris. Answer and reply as warranted. This is all for show, just something to trace if your department finds out. I can probably get this information for you tonight. I can cross-reference it too and try to get current addresses and phone numbers."

"You can do that?"

"Of course."

"Thanks, Simon. I'll owe you."

He smiled at her. "You're right. I love doing shit like this." He took a big bite of his sandwich, still smiling. "And yeah, I do it for fun too."

CHAPTER SIXTEEN

Tori felt restless as she paced in the living room. She wanted to call Casey, wanted to tell her what she'd done. She didn't pull her phone out of her pocket, though. Instead, she went into the kitchen and opened the fridge, thinking she might surprise Sam with dinner. There were chicken breasts and some pre-chopped veggies. Sam already had something planned, it seemed.

"What are you doing?"

She jumped, finding Sam standing behind her. Sam smiled and came closer, leaning in for a kiss.

"You're either slipping or you're preoccupied. I'm never able to sneak up on you."

Just one look into her eyes and Tori knew that Sam knew. Knew what, she wasn't quite sure.

"I was going to start dinner, but I didn't know what you had planned."

"What I had planned doesn't sound appealing right now." Sam moved past her and opened the fridge, taking out a beer and handing it to her. She also took out a bottle of chardonnay. "Want to be lazy and order something?"

"Sure. What do you have in mind?" she asked as she twisted the cap off the beer bottle.

"Mexican food, I think."

Tori leaned against the counter, watching her. "You know, don't you?"

Sam met her gaze. "Know what?"

Tori shifted. "You're home early, aren't you?"

Sam poured wine into a glass. "Well, I gave my notice today. I was going to wait until tomorrow, but…" she said with a shrug. "Anyway, other than wrapping up a few things, I don't have much to keep me busy."

"How did they take it?"

"Not shocked. They had apparently heard through the grapevine that I'd been offered the job." Sam took a sip of her wine, then moved closer, mimicking Tori's position against the counter. "What is it that I know?"

Tori hesitated. "I'm home early too."

"Yes, you are. Two days in a row."

Tori finally smiled. "I know O'Connor called you. She probably called the minute she read my note."

Sam smiled too. "The note that said you were taking a few days off? That note?"

"I…I just need some time." She hated lying to Sam and she couldn't meet her eyes. "It didn't feel right."

Sam turned to face her, reaching out a hand to touch her cheek, forcing Tori to look at her. "Sweetheart, whatever you've got to do, I'll support you. You know that."

Tori let out her breath. "I couldn't go to Malone with what I had."

Sam nodded. "I know that now. Yes, I spoke with Casey. She seemed to think that whatever you gave Malone would have been shifted over to CIU."

Tori nodded quickly. "Exactly. And it would have either gotten buried or tossed to the side and ignored."

"Probably so. Everyone has a caseload. Pulling someone to investigate something that happened that long ago would not be a priority."

"I know. And I need it to be a priority."

"I know you do." Sam picked up her glass again. "So, what are you going to do?"

Tori again hesitated. Should she tell Sam about Simon? She could only imagine what her reaction would be. She closed her eyes for a moment. When she opened them, Sam was there, looking at her, waiting.

"I'm going to try to talk to the guys on the list. I'm going to start there."

"And what will you ask them?"

"I haven't really worked that out yet." That much was true. "And I've been thinking about the notes that he left, the ones that I can't read. I'm wondering if they could be deciphered somehow."

"By whom?"

"I don't know. Somebody smarter than me." Again, she was thinking of Simon, and she wished she'd brought it up to him. Maybe she'd try to talk to him about that tomorrow.

"I guess it's worth a try. Have anyone in mind?"

The question was asked casually. Almost too casually. Christ, if Sam had talked to O'Connor, then she already knew about Simon. She sighed.

"So you know, don't you?"

Sam laughed. "Why are we talking in circles? Yes, I know. Did he agree to it?"

"Yes. He's going to do it tonight. But I forgot about the notes."

"And who is this hacker you know?"

"Simon. I worked with him a few times. He—"

"Oh my god! Is he the one who got suspended? I'm surprised he's even speaking to you," Sam said with a laugh.

"Yeah, that's him. He was quite nice about it all. Which reminds me, I'll owe him another bottle of scotch. Or two, I believe he said."

"You trust him?"

"Yes. I have to."

"Okay. Like I said, whatever you've got to do, I'll support you. I'd just rather you not do anything that's going to get you fired." Sam met her gaze, holding it. "Or worse."

Tori put her beer down and pulled Sam into her arms. She held her tightly. "I love you."

"I love you too, Tori." Sam pulled away a little, looking at her. "Don't shut me out, please. You don't have to keep things from me."

"I know. I'm sorry, Sam."

Their kiss was slow, lingering and they both sighed contentedly when they pulled apart. Sam smiled at her, then leaned closer for another quick kiss.

"I want to shower before we order dinner." Another kiss. "Share?"

Tori relaxed, feeling her world spin back to normal. "Yeah. Share."

CHAPTER SEVENTEEN

Tori had been disappointed that there was no email from Boris first thing that morning. Maybe Simon ran into issues. Or maybe it hadn't been as easy as he'd thought. She picked up the notes—the ones that were in code—and stared at the gibberish, trying to make sense of it. Why? Why had her father felt the need to keep some of his notes this way? Especially since they were left at home. Who was he afraid would see it?

She tilted her head, studying them. Could he read this? Did he know what it said? Was it like a second language to him? She looked up, staring at the wall. She'd never seen this before. Ever. Had he used it in other cases or was this a one-time thing? All questions she wouldn't get answers to. Maybe she could locate his old partner, William Vasher. She could show it to him, see if he knew what it was.

Once again, she picked up her phone, checking email. Still nothing from Boris. With a sigh, she was about to pocket it, then called Casey instead.

"Hey, Hunter. You okay?"

"Yeah, O'Connor. I'm fine. I need a favor, though."

"Sure."

"Can you pull up an address for someone? William Vasher."

There was only a slight pause. "That's your father's old partner?"

"Right."

Another pause. "Yeah, well, I'm not exactly at my computer. But I think Les and Sikes were still there. Give Les a call. I'm sure she'll look it up for you."

Tori frowned. "Where are you?"

"Just, you know, out and about."

Tori shook her head and smiled. "You're getting something to eat, aren't you? I swear, you should be as big as a house the way you eat."

"Yeah, yeah. You want me to call Les for you?"

"Okay, sure. Ask her to email it to me."

"Will do."

She stared at the phone after Casey had disconnected, wondering at her hurry. Wondering why Casey hadn't asked questions. With a shrug, she went into the kitchen to refill her coffee cup. A minute or two later, Leslie sent an email. William Vasher lived in Northeast Garland now, almost to the Bush Toll Road. She dumped her coffee into the sink and took a water bottle from the fridge instead.

By the time she got on Garland Road and merged into traffic heading north, she had spotted Casey's truck following her. She looked in the rearview mirror, seeing her about four vehicles behind. She pushed the phone icon on her steering wheel, planning to ask Casey what the hell she was doing. But she knew what she was doing, didn't she?

"Damn fool," she muttered. No, she wouldn't call her. She'd talk to her in person. But now she sped up, passing two cars in the left lane. She smiled as Casey appeared to be boxed in by a truck. Didn't matter really. Casey already knew where she was going.

Fifteen minutes later she exited the highway on Buckingham Road to the right. She glanced at the map on her console, then took a left on Mars, going north again. She was thick in a residential neighborhood, and she slowed as she approached Melissa Lane, then she turned right. Vasher's house was nearly at the end where Treece Trail intersected. Instead of pulling into his driveway, she took Treece, going down a few houses and making a sharp U-turn, heading back toward Melissa. She stopped along the curb, seeing Casey creeping along at a snail's pace. With what she was sure was an evil grin on her face, she sped out onto the street, causing Casey to slam on her brakes.

Tori got out and sprinted around her car, hoping she had an appropriate glare on her face as Casey lowered her window.

"What the hell, Hunter? I almost hit you!"

"You're asking me what the hell, O'Connor? Why are you following me?"

"What makes you think I'm following you?"

Tori put her hands on her hips. "O'Connor, I love you. I really do. But you're pissing me off!"

"You might need backup."

"I don't need a goddamn babysitter." She stomped back to her car. "Now leave. I can handle this."

"You shouldn't be doing this alone," Casey insisted. "Hell, Hunter, you shouldn't be doing this at all. If Malone—"

Tori held up her hand. "Look, I'm simply visiting with the man who used to be my father's partner. Thought maybe I'd let him know about Charles Griffin. That's all."

"I should come with you."

"No. This is personal business. It has nothing to do with you."

"You're being a stubborn, hardheaded ass!"

Tori rolled her eyes as she walked away. "Whatever."

She backed her car up, swinging around Casey and pulling into Vasher's driveway. As expected, Casey pulled along the curb and parked. Tori slammed her door shut, thinking how funny the situation would be if Vasher wasn't home. She and Casey had been practically yelling at each other in the street.

She heard the chime of the doorbell after she pressed it, then she heard a dog begin to bark inside. A short time later, the door opened—a security chain in place—and a woman peeked through the opening.

"Yes? May I help you?"

Tori smiled. "Mrs. Vasher?"

"Who are you?"

"I'm Tori Hunter. My father was—"

"Jason Hunter. Of course. You favor him."

The chain was released, and the door opened. The woman's gaze had lost its wariness, and she gave Tori a smile now.

"Come in, please," Mrs. Vasher beckoned.

Tori nodded and stepped inside. "Sorry to come by unannounced. I suppose I should have called. I wanted to speak with your husband. Is he available?"

"William is in his recliner, where he spends most of his days. Come."

Tori followed her inside a formal—and apparently little used—living room, past the kitchen and into a small, comfortable-looking den. The TV was on, a large flatscreen hanging above the fireplace. A shell of a man was in a recliner, covered to his waist with a blanket. In his lap sat a small, white dog, its fur a tangled mess around its face. The dog barked at her, and the man hushed it.

"William? You have company."

The man turned and stared at her. There seemed to be a flicker of recognition in his eyes. She, on the other hand, wouldn't have known this man to be William Vasher if she'd bumped into him on the street. The tall, robust man she remembered was thin and frail, his few remaining hairs a dull gray stubble on his nearly bald head.

"Mr. Vasher, I'm Tori Hunter. Jason's daughter."

He nodded slowly. "Well, I'll be. The last time I saw you was that night…"

Yes, William Vasher was one of the dozens of cops who had filled the house that night. The bodies had been taken—her family. But the blood remained. She remembered seeing him, remembered thinking that he was a familiar face, at least, even if she didn't really know him.

"Actually, I spoke with you once, many years ago. I was still pretty new on the force."

He nodded slowly. "Yes, I guess we did speak. What brings you around now?" he asked, his voice weak and raspy.

Mrs. Vasher motioned to the couch. "Please sit, Tori. Can I get you something? Coffee? Water?"

"No, ma'am, thank you. I'm fine."

She nodded, then left them alone, heading back in the direction they'd come. Tori sat at the edge of the couch, leaning forward. She rested her elbows on her thighs, wondering what all she should ask him.

"I found some old papers of my dad's," she began. "Notes and stuff about a case he was working on."

"A case? I think we had three or four open cases back then. I don't remember there being anything missing."

"Could he have been working on something without your knowledge?"

Mr. Vasher shook his head. "I doubt it. Why would he?"

Tori debated on how much to ask him, how much to tell. But she had to start somewhere. "Have you ever heard of the Blue Dragons?"

His brows drew together. "Blue Dragons? Now that was before my time. Before Jason's too. They had put an end to that nonsense before I even joined the force. It was in the early '70s that they shut it down. Maybe late '60s even, I can't remember for sure."

"What was it?"

"Just hearsay and rumors, best I recall. A bunch of cops playing the system. Taking evidence, weapons, money from crime scenes. Mainly money. That's how it started. Petty stuff, mostly. Then drugs came into play. That's when they shut it down."

"They?"

He coughed once, then waved his hand. "The powers that be. They came down hard on those poor guys. Most of them lost their jobs." He coughed again. "Just rumors. I couldn't honestly say that I ever met anyone who actually knew what went down." He narrowed his eyes at her. "Why are you interested in that?"

She shrugged. "Trying to get a history lesson, that's all." She stood then. "I wanted to let you know that we found a gun. Ballistics matches it to my father's killing."

His eyes widened at that. "After all these years?"

"Yes. It belonged to Charles Griffin. Does that name ring a bell?"

She could tell that he was going back in time, running through his memory bank. He finally shook his head.

"No. I don't recall that name. Was he the killer?"

"We're not sure. Charles Griffin was killed at his home. The gun was in a safe. No way to know really." That, of course, would have been the truth had Charles not left her his confession letter.

"That was a rough time for you. Rough time for all of us."

She took a deep breath. "Yes. Yes, it was." She moved away from him. "I've taken up enough of your time."

At that, he smiled. "Time? All I've got is time." Then he coughed. "But it's running out finally, I think. Lung cancer got me. I've done my last chemo. Months ago, they stopped that, thank god. If the cancer didn't kill me, I thought for sure the chemo would." He coughed again. "They said it's spread too far now. Nothing more to do but wait for the end."

"I'm sorry to hear that."

"It's been a good life. Can't complain too much." He held a hand out to her and she reached for it, giving it a gentle squeeze. "Nice to see you all grown up, Tori."

"Thanks." She touched his thin shoulder as she moved past him. "You take care now."

Mrs. Vasher was in the kitchen and Tori stopped on her way out. "Thank you. I'm sorry I intruded without notice. I didn't realize he was sick."

Mrs. Vasher gave her a gentle smile. "He's been fighting it almost two years. They only gave him nine months to begin with, so I've been blessed to have him a little longer than that." That smile faded. "It won't be long now, they say. A few weeks at most."

"I'm very sorry."

"No need. It is what it is. Come. I'll show you out."

CHAPTER EIGHTEEN

"So? What did you find out?" Casey asked as soon as Tori walked over to her.

"Nothing."

Casey stared, eyebrows raised. "Nothing? You got nothing, Hunter?"

"He's got cancer. He's dying. He never heard of Charles Griffin." She stopped beside Casey's truck. "You're wasting your time following me around. Does Malone know?"

"Of course not."

Then she arched an eyebrow. "Does Sam?"

Casey looked away and scratched the back of her neck.

"Good lord. So the two of you hatched this plan to follow me?"

"Sam's afraid you're going to get into trouble and I'm afraid you're going to do something stupid. So yeah, we decided that you needed a goddamn babysitter," Casey said with a grin, repeating her earlier words. "And don't act like you're pissed at me."

"I *am* pissed at you."

"No, you're not. You can't be pissed at me. It's not allowed, and you know it."

Tori blew out a breath. "You're right, O'Connor. Okay. Follow me to the house. I'll show you what I found."

No, she wasn't mad at Casey. And she certainly wasn't mad at Sam. They were just looking out for her. And she was trying to look out for Casey by keeping her out of this. Because yes, if Malone found out—especially about her dealings with Simon—he'd totally flip out. She could picture the steam coming off his bald head, see his red face as he yelled at them. She smiled at that thought, knowing he'd have a bottle of antacids in one hand and ibuprofen in the other. So yeah, she was trying to keep Casey out of it. As much as Casey would let her, anyway.

Once they got to the house and after Casey parked in the driveway, she walked into the garage and gave Tori a tight hug.

"I hate it when we fight."

Tori rolled her eyes. "You're such a girl sometimes."

Casey laughed. "Yeah. Don't tell Les."

Tori led her inside, then went directly to the spare bedroom that she and Sam had converted into an office. She sat down at her desk and motioned for Casey to use Sam's chair. Casey rolled it over beside her.

"Found these notes," she said, handing Casey the papers.

"What the hell language is this in?"

Tori gave a quick laugh. "Yeah. Best I can tell, it's some kind of code."

"What makes you think this has something to do with it all?"

She opened the top drawer and pulled out the other notes. "Because this was all together. Hidden in a folder that was supposed to be tax records."

Casey looked at them, nodding. "These are the names you found." Then she frowned. "What's Blue Dragons?"

"My initial thought was a fraternity or club of some sort. I asked Vasher. He said cops would take weapons and money from crime scenes. Said it was before his time, though."

"Well, if that's the case, then—" Casey shrugged.

"Then why was my dad interested in it?"

Casey met her gaze. "Maybe they had a resurrection."

"Maybe so. He was following them." She picked up the notes that were legible. "These notes are recaps of stakeouts—or surveillance—it seems." Tori put those down and took the notes that were in code, looking at them. "But what the hell does this mean? Why put some of his notes in code but not the others?"

"Maybe he knew someone was watching him. Maybe he was paranoid about the case. Maybe—"

"Maybe he knew he was delving into something that would blow up on him," Tori said. "Maybe he knew it went higher up than just a few cops on the street."

Casey shook her head. "But why, Tori? If his captain or lieutenant or whoever had him investigating these Blue Dragons, then why wasn't it brought to light when he was killed?"

"Maybe they didn't think it was related."

"Oh, come on. You've got one of your detectives secretly investigating this, surely you're going to think it's related. Especially an unmotivated murder that takes out a whole goddamn family."

"I've got copies of the file. I've been over it a hundred times. There was no evidence whatsoever. Speculation was that it was a current case or a past case. And current, meaning the four that we pulled. There was never even a hint of anything else. All that's in the file is interviews with those cases that obviously turned up nothing. There are a few lists of really old cases that they thought could have been linked—revenge killings—but nothing panned out. And as you know, I made a horrible witness." She leaned back in her chair. "That always haunted me, you know. Like if I could have described the guy, could have told them more, then maybe…"

"You were a twelve-year-old kid in shock, Tori. The fact that you turned out so great—and I mean that sincerely—is a miracle in itself."

Tori smiled at her, this woman who had become her best friend. "Thank you. But great? I don't know. If Sam hadn't come into my life, if you hadn't, I may still be that bitter, jaded person who no one liked and no one wanted to work with."

Casey squeezed her arm. "But you're not." She pointed to the notes. "So, what are you going to do?"

"The guy that's hacking into our system, I—"

"You actually went through with that?"

"Yeah." She'd forgotten about Simon. She quickly opened her laptop and pulled up her email. There was one from Boris with an attachment. "He got it already."

Casey frowned. "Boris? Who the hell is Boris?"

"He's a hacker. In Russia, I believe."

"Oh my god! You've lost your freakin' mind! In *Russia*?"

Tori laughed. "It's a fake name, O'Connor. He's just covering his tracks." She hesitated before opening the email, then decided against it. She wanted to look over it on her own before filling Casey in. "Anyway, this guy is super smart. I'm going to give him these notes and see if he can decrypt it or decode it or whatever."

"You trust him? I mean, what if it reveals something. Like—"

"I've got to trust him."

"And he works for the FBI?"

"I can't say."

"Come on, Hunter. You already said you had a friend at the FBI. What I'm saying is, why the hell would he do this for you? He could lose his job. He—"

"That's why it's Boris from Russia that I'm dealing with. So that if somebody finds out, they won't know it's him."

"They'll trace it back. Hell, they can find out anything."

"They who, O'Connor? CIU?"

"I don't know. Maybe."

Tori pointed at her. "This is why I didn't want you involved. If I get busted, if something happens, there's no need for you to take any heat for it. Because I'll say it again, I don't need a goddamn babysitter."

"And I'll say it again, you're being a stubborn ass."

"I'm going to interview these guys. Alone, O'Connor. If you feel like you need to follow me and keep watch, then do what you've got to do. But you're not going to be involved. Period."

Casey stared at her. "Fine. I'll follow from a distance."

"Suit yourself. Now, shouldn't you be doing some real police work. I don't want Malone getting suspicious."

Casey pointed at the laptop. "Aren't you going to open the email?"

"Yes."

They stared at each other in silence, then Casey smiled. "Oh, I see. You want to wait until I'm gone."

"I want to go over it uninterrupted, yes. And decide my plan of action. I want to start interviewing them today, if I can."

"Then what?"

"Then I'll see what I've got."

"And you'll let me know what's going on?"

"Yes."

"Okay, Hunter. You're probably right. If I'm following you around, Malone's going to wonder where the hell I am." Casey stood up. "I'm going to swing by Griffin's place again, interview the neighbor one more time."

"Why? You got something new?"

"No, no. Just to say I did. Got to account for my whereabouts today, you know." Casey went to the office door, then turned around and pointed her finger at her. "Don't you do anything stupid, Hunter."

Tori gave a quick smile. "Promise."

Casey grinned. "Yeah, right. See you later."

As soon as she was gone, Tori opened the email from Boris. It was short and straight to the point. "Attached is the information you contracted for." Nothing else. She clicked on the attachment. It was a spreadsheet with three tabs. The first was the list of names, their current addresses and phone numbers and a brief account of their retirement and subsequent working history. One was highlighted in yellow—Casper. Deceased. The second tab was their shift schedule during those years and what division they fell under. Curiously, there were only three divisions. Central, which covered downtown and the Deep Ellum entertainment district. Southeast, which encompassed Little Mexico. And South Central, a high crime area.

She glanced over it, then opened the third tab. This one was a list of commanders and where her guys fell under them. There were five—four lieutenants and a captain. She noticed her uncle's name—James Hunter. He had been a lieutenant at the time. One of the five was in yellow—Harken—now deceased. But another two were highlighted in blue. A lieutenant, Adam Staley. There was a note beside his name. *Killed in his home. Very recent.* She frowned, then went to the second name in blue. A captain. Robert Brewster. There was also a note beside his name. *Killed two weeks before your father. Car accident. Suspicious.*

"Brewster?"

She leaned back in her chair. *Brewster.* The name had been in her father's notes, yes, but there was something else familiar about it. Then she got up, hurrying over to the drawer where she kept the copies of her father's file. She flipped through the pages, pages she'd gone over hundreds of times over the years. She stopped when she saw it. Captain Brewster was over homicide.

She stared at the wall, seeing the pieces fall into place. Captain Brewster had her father investigating the Blue Dragons. But Brewster died. That's why no one suspected a connection between the Blue Dragons and her father's death. Brewster was the only one who knew about the investigation.

"Son of a bitch," she murmured. "Did they kill Brewster too?"

She flipped back through the file, going to the beginning, finding the two detectives who were assigned to her father's case—Hamilton and Jaworski. She went back to her laptop, finding them on the spreadsheet. Homicide. They reported to Lieutenant McMillan. Lieutenant McMillan reported to Captain Brewster. Stood to reason her father would have also reported to McMillan. And what about this Lieutenant Staley? He was in narcotics, not homicide. She grabbed the bridge of her nose. Killed in his home? What kind of killed?

She needed to get in touch with Simon but didn't dare email. Could she chance a call? No. She was just paranoid enough of getting caught that she didn't want anything to trace back to him. Instead, she called Sikes.

"Hey, Hunter. Thought you were taking a few days off."

"Yeah, I am. Listen, can you do me a favor?"

"Sure. What is it?"

She paced in the room, wondering how many questions John would have. "I need you to call someone for me. From the office phone, not your cell."

He paused, then replied slowly. "Okay. Who?"

"Look, I'm going to give you a number. Just call it, ask him to meet me for lunch. Same place. Got it?" She could picture John's face in a frown.

"That makes no sense, Hunter."

"It'll make sense to him."

"What's going on? Why don't you call him yourself?"

She blew out her breath. "Can you do this for me, Sikes? Without all the goddamn questions?"

"Jesus. You don't have to bite my head off. What's the number?"

"Thanks." She paused before giving it to him. "And don't tell anyone."

CHAPTER NINETEEN

Casey rang the doorbell, then knocked several times. "Mr. Alton? You home?" She didn't really anticipate getting any new information from him, but she thought after a couple of days, maybe he might have remembered something.

"Who's there?" came a suspicious voice from behind the door.

"It's Detective O'Connor, Mr. Alton. I have a few more questions, if you don't mind."

Steve Alton peeked from around the door, smiling slightly when he recognized her. "Since the thing with Charlie, I'm afraid I've been extra careful," he explained. "Come in, please."

"Thank you. I just need a minute of your time."

"It's no problem, Detective. Truth be told, since Charlie's been gone, I don't get to visit with people much."

"He was your closest friend then?"

He nodded. "At my age, friends are harder to come by."

She followed him into his kitchen where it looked like he was making lunch. A wooden cutting board containing a bright red tomato and some onion slices sat near the sink. "Oh, sorry. I guess I forgot about the time. Didn't mean to interrupt."

"No worries. I make a ham sandwich every day for lunch. That's been my menu ever since my wife died." He began to rinse some lettuce that was in a colander in the sink. "I can make you one if you like," he offered.

"Oh, no. Thanks, though. I'll need to get back soon." She leaned against the counter with her hip, watching him. "Have you seen any strangers around? Like maybe a silver car that doesn't belong?"

He looked at her and shook his head. "No. But then, I haven't been out as much as I normally am. I did see some police officers earlier taking down the crime scene tape."

"Yes. The forensic team got everything they needed. I believe Mr. Griffin's closest relative was a nephew. I imagine he'll get the house."

"He didn't talk much about his family, but I know he had a sister die recently. Charlie was gone four days, I think it was, for the funeral."

"After his sister died—which I believe was only a month or so ago—did anything out of the ordinary happen? I mean, did anything strange start happening?"

"Strange?" Mr. Alton paused and stared out his kitchen window, apparently thoroughly thinking back over the last month. "Well, his doctor visits became more frequent but that had been going on for six months or more already."

"Did he mention anyone calling him? Or watching him?"

"No. But I will say, he became a little different. Not his normally cheerful self. Like he was preoccupied with something." He plucked two pieces of bread from the loaf and put them on the cutting board. "We'd visit across the fence if we were both out in the back yard. Or out front there too. I don't guess a day went by that we didn't chat about something." He slathered mayo on the bread methodically. "It seems like the last few days before he was killed, he didn't really want to stay out and talk. Like he was nervous about something. I blamed it on all those doctor's visits. He never wanted to talk about that."

"Did he ever mention people he used to work with? Or did anyone come around to visit?"

He shook his head as he placed two thick slices of ham on the mayo. "Never had any visitors that I recall. And he'd been retired for a while now. Even when he worked, he wasn't very talkative about his job."

Casey felt her stomach rumble as she watched him assemble his sandwich, adding lettuce, tomatoes, and onions to the ham. He was doing it so carefully—meticulously—that she knew this must truly be his daily noontime ritual as he'd said.

"Well, I've taken up enough of your time, Mr. Alton. I don't want to interrupt your lunch."

He turned then and she glimpsed a touch of sadness—loneliness—in his eyes. "Call me Steve. And it's been no bother."

No, she imagined it wasn't a bother. Since his friend Charles Griffin was gone, she guessed his days were indeed lonely. She touched his shoulder lightly.

"I can see myself out, Steve. Thank you."

"Anytime, Detective O'Connor."

She smiled at him. "It's Casey."

CHAPTER TWENTY

Tori waited beside the tree, same as last time, hoping that Sikes had gotten through to Simon. And hoping that Simon would meet her. She assumed he would. Why else had he mentioned that Brewster's death had been suspicious? She did feel a little bit incognito, though. She had on dark sunglasses and a ball cap, much as Simon had worn yesterday.

She glanced at her watch impatiently, then peered down the sidewalk. He was a minute late, but there he came, wearing the same blue cap, minus the sunglasses this time. As before, he walked past her, and she fell into step beside him.

"Thanks for coming."

"Thanks for not calling me directly."

She smiled. "Maybe we need a secret hotline."

His eyes actually lit up. "We should get burner phones, Hunter. That's what we should do."

She was surprised at his suggestion and even more surprised that he was serious. He held up a small paper bag.

"I brought my lunch today."

"That's fine. I had a late breakfast anyway," she lied. She simply didn't want to take the time to order something.

The table they'd used yesterday was occupied so they found another nearer the playground. It was mostly empty, only two kids swinging while two women stood nearby, chatting and laughing.

"You have questions?" he asked as he unwrapped his sandwich.

"Let's start with Brewster. He was my father's commander. You think suspicious death?"

He stared at her for a moment, then picked up his sandwich. "I hope you don't mind, but I did a little digging into your past. Well, not yours exactly."

"My family?"

"Yes. By all accounts, there were no leads. But the two detectives who were assigned the case are on your list."

"Yes, they are."

"What is this list of names anyway?" he asked before taking a bite.

Tori sighed. Should she confide in him? She didn't really know him. When she'd worked for the FBI, she'd had a handful of dealings with him, one of which got him suspended. Did she really trust him? He seemed to sense her hesitation.

"The more I know, the more I can help you."

She arched an eyebrow. "Why do you want to help me?"

It was Simon's turn to sigh. "My job is boring. I don't really get to do any of the fun stuff. I gather information and someone else gets to play with it, not me. And, well, call me a softie but reading about your family kinda made me see you in a different light."

Tori took her sunglasses off. "Not the bitch from hell?"

He laughed lightly. "Don't worry. Your reputation is still intact."

"Ask anyone—I've mellowed."

He shrugged. "Right. But I don't care if they call you a bitch. You haven't been one to me."

She met his gaze and nodded. "Thanks."

He took another bite of his sandwich. "So? The list?" he asked as he chewed.

She leaned her elbows on the table, staring at him. "My father was secretly investigating something. I say secretly because his partner didn't know, and he kept notes at home. I think Brewster ordered the investigation."

Simon nodded. "Brewster died in a car accident, and two weeks later your father is killed."

"Yes."

"What was he investigating?"

"I'm not sure, really. Some of the notes that I found were in code. Only a few pages were readable. Then the list of names. And he had other notes, like reminders or questions to himself. But he had written Blue Dragons several times."

"What is that?"

"According to Vasher—that's my father's old partner—the Blue Dragons was a group of cops. They took cash from crime scenes, drug money probably. They took the drugs too. Other stuff. But he claims the upper brass shut it down in the '70s or even earlier than that." She shifted a little, pulling out the folded notes from her jeans pocket. "These are the notes that are in some sort of code. I was hoping maybe it might make sense to you."

He put his sandwich down and took them. As he studied them, his eyes moved quickly over each page as he nodded. "Cool."

"Cool?"

"Yeah. It is in code. You can tell they're words. We just have to find the key."

"How do we do that?"

He grinned. "Back in the old days, it would have taken a little time. Today? I can just feed this into an algorithm, and it'll translate it."

"Really?"

"Sure. But I don't want to do it at the office. I'll do it tonight at home."

"Are you married?"

He looked up, seemingly surprised by the question. "No. Well, not anymore."

"I see. Kids?"

"Nope. We weren't married long enough for that. She said I loved my computers more than her." He gave a sheepish smile. "What can I say?"

Tori laughed. "Great. Then I'll bring dinner."

"Dinner?"

"Yeah. I want to be there when you crack this. If that's okay."

"Yeah, okay. Sure."

"Good. Now tell me about Brewster." She pulled the notes from his hand. "And I'll keep these."

He picked up his sandwich again. "Brewster's car hit a concrete median at a high rate of speed. It was a fiery crash and there was an explosion."

"Why do you say it was suspicious? Was it investigated as such?"

"No. But I looked at the newspaper archives and read through the articles. There were three articles that I could find. One was simply a recount of the accident. Another was a writeup on the funeral. And a third was just a compilation of the three, really. But witness accounts of the accident said it appeared he was unable to steer the vehicle." He took a sip of water before continuing. "That could mean it locked up and he couldn't turn the wheel or else the steering column malfunctioned or something and he *could* turn the wheel, but he couldn't steer the car, couldn't control it. Just guessing at all that. As far as I could tell, I don't think there was ever any question that it was anything other than an accident. But with that kind of a fiery crash, I'd suspect some kind of an accelerant was used."

"Are you thinking someone jacked with his car?"

Simon gave a quick smile. "That's what happens in the movies. But I couldn't find where anyone questioned it. There was no mention of a lawsuit or anything like that."

She nodded. "Okay. I'll buy it. What about the other two? Harken? Staley?"

"Yeah. Strange. Harken died last week. I assume natural causes. All I read was his obit. Nothing out of the ordinary and he was in his early 80s. Now Staley? That's different. He lived in Denton. I didn't have time to dig a lot, only what was in the newspaper. I thought, if you want, I could get into the Denton PD's servers and try to read the file."

"What did you find from the paper?"

"Home invasion gone bad. Very sad, actually. His wife had a stroke and isn't expected to make it. He'd just come back from the hospital. Police think it was intended to be a burglary and the killer thought the house was empty."

"When was this?"

"Let's see. I think it was Monday."

Her eyebrows shot up. "This *past* Monday?"

"Yes. Why?"

"Because that's when Charles Griffin was killed."

It was Simon's turn to arch an eyebrow. "Who is Charles Griffin?"

She shook her head. "Too much to go into now, but if you could get some more info from the Denton PD, that would be helpful."

"Okay. I can do that."

She glanced at her watch. "I should go. I want to try to hit up a couple of these guys today. Get their story."

He nodded. "What time do you want to crack that code?"

"You tell me. I'll be there."

"How about you pick me up at five? I usually ride the bus."

"Sure. Out front?"

"No. Here at the park. It'll be safer. No one should see us."

She got up and nodded. "I'll be here. Thanks, Simon." She paused. "Pizza?"

He shrugged. "That's fine, sure."

She gave him a pat on his shoulder as she walked away. "See you at five."

CHAPTER TWENTY-ONE

Tori parked on the street under the shade of a large tree. She double-checked the address on the spreadsheet she'd printed out. Peter Dewberry. He retired from the force at age fifty-nine as a sergeant, after thirty-six years on the job. He then worked as a security guard until age sixty-six, when he retired for good. He was currently seventy-two.

She folded the spreadsheet and tucked it into the console before getting out. She'd rehearsed questions in her mind on the drive over, but right now, as she headed to the front door, she couldn't remember a one of them. For that matter, she didn't know why she picked Peter Dewberry to start with. He wasn't the first name on the list nor the last.

She pushed the doorbell, then waited somewhat patiently. No, that was a lie. She waited only a few seconds before pushing it again. She finally heard footsteps, then a man's voice.

"Who is it?"

She held her shield up to the peephole. "Police."

The door opened fully, and a rather tall man stood there, his hair an attractive salt-and-pepper mix with a neatly trimmed and matching goatee. He gave her a friendly smile.

"A lady detective. How nice. What can I do for you?"

"I'm Detective Hunter. Are you Peter Dewberry?"

"I certainly am." He held his hand out and she shook it. "Pete. Call me Pete."

"I'm wondering if you have a few minutes?"

"Sure do. You're saving me from heading out back to weed that new flowerbed I put in. That's the thing about being retired," he said as he went back into the house. "Got time on your hands and the next thing you know, you're digging out a huge ass chunk of grass to put in flowers 'cause you know the missus would like that."

She followed him inside, closing the door as he'd already disappeared from sight. She hurried after him, finding him in the kitchen.

"I was about to have a beer. You want one?"

"Better not."

"Ah. Yeah. On duty and all."

"Well, technically not on duty."

"No?" He took two beers from the fridge and motioned for her to sit. "I drink one beer each afternoon about three o'clock, sometimes earlier like today. Usually take it out to the back porch and visit with the missus then. Just one. Well, unless it's godawful hot and I'm out working the flowers, then I'll have two." He placed the second beer in front of her. "At six o'clock, after I have my dinner, then I have a splash or three of whiskey. It gets me through."

"I see. Well, I hope your wife won't mind that I'm here. I won't stay long."

Pete Dewberry gave a hearty laugh. "Don't know if she'll mind. Probably not. Don't know if she even hears me, but it makes me feel good."

She arched an eyebrow, not knowing what he meant by that.

"My Dottie passed on just last year. Had a nasty case of the flu that she couldn't shake."

"I'm so sorry."

"Hit me hard, I don't mind sayin'. Got no kids." He winked at her and laughed again. "Not for lack of trying, I'll say that."

She couldn't help but smile. While his eyes held that faraway sense of grief—loss—his demeanor showed none of it. He seemed inordinately cheerful.

"Now, Detective Hunter, what brings you around? You're not on duty, you say, so I don't guess it's police business. You doing some fundraising or something? Looking for volunteers?"

She shook her head at that. "No, no. Nothing like that." She took the beer bottle that had been placed in front of her and took a sip. "I'm actually interested in some old history. Back when you were in your early days."

"On the force?"

"Yes."

"Well, fire away with questions. I'll see how much I remember. Because the truth is, I tried to leave all that behind when I retired."

She thought she'd start with the most important thing. "Have you ever heard of the Blue Dragons?"

His eyes widened. "Blue Dragons? That's some ancient history for sure. To hear the old-timers tell it, it was a club of scoundrels was all. Started back in the 1950s, I think. Could have been even earlier than that. Record keeping wasn't so good back then, you know. It would be easy to take something from a crime scene." He rubbed his goatee absently. "Wasn't so good when I was first there either. Anyway, it started with street cops, I hear. If they stumbled upon some cash—drug money, mostly—they shoved it into pockets, and everyone looked the other way. That went on for years. By the mid '60s, there were more checks and balances, but still, drug money flowed, and cops skimmed off the top, then logged what was left. The Blue Dragons is what they were known as. It didn't take no time before sides were drawn."

"Sides meaning good cops, bad cops?"

"Yeah. They knew who they could trust and who would go to the brass if something was amiss. They even had a clubhouse. A rickety dive of a bar in old Deep Ellum."

"How do you know all this?"

"That ancient history came up because some fools tried to start it up again when I was on the force."

She nodded. "Okay. So go on. They had a clubhouse."

"Yeah. Had a back room set up for them. Pool table, a jukebox, and bottles of booze. And whatever drugs they confiscated. Big ass party, to hear it told."

"How many cops?"

"Back then? Forty or fifty, they claimed. But it was a strain on the morale, not to mention the drug use that started up. The brass shut it down. Cops got suspended, cops got let go, cops got transferred. They broke up the gang, so to speak. By the early 1970s it was shut down for good. I started on the force in 1974, and it was still fresh enough that nobody wanted to even talk about it."

"So that was the end of the Blue Dragons?"

"For a while, yep. It was in the late '80s that whispers were going around that the Blue Dragons had formed again. But it was real hush-hush this time. Before, they were all out in the open. An unguarded secret, as they say. This time, though? Like I said, secret, mostly rumors. So much so that everyone thought that was all there was to it. Rumors. You couldn't find a single officer who would admit to being a part of that gang. But then it started happening. Drug busts where the anticipated cash was less. Or where they were expecting so many kilos of cocaine or weed and there'd be half that."

"Did you know anyone involved?"

He cocked his head sideways at her. "Heard rumors, heard names mentioned, but like I said, no one would fess up to it." He stared at her. "I also heard they were doing a low-key type of investigation, trying to find out who the ringleader was of this new version of the Dragons."

She nodded. "So what happened with that? They bust up the gang again?"

"Can't rightly say. Heard rumors of murder for hire, extortion. Heard there was tampering of evidence. Or worse."

"Worse?"

"Planted evidence."

"So basically dirty cops."

"The dirtiest of the dirty. Money has a way of changing people. And influencing them, if you know what I mean."

"You think it could still be going on?"

He shrugged. "Don't know that it ever stopped. But guys move on, guys retire, new blood comes in. Hell, got cameras everywhere now. A cop would be taking a chance nowadays, that's for sure." He drained the last of his beer and put the bottle down. "Why so interested?"

"I told you, just wanted a history lesson."

"Bullshit. I've been a cop too long." He leaned forward. "What's really going on?"

She ignored that question, asking one of her own instead. "Who was your partner?"

"Partner? Had a few different partners over the years."

"During this time. Say early '90s."

He looked up as if thinking back that far. "That would have been Paul Douglas. They used to tease us. Peter and Paul. All we needed was a Mary," he said with a laugh.

Paul Douglas was also on her list. "Was he involved?"

"With this gang?" He rubbed his goatee again. "Not out in the open, no. I never saw him do anything. But I will say that before we rode together, he worked a beat in Little Mexico. Might have had an opportunity there." He shrugged. "We didn't ride together too long. Not even a year, if I recall."

"Do you remember when Jason Hunter was killed?"

He had a slight frown on his face. "Jason Hunter? Oh, the detective. He and his family…" His eyes narrowed. "Wait a minute. You're—"

"His daughter."

"Well, I'll be." He nodded. "Yeah, sure. I remember that. Case went cold real fast."

"Yeah, it did."

He stared at her thoughtfully. "You think this is all related?"

This man—Pete Dewberry—was a complete stranger to her. She knew nothing about him, didn't know his character. Yet something in his eyes conveyed his true self. This man was trustworthy.

"I came upon some notes that my father had. He was the one investigating the Blue Dragons."

Pete leaned back in his chair, once again fingering his goatee. "And then he's murdered."

"Yes."

"If I may ask, Detective Hunter, how did you come looking for me?"

Tori smiled. "My father had a list of names. You were one of them."

At this, Pete laughed heartedly. "My oh my. You mean he thought I was part of this gang?"

Tori shrugged. "I just have a list of names. I thought I'd interview them—like I'm doing you—and see what happens."

"See if you can shake somebody out, you mean?"

"Something like that."

"But you're doing this on your own? You said you were off duty."

"My lieutenant doesn't know. I haven't shared with him the notes I found. If I did, he'd have to hand it all over to CIU—Criminal Investigative Unit."

He snorted at that. "Yeah, I remember CIU. Never had any use for them. Thought they were all better than everybody else."

"Still do." Even Sam would have to agree with that.

"Who were some of the names?"

"Paul Douglas was one."

"You don't say. He had a friend he hung with. Bexley was his name. Thomas Bexley. I never trusted him. Shifty eyes."

Tori nodded. "Yeah. He's on the list too."

"Well, you should be careful. We're all old men now, but don't think for a minute that any one of us have forgotten how to use a gun."

"Do you ever keep in touch with any of them?"

"At first I did, sure. Meet up at the bar for a quick drink sometimes. When I retired from the force, I went to work as a security guard. Ended up at a bank. Godawful boring job, that was." He smiled, then laughed. "I kept hoping some fool would come in and try to rob the place. But I lost touch with the guys after a while. Me and the missus liked our own company, I guess."

"She's been gone a year now, you said?"

He nodded slowly. "Last month it was a year. On the twenty-first." He glanced to the window, a wistful look on his face. "Had me a hard time of it that day. You don't know how much you're going to miss someone until they're gone."

"I'm sorry."

He raised an eyebrow. "You married?"

Tori nodded. "Yes. Her name is Sam. She's a cop too."

"Her? I see."

Tori stood. "I should go. Thanks for the beer. And for your time."

He got up too. "I enjoyed the visit, Detective Hunter."

"Please, call me Tori."

"Okay. If you have more questions, come on back around. I'm usually always here." He jerked his thumb toward the window. "Or out back keeping up Dottie's flowers."

"Thank you, Pete. I appreciate it." She held her hand out, shaking his firmly. "Perhaps I'll swing by sometime."

He smiled and nodded. "I'd like that."

She'd taken an instant liking to the man and figured she'd come back whether she had more questions or not. She got back inside her car and pulled out the spreadsheet, putting a checkmark beside Peter Dewberry's name. She glanced over the others, trying to decide who to go see next. She flipped the page over, staring at the commanders. Maybe she should go visit her uncle. He'd been a lieutenant then. Surely if there were rumors going around, he would have heard them.

Of course, she and her uncle didn't really have a relationship. He'd most likely be shocked if she dropped by. Didn't matter. She'd go see him and then call it a day. She'd start fresh in the morning. Because if Simon could decipher her father's notes, it might lead to a clearer path instead of randomly interviewing these guys.

CHAPTER TWENTY-TWO

Her call went to voice mail, and she smiled as she drove, listening to Sam's familiar voice before speaking. "I'm going to miss dinner tonight. I'm on my way to see Uncle James, then I'm going to..." She paused. "Well, I'm going to meet someone for pizza. He's going to try to crack the code on those notes my father left." She paused again. "I love you, Sam. I'll see you tonight. Hopefully I won't be too late."

As she pulled into her uncle's driveway, it occurred to her that not only had she never been to this house before, but she also hadn't been to his previous house either. This was in an older, well-kept neighborhood with large trees and equally large homes. Best she recalled, they'd moved here the year he'd retired from the force. She'd gone to his retirement party, thrown by his kids at some fancy restaurant. It was the last time she'd had any conversations with them, her uncle included. How long ago was that now? Ten, twelve years? More?

She paused at the door, taking a deep breath. Her Uncle James and his kids were the only family she had left, yet she had a hard time considering them family. Her mother had had one older brother who never married. He'd been living in Arizona when her family had been killed. He was gone now too. Aunt Carol and Louise were long gone too. But no. This was blood family only. Not *family*. Sam. Casey and Leslie. They were her family. James Hunter was nearly a stranger to her now. In fact, he'd always been a stranger, hadn't he? She could count on one hand the number of times their families had mixed when she'd been a kid. No wonder they hadn't wanted to take her in permanently.

She punched the doorbell without another thought. It opened quickly, and Aunt Judith stood there, a surprised look on her face.

"Why, Tori. My god, how long has it been?"

Tori took in her smart suit, her graying hair, still neatly styled as she'd always worn it. "Been a while, yes."

"Well, come in. I was actually on my way out. Shopping. Then I'm meeting Lee Ann for dinner. But James is here."

"How is Lee Ann?" she asked politely, not really caring one way or the other.

"Oh, she's as busy as ever. She's a grandmother now herself, if you can believe that. It's so exciting for me and James to be great-grandparents."

"I'm sure it is. Well, don't let me keep you. I just wanted a word with Uncle James."

"Of course. Come in," she said again, moving aside for her to enter. "You'll find James in his recliner. Never thought the day would come that he'd be hooked on daytime talk shows."

Tori simply gave her an appropriate smile and followed her inside. The foyer opened up into a formal—and pristine—living room. She glanced around, seeing nothing personal. Everything matched perfectly and seemed to fit a theme. White.

"A waste of space, James likes to say," her aunt commented. "Truthfully, we only use this room during Christmas." She pointed to a corner. "The tree goes there. I'll admit, I go a bit overboard on decorations, but the kids love it. Our grandkids are mostly all grown up and, of course, starting to have babies of their own now. Dawn's kids are the youngest with Kyle a senior in high school, but it's quite a houseful."

Tori nodded but said nothing. Down a hallway—with a half-wall on one side separating it from a dining room—and past the kitchen, she followed Aunt Judith into another room. This room was too large to be a den. Not one but two sofas, arranged in an L-shape, framed a fireplace. Four recliners were in a semi-circle facing a large TV. A game show of some sort was on, and her uncle was watching with rapt attention.

"James? You have company, dear."

He turned then, shock showing on his face as he spied her. "Well, I'll be goddamned," he muttered.

He got up, his shoulders a little more stooped than she remembered. He would be in his late seventies, she guessed. Seventy-eight, seventy-nine even. He held his hand out to her and she shook it.

"Hello, Uncle James."

"What brings you around? Or is it about the gun you found?"

"You heard?"

"Oh, sure. I'm out of the loop now for most things, but I still keep in touch with some of the fellas." He motioned to one of the other recliners. "Come. Sit."

"I was about to head out, James, but I can get you something to drink first, if you'd like," Judith offered.

"I can get us something if we need it. You go on," he said as he muted the TV.

Aunt Judith glanced at her. "Good to see you again, Tori. You should come around more often."

Right. But she offered a smile. "Sure. Good to see you."

Instead of sitting, Tori stood next to the TV. Uncle James resumed his seat in his recliner. He'd aged a lot since she'd seen him last. His face was lined with wrinkles, and she recalled that he used to be a heavy smoker.

"So you found the killer?"

She met his gaze, nodding. "It appears so. Circumstantial, of course."

"What was his name?"

"Charles Griffin. We can't find any connection to my father, though."

"Why would there be a connection?"

"A motive for the killing," she clarified.

"Ah, yes. Are you still convinced it was a hit? There was never any evidence of that," he reminded her. "Random killing is what the detectives thought."

Right. Hamilton and Jaworski. Two men on her list. She finally moved to sit down, getting right to the point. "What do you know about the Blue Dragons?"

His eyebrows rose, then he laughed. A nervous laugh, she thought.

"Now that's a name I haven't heard in a while. That got started back in the day, before I came on board. What we learned about it was mostly rumors—gossip—and probably mostly exaggerated at that. Most of those guys got kicked off the force. To hear most tell it, it started in 1952."

"What did they do?"

"Stupid shit from what I heard. Padding their pockets with drug money. Doing a bust, then taking the drugs for themselves. Or busting up a gang of thieves, then taking what they wanted before logging in anything. Weren't cameras on everything back then. They could get away with that shit."

"So what happened to the Blue Dragons?"

"Shut 'em down. Like I said, most of them lost their jobs."

"What about later?"

"Later?"

"Any rumors that it started up again back when you were a lieutenant?"

He stared at her for a moment, finally nodding. "Oh, yeah, I heard some things. But it was nothing. Mostly guys getting together for poker and whiskey, nothing more. After what happened the first go 'round, guys would have been crazy to start that shit up again." He shook his head. "No, I don't think it was anything more than rumors."

"You remember any names?"

"Names?"

"You know, names mentioned in those rumors."

He met her gaze, his brows drawn together. "What's all this about, Tori?"

"Nothing really. Came up in an investigation, that's all."

"What came up?"

"The Blue Dragons. No one seems to know what it was or who was involved."

He picked up the remote, flipping it around in his hand. "They busted that up way back in the early 1970s, Tori. It had already been going on for twenty years or more by then, I heard. Like I said, I doubt anyone would have been stupid enough to start that up again. Besides, what could they do? Everybody's got goddamn cameras now."

"Not in the '80s, early '90s."

"I was a lieutenant then, Tori. I would have known if that was going on. Like I said, guys might have *called* themselves Blue Dragons, but it was poker and whiskey, nothing more." He shook his head and she noticed that he didn't meet her eyes. "There's nothing to look into there."

"Yeah. Probably." She got up. "But I thought if anyone would know, it would be you. Especially when you transferred to CIU. They're always in the know about everything, right?"

He smiled at that. "Yeah, they like to think they are. I never fit in over there. They had a different way of doing things than what I was used to."

"Yes. That's what Sam tells me."

"Sam?"

"My wife. Samantha Kennedy."

"Wife?" He shifted his eyes away from her. "Oh. Right. I had forgotten. I guess with Carol and all, you never stood a chance."

"Excuse me?" she asked sharply.

He held his hand up. "Nothing. Your Aunt Carol was always an odd bird, that's all I'm saying."

Tori squared her shoulders. "Aunt Carol and Louise took me in when you would not. They gave me a home." Her eyes narrowed. "Don't you dare denigrate them."

"I meant no disrespect, Tori. I—"

"Didn't you? Carol and Louise gave me a loving home. I couldn't have asked for more." She met his gaze. "They were always supportive of me."

He held his hands out. "We had a house full, Tori. There wasn't room for another. You know that."

She gave him a half-smile. "I'm thankful, actually. God knows how I would have turned out if I'd lived with you instead." She moved away from him. "I should go. Thanks for your time."

He followed after her. "Carol was my only sister. The oldest of us kids. I wasn't trying to denigrate her, as you say. I—"

"Spare me the bullshit. Because you know what? It doesn't really matter, and I simply don't care. You made it clear all those years ago that you wanted no part of me. And when I came back and joined the force, you made it doubly clear that I wasn't a part of your family or your life. I'd lost Carol and I'd lost Louise." She raised her hand. "And of course I'd lost my whole family. It was just me back then. No one else. Yet you couldn't be bothered. So I know you and I aren't *really* family."

"Tori—"

"No. I'm sorry I came by, actually. I thought maybe you might have some information that would help. Sorry to have wasted your time." She paused, meeting his gaze. "And mine."

She retraced her steps through the house, hating that she'd let him get to her. She slammed the front door a little too loudly. "Fucker," she muttered as she walked away. Why the hell had she even bothered? She didn't need him.

She'd find out the answers herself.

CHAPTER TWENTY-THREE

"You heard from her?"

"She left voice mail," Sam said, tucking her phone against her shoulder as she dried her hands. "She said she was going to see her uncle, then out for pizza with someone."

"What? Her uncle? I didn't think she ever talked to him," Casey said.

"She doesn't."

"Should we be worried?"

Sam smiled as she put her phone on the counter and switched it to speaker. "Because she went to see her uncle?" She opened the fridge, hoping there was something inside to eat.

"No. Because she's going out for pizza with somebody besides us."

"I assume it's her FBI hacker friend."

"Yeah, who is that guy, anyway?"

Sam hesitated. "I shouldn't say. They're being all secret about it."

Casey laughed. "Yeah. Boris. From Russia."

"Yes. His idea. Say, what are you and Les doing for dinner?"

"She's not home yet. But I was contemplating whipping something up."

"Really?"

"No, not really. I was going to order something. You want to come over?"

"Can I?"

"Of course. Come on."

"Thanks. I'll bring wine."

She stared at her phone for the longest time, wondering if she should call Tori. She'd sounded fine on the voice mail. But her uncle? What in the world had possessed her to go see him? They had no relationship whatsoever. In fact, since she and Tori had been together, she couldn't recall a single time that they had even spoken. He'd already been retired by then, so it wasn't like they had ever run into him.

But no, she wouldn't call her. Tori was working. Tori was in her own space right now, and Sam needed to let her be. Whether anything would come of this or not, she didn't know, but she knew she needed to give Tori this time. If it ended without Tori finding the answers she sought, Sam at least hoped it would give her some closure. Even if she never found out who had ordered the hit, the man who had been in her house that fateful night—the man who had pulled the trigger—was now known. And he was dead. Would that be enough for Tori?

Sam stared at the wall, slowly shaking her head. No. It wouldn't be enough, she knew. Tori needed to know who was behind it. In all these years, this was as close as she'd ever been. Sam didn't think she'd rest until she knew the truth.

CHAPTER TWENTY-FOUR

Simon got in and slammed the door. "Did anyone follow you?"

Tori rolled her eyes. "Who?"

Simon glanced behind them as she drove away. "I work for the FBI. I know what all goes on. I hear things."

"This isn't a spy movie." She made the block, then pulled into traffic. "And order the pizza, would you? I'm starving." She punched in her passcode before handing him her phone. "Use the app on my phone, just change the address to yours."

"What kind of pizza?"

"I usually get the one with everything. Get what you want."

"They've got your usual order saved. That'll be fine I guess."

Tori's stomach rumbled just thinking about food. She'd had a bite of Sam's toast that morning, nothing more.

Five o'clock traffic had them practically crawling, and she sighed heavily. "I interviewed a couple of guys today."

"Oh yeah. Did you find out anything?"

"One guy, Pete Dewberry, was very forthcoming. Knew a little history on the Blue Dragons. Said pretty much what Vasher had." She paused. "Then I went to see my uncle. James Hunter."

Simon's eyebrows rose. "He's on the list. I wondered if he was related to you."

"My father's brother. They were never close. Therefore, I'm not close to him."

"After your family...well, after they were gone, where did you go?"

"Not with him," she said quickly. "They didn't want me. I stayed there on and off." She paused before continuing. "I was...well, in counseling. In and out. Eventually his sister, my aunt Carol, took me away. Houston."

He nodded. "So did you learn anything from him?"

"No. He didn't think the Blue Dragons were active during that time. Said it was only rumors."

"But your father was investigating them?"

"Yes."

"So is he lying or he just didn't know?" Simon pointed up ahead. "Turn right at the light."

Tori changed lanes. "He was a lieutenant at the time. May have been out of the loop."

"Have you considered he was involved?"

"In the Blue Dragons? No. From what everyone says, it was street cops."

She turned at the light, and he motioned for her to keep going.

"I got into Denton PD's servers this afternoon."

She looked at him sharply. "From your office?"

He smiled "Had some downtime."

"What did you find out?"

"Not much more than what the paper said. They've got a vehicle on a security feed from the neighbor. Partial plate. No hits." He motioned with his hand. "There. On the left. Emerald Ridge."

"What kind of vehicle?"

He shook his head. "I don't remember. Sorry."

She turned into the entrance. "Why do they give apartments names like that?"

"Well, it's better than most. Lots of trees and plenty of greenspace." He held up a remote and the gate opened. "I'm in Building Three. Hang a right."

"Do you own a car?"

"I do. It's just easier to take the bus. They drop me off right in front of the building at ten minutes to eight each morning. There…park over there."

She did as he instructed. "Do I need a permit?"

"They only come around and check it at night. You'll be fine."

She followed him through some hedges and up a set of stairs. "How long have you lived here?"

"Oh, two years or so."

"After your divorce?"

"Yes."

She stood behind him while he unlocked his door. The inside was immaculate and hardly looked lived in. Until she spotted his desk, which took up half of his living room. While she wouldn't say it was cluttered, it was obviously where he spent most of his time. The chair looked to be as comfortable as a recliner. The desk held no less than four monitors.

"There's stuff in the fridge if you want something to drink," he offered. "I'm just going to change real quick."

"Okay. Sure."

The fridge, too, was neat and orderly. It also contained beer. She took out a bottle and twisted off the top. After her first swallow, it hit her that she'd had nothing to eat all day, but it tasted good all the same.

"I'll have one too," Simon said as he headed to his desk. He was wearing shorts and flip-flops, so unlike the computer geek she'd come to think of him as. That is until he slipped on the black-framed glasses that were lying there.

She brought him a bottle and placed it on the stone coaster that was to the left of his keyboard. She looked around, noting that the TV was strategically placed so he could see it from his chair.

"Your couch doesn't get much use, huh?"

He took a swallow of his beer. "I pretty much live right here."

"You're on a computer all day at work, then come home and do it some more?"

"This is fun stuff."

"What? Hacking into things?"

"Yeah. I actually get paid for some of it. I work for a penetration testing company."

"What's that? You try to hack into servers to see how secure they are?"

"Pretty much, yeah."

"And are you successful?"

He smiled. "Tops in the company."

"So why the FBI then?"

He pulled his keyboard closer and began typing. "They recruited me out of college. Good benefits. This other is just a parttime thing, for fun really." He held his hand out. "Let me see the notes."

She pulled them from her back pocket. "How are you going to do this?"

His fingers were nearly flying over the keys. "I have a tool for decrypting passwords. I modified it today to fit what we want. I'm going to try that first. If that doesn't work, I'll try an algorithm."

"Why do you have a tool for decrypting passwords? Is that legal?"

"Sure it's legal. Anybody can download one. Now if you want a really good one, you'd go out to the Dark Web for that."

"Is that what you do?"

"No. The company I work for supplied it. And of course, I've got access to one at work. But there are a lot of different ways to get into a server. You don't always need a password."

She stood behind him as he put in a couple of lines from her father's notes. It seemed like only a matter of seconds before the gibberish was rearranged into readable words.

"Bingo. Piece of cake," he said with a grin. "Let me put it all in and we'll see what we have."

"How did you do it so fast?"

"Do you really want to know how I rewrote the program?"

"No." She read the few words that did come up before Simon clicked out of it.

Felt someone following me today (it's Wednesday). Couldn't shake it. I—

A knock on the door made her jump, then she realized it was most likely the pizza. Instead of just opening the door though, she asked, "Who is it?"

"Pizza delivery."

She opened the door then, giving the young guy only a cursory glance as she took the box from him. "Thanks. Your tip was included on the order."

"Yes, ma'am. Thank you."

She closed the door quickly, then locked it. She placed the box on the short bar that separated the kitchen from the living room. "Plates?"

"Cabinet by the stove," he said without turning around.

She took out two plates, then grabbed a handful of napkins. She put two slices on each plate and took his over to him. He didn't seem to notice. Her stomach was rumbling by the time she took her first bite, and she moaned out loud.

"Is it that good?"

"I'm starving," she said around a mouthful. "First thing I've eaten all day."

He absently took a slice, biting off a large piece before putting the slice back down. Unlike her, there was no verbal indication that he even tasted it. His concentration appeared to be solely on his computer.

"Are these in order?" he asked, meaning the notes.

"I have no way of knowing. They're gibberish to me."

"Okay. This is what I've got so far," he said, pointing to the screen. "I'm just going to put in one page at a time, then we can try to get them in order."

"Okay. Would you print that out for me?" She waited by the printer, snatching the paper as soon as it was spit out.

Felt someone following me today (it's Wednesday). Couldn't shake it. I pulled into a pharmacy and went inside. Sure enough, spotted Jenson in his personal car. He parked at the far edge of the parking lot. Do they know I'm investigating? I've been so careful. My weekly meeting with Brewster is in the morning. Has someone been watching us? Do they know we've been meeting at the diner that early? (I think I'll call him and request a different meeting place and perhaps an hour earlier, although finding a diner open at 4:30 a.m. might be difficult.) (I'm being paranoid, thus using my old code when writing this! Surprisingly, it's still easy to read.)

Ran into James today. It was unusual as I haven't seen or spoken to him in several months. I still have a hard time believing he's involved in all this but maybe that's wishful thinking. He and McMillan are tight. And as I told Brewster, why would all four lieutenants meet? In the last three months that I've been following them, there is nothing to indicate that they have a relationship, other than McMillan and James, who have been to lunch several times. The others? No. While I have enough evidence on the officers (and Hamilton and Jaworski), there's little to point to the lieutenants, other than circumstantial. (And Staley and McMillan meeting after the drug bust.)

Tori rubbed her forehead. So her father thought Uncle James was involved. Maybe he was. Maybe that explained his nervousness today. She took out her phone, bringing up email. She opened the one from Boris, then enlarged the spreadsheet. Jenson reported to Harken. Lieutenant Harken had been in the robbery unit. He was highlighted in yellow. Deceased.

She heard the printer come to life again and she went over, taking the paper from it.

Brewster is dead. My gut says it wasn't an accident. McMillan took the news too easily. So did Hamilton and Jaworski. There was no shock on their faces. I don't know if I continue this investigation or not. Who do I bring these findings to? Everything I've reported to Brewster thus far, has he kept it to himself? Or did he go to the chief with it? Do I drop it? How did they know Brewster ordered the investigation? They had to have seen us meeting. Maybe they've been following me for longer than I suspected.

Am I in trouble? If they took out Brewster, would they be willing to do the same to me? (Maybe I'm off base. Maybe it really was an accident.)

I'm tempted to go to Vasher with all of this, but honestly, I'm not sure who I can trust. Vasher and Hamilton have known each other since the academy. Their families are friends. I think I should take all of this to the chief. Problem is, all of the physical evidence (pictures and most of my notes) has been handed over to Brewster. My fear is that he kept that with him. And it probably burned, just like he did.

"Jesus," she whispered.

"Something good?"

"I guess it depends on how you look at it."

She pulled another page from the printer. This appeared to be the first one written in this code.

Reverting to an old written code of mine, one I first used way back when I was a kid to hide things from James (and Mom). It took longer to get it all to make sense (this is my 3rd attempt at writing this!)

The names I've given to Brewster are all involved, some deeper than others. Dewberry is completely clean. There's no evidence linking him at all, and the others don't trust him. That's telling. His partner requested a transfer—Paul Douglas—back to Little Mexico. Douglas is also big pals with Bexley. And Bexley is one of the few I have photos of at that last bust. Bexley and Douglas took the money. Sawyer the drugs. I stayed with them all night, following Bexley from the scene. They all met up with Staley at 3:15 a.m. (behind a warehouse on Bonham). I followed Staley from there. Not surprised to see him meet with McMillan half an hour later.

Odd thing here—Sawyer is under Sergeant Walsh. Sergeant Walsh reports to James. In assault. Why was Sawyer even at this bust in the first place? This is the 3rd or 4th time that an officer was at a scene where he shouldn't have been. Brewster is concerned this goes from officer to sergeant to lieutenant, but I can't find anything to indicate that any of the sergeants are involved. It pains me to link James to the others, but I must. My gut says Staley is the top dog in the (new) Blue Dragons. He's got the most access being in narcotics. Easy to have money/drugs disappear. That's just my gut. No proof of that at all.

It's all coming to a head though. Brewster said a few more weeks, then I'm done. I'll be glad to get off this detail. I haven't devoted as much time to my cases (and Vasher surely can tell) and I'm preoccupied at home. While Donna hasn't complained (I've explained what I'm doing), me going out most nights is wearing thin, I'm sure. (To be honest, I'm very tired.)

Tori slowly put the paper down, then looked over at Simon, who was watching her. She glanced to the printer where the fourth page had printed.

"That's the last one," he said.

She handed him the one she'd just read. "This was page one." She took the other two pages she'd read, handing them one at time to him. "This is page two, I guess. And this is three, where Brewster died."

He took them and started reading. She took the final page from the printer.

Something's going on. McMillan is avoiding me, barely speaks. Hamilton and Jaworski haven't been around much and when they are, they don't speak or look at me. I noticed at Brewster's funeral that Staley and McMillan never once made eye contact. Harken either. I didn't even see James there.

I've got an appointment with the chief in three days (Friday). I'll tell him everything I know and let him take it from there. I want out of it. I only hope it's not too late. I fear McMillan is in too deep.

There was a man found shot to death outside the bar they go to (Breaker's) four nights ago. Me and Vasher should have caught the case, but he put Hamilton and Jaworski on it. The first two officers on the scene were under James' command—Sawyer and Casper. I heard rumors that the dead guy was a known drug dealer, yet narcotics was never contacted. Strange, considering how close McMillan and Staley are. Here's the thing. Some "witness" claimed he saw two guys in a fight after they'd exchanged "drugs for money" first. One shot the other. The witness couldn't describe the guy who ran off. No other witnesses came forward. (Is it a coincidence that Bexley and Jenson were inside the bar at the time?)

Did some more snooping around. The dead guy was Hector Velasquez, a low-level dealer who works exclusively in Little Mexico. No way should he have been in that part of the city. My thoughts on it? He was an informant who wanted a cut of the money (or drugs) from a bust. Nothing will come of this case, of course. My guess (and fear) is that Velasquez was killed by one of our guys. Bexley maybe? Jenson? Sawyer and Casper were first on the scene. Easy for them to ignore Bexley and Jenson being there, especially if they were already in the loop.

Yeah, I'm grasping here, I know. And I'm damn paranoid. I didn't tell Donna, but a truck tried to run me off the road this morning on the way to work. Not an accident. And because I'm so paranoid, I didn't report it. I think that may have been a mistake on my part. By not reporting it, it means I didn't want to call attention to it (or I wasn't surprised by it). If McMillan had any questions about me, that probably told him all he needed to know (provided he was involved). I got a bad feeling that I can't shake. Makes me want to barge into the chief's office in the morning instead of waiting until Friday.

Regardless, I'm done with this case. After I talk to the chief, I'm taking some time off. A week or two. Need some rest. Need to spend time with the family. Maybe take the kids out somewhere fun. A camping trip? I know Donna would like that and the kids would love it.

Tori felt a lump in her throat as she read the last of it. This was most likely written on Tuesday night. He was set to meet with the chief on Friday. But he never got that chance. He was killed on Thursday evening, during dinner with his family.

"Does this all make sense to you?"

She handed him the last page. "More sense now, yes."

Simon started reading, then stopped. "I guess after reading this, you now think your uncle was involved?"

"My father apparently thought so." Tori sat down on the couch and leaned back, eyes closed. "They called themselves the Blue Dragons. A name they stole from a previous generation. This second version of it was apparently in a little deeper than the first. I don't believe murder ever came into play the first time around." She rubbed her eyes. "Of course, who knows? I only know what a couple of old men remember from that long ago."

Simon read the last page in silence, then stacked it neatly with the others, placing it on the bottom, in order.

"What can I do to help?"

She shook her head. "You've done enough. I don't even know what the hell I'm going to do."

"Take it to your captain? Lieutenant?"

"No. I don't think so. With what I've got? It would go to CIU, who wouldn't do a damn thing. They'd probably take it to the DA's office to see if they wanted to investigate. They've got their hands full with current cases. You think they're going to pull someone to look into alleged misdeeds from over thirty years ago?" She pointed to the papers. "With only that as evidence? It wouldn't go anywhere except to the bottom of the pile."

He shrugged. "So now what?"

"I'm going to continue to interview these guys. See what shakes out. He's named the main players in these notes, but there's one that he didn't mention who is on our list. Cunningham. I think I'm going to start with him."

"What about your uncle?"

"When I talked to him today, he acted like he'd only heard rumors. Said he heard it was some guys getting together for poker and whiskey, nothing more."

"You don't believe him?"

She stared at Simon, thinking back to her uncle's reaction to her mention of the Blue Dragons. Shock? Surprise? Maybe a little. He was certainly nervous. She sighed.

"No. I don't think I believe him."

Simon scribbled something on a piece of paper and handed it to her. "Email Boris with that message. I'll meet you at our usual place. I'm going to get a couple of burner phones tomorrow. I'll—"

"Simon, no. This is my deal, not yours," she protested.

"You're probably going to need my help with something." He gave a crooked grin. "I ain't got nothing else to do, Detective."

She didn't return his smile. "I don't want you to lose your job, Simon. Or worse, get brought up on charges."

"I know how these things are done, Hunter. I'm in the business. I can guarantee you it will not trace back to me. And I'm talking about the Boris email. As far as me snooping in their records, they'll never find that."

"You can't be positive, Simon."

"Look, there's no reason for them to know. I was very quiet—under the radar. I didn't run any programs that would trigger anything. I was in their data as if I was an end-user. I collected what I wanted, then deleted the log files."

She stared at him. "And that's that?"

"Well, I'm sure they use a third party where the logs are sent, but because there was no evidence of intrusion, there's no reason to even look at the log files. And even then, it won't trace to me. It won't even trace to anyone on this continent. Do you understand?"

She finally gave him a smile. "No. And I don't guess I want to." She looked at the paper he'd given her, then laughed. *I owe you two bottles of scotch. The good stuff. Let's meet.* "So when I email you this message—sorry, when I email *Boris* this message, you'll meet me at our spot?"

"Yeah. If I get the message in the morning, I'll assume it's for lunch. If it's after lunch, then…what? Five? Like today?"

"Okay. And you really want to get burners?"

"It'd be easier."

She nodded. "I really hope I don't screw up your life, Simon."

"No. I'll be fine. In the meantime, is there something you want me to do?"

"How about check into the death of Harken? Just to be sure."

"Okay. I can do that."

"Hopefully it'll be natural causes," she said with a shake of her head. "Because if it's not, then this thing is going to blow up. Which is funny, because I don't even know what the hell this thing is."

CHAPTER TWENTY-FIVE

Tori had hoped that Sam would be waiting up for her and she wasn't disappointed. She was on the sofa, the TV muted, and she held a book in her hands. She smiled when she saw her, tossing the book aside.

"Hey, you."

"Hey." Tori sunk down beside her with a weary sigh. "Did you get dinner?"

"I did. I went over to Casey and Leslie's place."

"And did you talk about me?"

Sam leaned closer to kiss her. "Yes, we did. And I missed you being there with us."

"Sorry. I...I have to do this."

"I know, honey. Did you learn anything today?"

"I learned plenty." She pulled Sam close to her. "But I don't want to talk about it now. I'm tired. I want a shower and bed." Then she smiled. "And maybe a backrub."

Sam kissed her again. "That can be arranged. Go on. Get your shower. I'll meet you in bed."

Tori got up and headed down the hallway, then paused, turning back around. As expected, Sam was watching her.

"I love you, Sam."

"I know. I love you too. Very much."

She turned to go, then stopped again. "We haven't had a lot of us time lately. None really. I've been so preoccupied with all this and—"

"Tori, I know how important this is to you." Sam got up, moving to her. "I just don't want you to push us away. And by us, I mean me and Casey. She's really worried about you."

"And she wants to follow me around. Did she tell you I caught her on the first try?"

Sam laughed. "She did. She also said she called you a stubborn ass." Sam's smile faded. "Don't be one, okay? Casey only wants to look out for you, to have your back."

"I'm trying to have hers by not getting her involved. It could get ugly." She swallowed. "We got the notes deciphered. They were...enlightening, to say the least." She sighed. "We'll talk in the morning. I'm so tired."

"Okay. Go on. Let me lock everything up. Be right there."

Tori nodded, heading slowly to their bedroom. The weight of the day hit her, crashing down heavy on her shoulders. She stripped off her clothes and let them land on the floor before going into the bathroom. She closed the door and leaned against it, her eyes shut.

Sam was worried about her. She could see that when she looked at her, could see the questions there in her eyes. Was she going about this all wrong? Should she bring all of this to Malone? Should she do it the right way?

She opened her eyes then, meeting them in the mirror. The right way? Was there a right way? She didn't care about that and that scared her a little. As she'd told Casey, she didn't care about justice. She didn't care about going through the proper channels or whether what she'd found today would be admissible in court. She didn't care about any of that. She wanted the truth. She wanted to look into the eyes of the man who ordered the hit.

"And I want to kill him."

She barely whispered the words, but they hung in the air, echoing over and over in her mind. Is that what she wanted? Really? What would that make her? A killer? No better than him? She'd lose her job. She'd lose Sam. She'd lose her life. Was she prepared for all that?

She realized her hands were clenched into fists, and she made herself relax. She stared at herself, seeing the few strands of gray showing in her dark hair. Her hair style hadn't changed much over the years although it wasn't quite as short as she once wore it. She stared at the gray for a bit longer, then moved to her face, seeing creases around her eyes. She turned away from her reflection then. No, it wasn't the gray hair or the pronounced laugh lines that made her turn. It was the look in her eyes. She wasn't sure she recognized it.

She wasn't sure she recognized *her*. And yes, that scared her too.

CHAPTER TWENTY-SIX

Casey shuffled papers on her desk, then practically stuck her nose against the screen as Malone walked over, hoping he wouldn't stop. He did.

"Got something interesting?"

She leaned back in her chair. "Just kinda going over everything. I visited with a couple of Griffin's neighbors again yesterday. Nothing new. It's a total dead end."

He stood by her desk, looking pointedly at Tori's empty chair. "You heard from Hunter?"

"No sir. Well, not exactly."

He raised an eyebrow. "What does that mean?"

"I mean—" She paused, knowing she didn't dare tell him anything. "I talked to Sam. And, you know, Tori is Tori."

"Does that mean we'll see her today or not?"

Casey stared at him, blinking several times. "I'm gonna say no. She said she was taking a few days, right?"

"Right. I just didn't think she could stand to be away that long. Got some news about her family's case. They're not going to close it, after all. Finding the gun in Griffin's safe is circumstantial evidence only, despite the many photos of Hunter that he had."

"And the confession letter?"

"As far as everyone is concerned, it doesn't exist. I don't think it much matters anyway. Tori knows who did it and that person is dead. I would think in her mind, the case is closed regardless if it's official or not."

God, did he not know Tori at all? *Closed?* Oh, in her mind, the case was *so* not closed. But she said nothing, simply nodding at him. He went back to his office, and she let out a sigh. The ringing of her cell—Tori's ringtone—made her snatch it up.

"You okay?" she asked quickly.

"I'm fine, O'Connor. Are you?"

"The lieutenant was just questioning me. Asking if I'd talked to you and if you were coming in today." She got up and headed down the hallway for some privacy. "Missed you at dinner last night."

"I had things to do. And I need a favor."

"Anything. What's up?"

"I need you to get with Denton PD. They responded to a murder on Monday, same day as Charles Griffin. Lieutenant Adam Staley. Retired. Dallas PD."

Casey looked around, making sure no one was watching. "Is he one on your list?"

"Yeah."

"Holy shit. That can't be a coincidence."

"No, it can't. See what they've got. See how similar it is to Griffin. From what I've been able to find out, they have a partial plate from a neighbor's security camera."

"How do you know that?"

"I just do, O'Connor. Will you look into it?"

"Yeah, of course." She paused. "What are you doing today?"

Tori gave a quick laugh. "You know what I'm doing, Casey. And you won't be there to follow me around."

"Will you at least be careful?"

"Promise. Talk to you later."

Casey blew out a heavy breath as she pocketed her phone, then walked nonchalantly back to her desk. She glanced once in the direction of Malone's office, but he was on the phone, his back to her. She quickly looked up the information for Denton PD and picked up her own phone.

CHAPTER TWENTY-SEVEN

Tori picked the one name not mentioned in her father's notes—Darrell Cunningham. He was the youngest on her list at sixty-two, although he'd been retired for a number of years already. After he'd left Dallas PD, he'd volunteered at a YMCA. No other employment history was listed.

She walked up to the front door—it was an older house in an older, rather shabby neighborhood—and knocked as she didn't see a doorbell. The morning was pleasantly cool and breezy, and she noticed two of the side windows were open. She knocked again, finally hearing a woman's voice—"Coming"—before she saw her shadow through the door's glass.

The door opened fully, and a woman stood there, a friendly smile on her face, and she held what appeared to be a dishcloth in one hand.

"Yes? May I help you?"

"Good morning," Tori said, remembering to add a smile to her face. "I'm Detective Hunter, Dallas Police Department." She automatically held up her shield. "Is Mr. Cunningham home?"

The smile left the woman's face. "Is something wrong?"

"No, no. Not at all. Just looking for some old history back when he was on the force. Won't take but a minute of his time."

"Okay, then. Sure, come in." She stepped back. "I'm Lila, his wife. We've just finished up breakfast and were having coffee. Would you like a cup?"

"Oh, no, ma'am. Don't go to any trouble."

She followed her into their modest home, the entryway opening into a living room, a space that looked lived in with two comfy recliners sitting side-by-side. The kitchen was in the back of the house and a man sat with his nose in the morning paper, a coffee cup within reach. Breakfast dishes were beside the sink, and she assumed she'd interrupted Lila's washing of them.

"Darrell, there's a detective here to see you."

His head jerked up, his eyes sharp. While he was only sixty-two, she wouldn't call it a youthful sixty-two. His hair was more gray than brown, and he was easily fifty pounds overweight, she guessed.

"I'm Detective Hunter," she said easily, holding her hand out to him.

He put the paper down and stood, shaking her hand firmly. "What's this about?"

"I have some questions from…well, years ago." She looked at his wife, then back to him. "Is there some place we can talk?"

He stared at her for a moment, uncertainty in his eyes. Then he nodded. "Sure. Let's go on out to the back porch. Got to take advantage of this cool weather before summer is upon us."

Tori nodded, then glanced over at Lila, taking the time to offer her a smile before following him out the back door. Unlike Charles Griffin's neat and manicured lawn, this one was in desperate need of a cut. Weeds grew around last year's flowers and crusty, dry leaves leftover from winter still littered the porch's corners. A small table with four chairs was against the side wall and she wondered how often it got used. The chairs looked worn and rusty. Nearer the door were two other chairs and she assumed this was where they sat, perhaps in the late afternoons, looking out at their weedy yard. She pulled her chair away from his, turning it to face him. She got right to the point.

"Tell me about the Blue Dragons." If he was surprised at her question, he didn't show it. In fact, he looked almost like he'd been expecting it.

"I hadn't thought about that in years. Hadn't heard the words mentioned since well before I left the force. Then in the last month or so, that's about all I've been hearing."

She leaned closer. "From whom?"

"Lieutenant Staley, mostly. And a couple of the guys have called."

She nodded, holding his gaze. "Tell me about the Blue Dragons," she said again. "Were you a part of it?"

He smiled. "I guess you could say that. Way down at the bottom of the pecking order, though. So much so that I don't even know who the top dogs were. Or I didn't. Staley obviously was one."

She had to bite her lip not to pepper him with questions. "How did you get involved?"

"I worked a beat in Central. We had our share of drug collars. We beat narcotics there a lot of the time. Mostly small stuff. But one time…wow. That was the first time I'd seen that much cash. I almost shit my pants," he said with a laugh.

"What happened?"

"Oh, it was just me and Bexley. He was my partner at the time. I'd been having some financial problems. Bexley knew it. He said we should grab some of the cash before the detectives showed up." He shrugged. "I knew it was wrong, yeah. But it was drug money. I didn't think anyone would miss a few hundred bucks." He laughed again. "I took a small wad and shoved it in my pocket, but Bexley was grabbing handfuls and shoving it inside his vest. So I shoved it in too, you know, following his lead. We didn't say a word about it until our shift was over. Then we counted it. Seventeen thousand and some change." He leaned back in his chair, a smile on his face. "I got drunk on my ass that night."

"That was your initiation into the Blue Dragons?"

"Yeah. Bexley told me he and some others did it all the time. Said they called themselves the Blue Dragons. To tell you the truth, I didn't ask any questions. But my share of that haul, over eight thousand, that sure came in handy."

"So you did it more than once?"

"Oh, yeah. Now and then. Drug money only. The drugs themselves? I didn't want no part of that, no sir. Bexley knew it." He paused, as if deciding whether he should say more or not. "But I heard things."

"Things like what?" she coaxed.

"Like they were getting involved in stuff other than drugs and money."

"Like what?"

"Like taking bribes to look the other way, like letting suspects walk for cash. I even heard they framed some innocent man for murder, planting evidence at the scene. I heard they did that more than once."

Her brows drew together. "For money?"

He nodded. "Don't know if that's all true or not. Could be just rumors. Jenson is the one who told me that. I never had the balls to ask Bexley. I didn't want to know."

She stood up, going to the edge of the porch. Was this all true? It certainly filled in the blanks to her father's notes. She turned back around.

"Tell me about Staley."

"Lieutenant Staley was in narcotics, but I ran into him a few times, late at night. Off duty," he said. "Figured he was one of the top dogs, seeing as how Bexley and the others treated him."

"Others?"

"Oh, there was Jenson, like I said. And Paul Douglas. And a couple of detectives from homicide. Jaworski was one. Can't remember the other."

"Hamilton?"

"Oh, yeah. Hamilton. Those were about the only ones I ever saw, but I heard that Casper and Sawyer were in the group too. They were in Little Mexico." He shook his head. "I never worked Little Mexico, but I heard stories. Douglas said you could cash in every night if you wanted to, there were so many drugs changing hands."

"Staley? You talked to him recently?"

"Yeah. It was the weirdest thing. Hadn't talked to the man in a decade or more and he calls me up out of the blue. Wanted to meet." He shrugged. "I didn't know what it was about, but I met him at a bar one afternoon. He was in pretty bad shape."

"How so?"

Cunningham narrowed his eyes at her. "Why all the questions? You never said."

"No, I didn't. It's actually for personal reasons. I'm sort of off duty."

"Personal?"

"Do you remember Detective Jason Hunter? Homicide?"

He nodded slowly. "Name rings a bell."

"He was my father."

Cunningham held her gaze for the longest time. "He was the one killed in his home."

"Yes."

As he stared at her, recognition seemed to set in. "I wonder if that's what Staley meant," he murmured, almost to himself.

"Tell me about your meeting with Staley."

"Well, like I said, he was in bad shape that day. His wife had just had a stroke, was clinging to life. The man was beside himself, said he had to make things right with God. Said he was being punished for what they'd done."

"You took that to mean what?"

"I didn't really know. Hell, I've been off the force going on ten years. Staley retired before me. I hadn't given all that stuff much thought in ages."

"What did he say?"

"Well, the first time we met, he said it was a mistake to get the Blue Dragons up and running again. That was news to me. I had no idea the Blue Dragons were this group from way back in the day. I didn't know all that old history. He told me some about that, told me they'd shut them down. When he said most of them had lost their jobs, I was just thankful that I made it out unscathed. Like I said, I knew it was wrong but what are you going to do?"

She simply nodded. "Go on."

"He kept knocking back shots and talking about how wrong it all had been. That's about all. Then a week or so ago, he called me up again. We met at the same place. This time he told me that he'd made a pact with God. Told me he was going to go in and confess all he'd done. Confess about the murders. Said he was warning me in case someone came to ask questions. Said he'd warned all the others too. I thought that's what you were here for."

"What murders?"

"I don't know. I don't know anything about that. I was low man on the totem pole."

Tori went back to her chair and sat down. "You know he's dead, right?"

His eyes widened. "No way."

"Yes. Shot. In his home. Monday."

He leaned back heavily in his chair. "Oh my god. What do you think happened?"

She tilted her head. "What do *you* think happened?"

He held her stare without blinking. "Someone didn't want him to confess."

Tori took a deep breath and nodded. "Yeah. That would be my guess. But who?"

CHAPTER TWENTY-EIGHT

"Yeah, Detective Anwar? This is Detective O'Connor, Dallas PD. I understand you're working the Staley murder case."

"I caught the case, yeah. We don't have much yet." He cleared his throat. "What can I do for you, Detective O'Connor?"

"I've got a case. Same day as yours. That same morning, actually. It was a hit. Used a 9-millimeter. Got nothing except a description of a vehicle. Silver Chevy. Impala."

"Yeah. That matches our vehicle."

"Great! You get plates?"

"Partial. H-W-R. Can't make out the rest. But we ran it. Got no hit on an Impala with plates that started with that."

"We only got a fuzzy first letter. The choice was E or H."

"We're running stolen plates now. Not sure how that will help us."

"Okay. What else you got? Because we got shit," she said bluntly. "White male, slim build. He was seen only from the back, running away. Jumped into the Chevy and sped off. The only surveillance we have on the vehicle is from traffic cams.

But they were smart. Like they knew where the cameras were. Never got a clean shot of them."

"Them?"

"Yeah. Two guys. One driving, one did the hit."

"You think it was a hit? Not someone breaking in?"

"No, no. It was a hit. Two shots. One to shatter the glass, the other a shot to the head. The victim was in his kitchen taking out the trash. Our killer never entered the premises."

"Our victim was found in his bathroom. Without anyone there to confirm—his wife is in the hospital—we don't know if anything was taken. We're going with the assumption that it was a home invasion and Staley surprised them by being there."

"He was retired from here. Lieutenant Staley."

"We're aware of that. Damn shame all around. And from what I know, they expect his wife to die any day now."

"They got kids?"

"Yeah. They were at the hospital when they got the news."

"Okay. Well, if you get a hit on the plates, I'd appreciate it if you'd let me know. And of course, we'd like to share ballistics on the bullet, see if we got the same killer."

"Right. I'll let the lab know."

"Great. Thanks, Detective. And if I happen to stumble upon something, I'll be sure to pass it on."

"Thanks."

She hung up, then jumped as a hand touched her shoulder. She relaxed when she saw Leslie walk past with John following.

"Hey, guys," she said. "What's up?"

"Been at that apartment trying to get people to talk. No one wants to be involved," John said. "How the hell are we supposed to do our job if no one will talk?"

"You mean you didn't use your charm on them?"

"They're scared," Les said. "Gang related. They're afraid they'll be targeted if they talk."

"Yeah, gangs are hard," she said absently, wondering if she should call Tori. She stood. "Gotta run. See you later."

She chanced a glance behind her, finding Malone still on the phone. She slipped out the door unnoticed.

CHAPTER TWENTY-NINE

"Yeah, O'Connor. What did you get?"

"Not a lot, Hunter, but enough to make me think it's the same killer. Same car, that's for sure. Their partial plate started with an H. Same as ours."

"I thought ours was an E," she said as she turned onto the Central Expressway, heading north.

"It was fuzzy. E or H, Mac guessed. I'm going to go with H now. And we'll do the ballistics thing. That'll confirm."

"Okay. Good."

"Where are you?"

"Heading to North Dallas. I wanted to speak with Pete Dewberry again."

"You find out anything?"

"Yeah. Plenty. Too much to go into on the phone."

She still wasn't sure how involved she wanted Casey to be. The less she knew, the less it would blow up in her face should things go south. She couldn't use that approach with Sam though. She'd let her read the notes. She'd seen the look in her eyes, had known she was concerned, especially that her uncle might be involved. Sam didn't have to say the words, but Tori knew she thought Malone should be briefed. And probably he should. But she wasn't going to. She was too close.

"I'll talk to you later, O'Connor."

"Yeah. Sure. Okay."

She paused, hearing the dejection in her voice. "Casey, if nothing comes up, maybe we could go out to the boat on Sunday, drown a few worms." She made the offer even though she doubted they'd get the chance to go. There were too many things to do.

"Really? You and me? You think Sam and Les would go for that?"

Tori laughed. "We'll try to sneak away without them."

"Okay. Deal." Casey paused too. "Thanks, Tori."

"Talk to you later."

She was smiling as she disconnected. Casey was her best friend. Her pal. She loved her like a sister—like family—yet more than that. Casey, much like Sam, could keep her grounded. And like Sam, Casey usually knew what she was thinking.

The smile left her face. Except now. Because *she* didn't even know what she was thinking. The Blue Dragons appeared to be a small group, unlike the first time. Staley had obviously been one of the leaders. But who else? Did all four lieutenants have a say in it? McMillan? Harken? Her uncle too? Were they the ones calling the shots? And what was the pecking order? If Cunningham was at the bottom, who was right above him? Casper? Jenson? Bexley? Sawyer? Maybe. She assumed Hamilton and Jaworski would rank higher, but maybe she only thought that because they were detectives. Did the Blue Dragons' pecking order mirror that of the police?

All those questions swirled in her head as she drove to North Dallas. Her gut told her she could trust Pete Dewberry. Her father's notes indicated the same—he was clean. She didn't know what else she could get from him though. If she went over the notes with him, would it jog his memory? Did she have any business involving him in the first place?

Too late now, she thought, as she pulled into his driveway. She couldn't explain it really, but she had a sense that she was *supposed* to trust Pete Dewberry. She waited only a beat, then opened the door, taking the folder where she'd put the papers— copies of the spreadsheet and the notes Simon had printed, as well as the original ones that she could read. Out of habit, she locked the car as she walked to the door. The doorbell went unanswered, however. She rang it twice more, then finally went back to the driveway.

On impulse, she went around to the side. A privacy fence blocked a view of the backyard, but she went to the gate. It was unlocked and she opened it. She found Pete on his knees, weeding a flowerbed. This must be the new one he said he'd put in for his dead wife.

"Pete?" she called, not wanting to startle him.

He turned his head, his face breaking into a smile when he saw her. "Detective Hunter. Come on back."

"Sorry to just barge in. When you didn't answer your doorbell, I took a chance you were out here."

He stood up and brushed the dirt off his jeans, then motioned her to join him on the back porch. "Starting to get hot already and we're not even through April." He sat down and pointed to the bed he'd been working on. "I started on that flowerbed last summer, a few months after my Dottie passed on. Picked all her favorite flowers to put in it. Should have had this year's flowers in already, but I got behind. The older I get, the less urgency I seem to have."

She knew his age from Simon's spreadsheet, but she asked anyway. "How old are you?"

"Hanging on to seventy-two. Got me a birthday coming up next month. The missus used to bake me a cake each year. A plain old yellow cake with this rich chocolate icing. Made it from scratch, she did. Moist as all get out." He sighed. "Last year I didn't even remember the date. I was still grieving. This year? I guess I'll have to acknowledge it. Don't have an excuse."

"The years do go by fast, don't they?"

He smiled at her. "You're too young to be worrying about that already. At least wait until you're sixty." He glanced at the watch on his wrist. "And if you'd been an hour later, we could have had a beer while we chatted. I don't dare open one before noon. Dottie wouldn't approve."

She returned his smile. "I wanted to go over a few things with you. If you've got the time," she added.

"Got nothing but time, Detective."

"Please call me Tori. And it's about the Blue Dragons."

He nodded. "I take it your interviews with these guys went well. No one clammed up on you?"

"I only interviewed Darrell Cunningham. Well, my uncle too. He was a lieutenant at the time. James Hunter."

"Oh, sure. I remember Lieutenant Hunter. Did he shed some light?"

"Actually, no." She took a deep breath, not even knowing where to start. "Look, I know you don't know me, and I don't know you, but I need someone I can trust. Someone who was on the force back then. Someone who knew these guys."

He leaned forward, his elbows resting on his thighs. "You thinking you might dig up something on these guys? Some ugly dirt or something?"

"You remember Lieutenant Staley?"

"Staley? Yeah, he was in narcotics."

"His name was on this list that I have. My father's list. He was murdered on Monday. In his home."

Pete's eyebrows shot up. "And you think it's related?"

"I interviewed Cunningham this morning. You knew him?"

Pete shook his head. "Can't say I knew him, no. Knew *of* him. He and Bexley rode together for a while, I think."

"Yes. Cunningham said that Staley contacted him recently. Said he wanted to confess all that they did back then. Said he wanted to warn him in case the cops came around asking questions. Said he was going to warn all of them that he was going to go forward."

"Okay, you lost me there. Confess what?"

"The Blue Dragons were involved in much more than drug money, apparently. Cunningham said they planted evidence.

Said they let suspects walk for cash. Said they framed people for murder. Again, for cash. Then Staley meets with him, says he's ready to confess about the murders. Made a pact with God or something."

"Murders? And then Staley gets whacked?"

"Yes. He lived in Denton. My partner talked to the detectives there. The shooter was in a silver Chevy. That matches the car that we've got in another murder on Monday."

Pete held his hand up. "Slow down there, Tori. I've been out of the business a while now. You got another murder on Monday? Someone else on this list of yours?"

"No. But it's what got this all started. The man—Charles Griffin—had a gun in a safe. Ballistics matched that gun to my father's murder."

"Whoa. So he was involved with these Blue Dragons?"

She shook her head. "No. I'll give you the short version. Charles Griffin left me his confession. He killed my father, my family. He was a pawn. Coerced. They threatened the lives of his family. He indicated that it was dirty cops who did it. So that's when I started digging. I found some old notes that my father kept at home. They were in a box all these years. I found the list of names. He had some encrypted notes too. Got those transcribed last night." She tapped on the folder she still held. "Got it all here."

"Can I have a look?"

"Yes. Since you knew these guys, it might make more sense to you."

He stood. "Let's go inside to the table. I'll see what you got there."

CHAPTER THIRTY

"O'Connor? Anything new?"

Casey looked at Lieutenant Malone, her mind a jumbled mess. Should she tell him about Staley? Was that new? Was it related? Would Tori kill her?

"Well?" he asked.

"Well...I might have something, yeah."

He raised his eyebrows, waiting. She chewed on her lower lip. Yeah, Tori would kill her. He noticed her hesitation and motioned with his head.

"My office."

Leslie was on the phone, but John was watching her. She gave him a weak smile as she followed Malone. He didn't wait for her to sit.

"Out with it."

"Okay, yeah. So, you know we had the first letter on the plates, the silver Chevy."

"Right. It was an E you said."

"Or H. Anyway, Denton PD had a murder the same day. Silver Chevy. Impala. They got the first three letters of the plates. H and something else. But I'm thinking maybe it's a match to ours."

He nodded. "Lieutenant Staley."

"You heard about it?"

"Captain mentioned it. I never knew the guy. Tragic, really. His wife had a stroke and is on life support. From what I hear, Staley was devoted to her."

Casey just nodded. "Don't know how this will help us, but it's something."

"Was there anything in Griffin's background to indicate he knew Staley?"

"No, sir."

"Yet you think the killings are related?"

"Same car, same day. Ballistics will tell us for sure, of course."

"You let Mac know?"

"Yes, I called him. He's going to be in touch with their lab up there."

"Okay. Good, O'Connor. Maybe something will shake out." He paused. "You let Tori know about this?"

"Actually, yeah, I called her." Technically, that was a lie. Tori had called *her.*

"And?"

"And…we're going to try to get out on the boat on Sunday, maybe do a little fishing." Thankfully her cell rang, and she snatched it out of her pocket. "Sorry. I've got to take this."

She left his office, phone to her ear. "Yeah, O'Connor," she answered.

"It's Mac. Found your silver Chevy."

"Found it where?"

"In the Trinity River."

Her eyebrows shot up. "What the hell?"

"It gets better. Two guys inside, still strapped in their seat belts."

"Drowned?"

"No. Shot. They pulled the car from the West Fork. Fort Worth is working it. But the silver Chevy caught my attention. Impala. I already gave them a call. They'll keep me in the loop."

"You get the plates?"

"Not yet. I'll let you know."

"That's great, Mac." She turned, heading right back to Malone's office. "They ID these guys yet?"

"No. There was nothing on them. They found a gun. Haven't gotten particulars on it yet."

"Okay, thanks. I'll be in touch with the detectives there. If you hear anything else—"

"You'll be my first call."

She met Malone's gaze. "Maybe a break. That was Mac. He said they pulled a silver Chevy Impala out of the river in Fort Worth. Two bodies inside. Both shot. I'm going to head over there, see what I can find out."

He nodded. "Good, O'Connor. Keep me posted."

"Yes, sir."

CHAPTER THIRTY-ONE

Tori paced in Pete's kitchen as he read through Griffin's confession letter. He'd already gone over her father's notes, giving a little insight into some of the instances. It was his opinion that Staley was the ringleader, but his death begged to differ. If not Staley, then who was it? McMillan? Harken?

Her uncle? She shook her head. No. Even though he and her father weren't close, he still wouldn't go along with a plan to kill him and his family. He wasn't that ruthless, surely. But he was most likely involved.

But if not Staley or her uncle, then who? Harken was dead. That left McMillan. Lieutenant McMillan had been over homicide back then. Hamilton and Jaworski reported to him. Hamilton and Jaworski were the detectives assigned to her father's case. A case that went cold quickly. Was that McMillan's doing? Had he ordered them to let it go cold? Is that why there was no evidence?

Again, she shook her head. There had been no evidence to begin with. There were no security cameras back then. No neighbors saw anything. No one heard a car squealing away. God knows she wasn't any help. She couldn't even describe the man—Charles Griffin.

"Hell of a thing for you to read after all these years."

She turned to Pete, nodding. "Yeah. Quite a shock."

"So these cops he mentioned, you think it's the Blue Dragons?"

She nodded. "Don't you?"

He placed the confession letter next to the other notes she'd brought with her. "There weren't as many checks and balances back then, no. But I can't imagine them arresting someone and holding him for a couple of days and there not being a record. You'd have to have a sergeant in your pocket too."

"What if they didn't arrest him? What if they just *told* him he was being arrested?" She sat down opposite him. "Detectives bring guys in all the time for questioning. So they put him in a holding cell. He's scared, thinks he's arrested."

"Don't you think he'd be asking for an attorney? For a phone call?"

"Who's he going to ask? And even if he does, you think anyone is going to pay him any mind?"

"You've got a point there. He'd be ignored."

"Right. So they leave him in there a couple of days, long enough to get pictures of his family, long enough to plan things. Then they let him out and the ball is in motion."

"And he has no clue who is calling the shots, but he knows the cops are involved. What's his choice? Go to the police with what he's got?"

"No way. He's scared," Tori said. "If he thinks it's dirty cops, who could he trust?"

Pete nodded. "He then does what they instruct him to do."

"He kills," she said thickly. "He kills my family. Then he lives in fear the rest of his life, always looking over his shoulder, always waiting for them to contact him again."

"And they finally do."

"Right. I think they wanted him to kill Staley. Staley was about to talk, to confess. They wanted to eliminate him. That was the target. So they go back to Griffin. Only this time, they don't have any leverage with him. His parents are deceased, his sister has just died, her kids aren't local. He's got cancer. They have nothing to threaten him with."

"And he turns the tables on them by saying he'll go to the cops this time."

"Right," she said with a quick nod. "So now they're panicking. They have Staley about to confess, they've got Griffin threatening to go to the police if they keep calling him."

Pete nodded too. "They hire a real hitman, take them both out."

She smiled, then it faded. "But I can't prove one goddamn thing of this. Not one."

"Who ordered the hit on Staley?"

Tori shrugged. "McMillan?"

Pete met her gaze. "Your uncle?"

Tori ran a hand through her hair, absently remembering Sam's fingers there just that morning, Sam telling her it was time for her summer cut. She sighed. "I can't even entertain the idea that my uncle was involved in my family's murder."

Pete stood up and went to the fridge. Tori wasn't surprised to hear the clanking of beer bottles as he pulled two out. "Not to be disrespectful to your uncle—because I didn't know the man—but money has a way of changing people. If he's involved in this little gang, if he's one of the higher-ups, then he most likely knew what was going on. From what you've been able to dig up, there was a lot of money involved. That's just drug money. All this other stuff? Planting of evidence, letting perps walk. Gotta be some big bucks there too. You're not going to risk your career for chump change. We're talking big, big bucks here."

"Yes, I agree. If it's just these few guys involved, that's a lot of cash to go around."

He handed her a bottle. "I remember an incident once. Early on when I was brand new on the force. Probably the first time I'd heard of Bexley. He shot someone after a traffic stop. Young Mexican kid. Caused quite a stir, but again, back then there weren't cameras everywhere. The kid was dead, and all you had was Bexley and his partner's take on things. Now like I said, I never trusted Bexley and I certainly never hung with him, but he was under your uncle's command back then." Pete took a swallow of his beer. "Bexley was a rookie cop at the time. It all blew over, but I think Lieutenant Hunter took a firm stance protecting his guys."

Pete paused a moment, then nodded. "Heard rumors after that. About the killing. The kid was unarmed. Heard they planted a gun on him." Pete shrugged. "That's how it used to be in the old days. I'm not trying to say that your uncle was a part of a coverup or anything, just that he stuck up for his guys."

"I don't have a relationship with my uncle, so don't think you're offending me by telling me this." Tori twisted off the cap on the bottle. "If Bexley was a rookie, that would have happened well before the Blue Dragons got up and running, I'd guess."

"You and your uncle don't talk?"

Tori shook her head. "He and my father were never close, and there was only a handful of times our families were together. But my lack of a relationship with him is more personal." Tori took a swallow of the beer. "He didn't want me. After…after they were gone, he didn't want me." She held her hand up, not wanting to go into all that. "So what I'm saying is, I'm not protecting him because he's my uncle. I simply can't see him signing off on having his own brother killed. And his wife and kids," she added quietly. "I don't believe he's that much of a monster."

Pete sat down again. "You're doing all this on your own?"

"I am. I don't know who I can trust. I don't know if the Blue Dragons are still around. And if I take all of this to my lieutenant, he'll have to go further up the chain with it. I'll be out of the loop, off the case. They'll get CIU involved, Internal Affairs. Probably take it to the DA's office to see if there's enough here to go back that far and investigate."

"You're afraid it'll disappear?"

Before she could answer, her cell rang. It was Casey's ringtone. She pulled it out of her pocket. "Yeah, O'Connor. What's up?"

"You won't believe this, Hunter. Fort Worth PD pulled a Chevy Impala out of the Trinity. Up on the West Fork, upstream of some park there."

"Is it ours?"

"Guessing. I talked to one of the detectives. They don't have much right now and the ME hasn't even taken the bodies yet. I'm on my way over there."

"Bodies?"

"Two. Males. Both shot."

Tori stiffened. "It's got to be our guys."

"Yeah. But don't forget, Denton PD is working a murder too. We might be fighting for the car."

"As soon as you get IDs on them, let me know."

"I will. And you need to call Malone. Just touch base. Tell him you'll be back to work on Monday." Casey paused. "You will, right?"

Tori figured if she stayed out much longer, Malone would come find her. "I'll be in touch with him."

She placed the phone facedown on the table. "That was my partner. She said a Chevy Impala was fished out of the Trinity. Two men inside. Both shot."

Pete nodded. "Looks like you found your hitmen."

"Yeah. But who in the hell killed *them*?"

CHAPTER THIRTY-TWO

Casey tried not to hover, but she used her phone to take as many pictures as she could. A loud clearing of a man's voice made her look up.

"You know, we'll be happy to share all of this with you, O'Connor."

It was the detective she'd spoken to earlier. "Yeah, I know. I'm just trying to get a head start. Sorry."

"The ME guesses they've been in the water several days already."

"You run prints? Or are they waterlogged?"

"Yeah, quite bloated. But we got a hit on one. The driver. Jeffery Scarsdale." Detective Weaver looked at his notes. "Last known address was in Phoenix, but he has ties to this area. Has priors. Been arrested both here and in Dallas."

"Age?"

"Forty-two."

"The other?"

"Nothing on him yet. He appears to be much younger. Mid-twenties, maybe. Hard to tell. Both shot in the back of the head."

"And the gun you found? We're hoping to get a match."

"Yeah. Glock, 9-mil."

Casey nodded. "The bullet pulled from our vic was a 9-mil. Denton PD has a similar case. If you don't mind, I'll call them. Give them your name?"

Weaver nodded. "Sure. I'll pass them on to our lab."

"Great. And I'll have my guys get with your guys. Appreciate it." She turned, then stopped. "If you get an ID on the other one, you'll call?"

"Sure, O'Connor. I'll try to remember," he said dryly as he walked away.

It didn't matter, she thought. Mac would be all over this one. She pulled her phone out and called Detective Anwar in Denton.

CHAPTER THIRTY-THREE

Tori had debated calling Malone, but she was afraid he'd be full of questions. Instead, she texted him. *I'm going to need a few more days.* And he replied with an equally short text. *I'll expect you Monday morning.* She sighed. She had no intention of going in.

She called in an order to Sam's favorite Italian restaurant. Then she texted Sam. *I ordered dinner. Would you stop at Fellini's on your way home?* She received a heart emoji as a reply, which made her smile.

And then she headed home. She was tired. Mentally, at least. After she'd left Pete Dewberry, she'd driven over to Thomas Bexley's house. No one answered the door. She then called him, but it also went unanswered.

She then thought she'd take a chance with McMillan. He was at home, but he wouldn't give her the time of day. As soon as she introduced herself, she'd seen the shield go up.

"Hunter?"

"My father was Jason Hunter. You may remember him."

"Rings a bell."

"I would hope so, considering he was under your command. Hamilton and Jaworski were assigned to his murder."

"Yeah, of course. I remember."

"I'd like to ask you a few questions, if you've got the time."

He'd stared at her for a long, uncomfortable moment, then he shook his head. "Actually, no. I don't have time."

He'd literally closed—slammed—the door in her face and she heard the lock engage from the inside. She'd left then, a little curious as to the nervousness that he'd shown. Did he think that maybe Staley had talked before he was killed? Or did he know that she'd been to visit Cunningham? Or even Pete? She didn't know how he would know unless Cunningham called to warn him. She knew Pete would not.

She had too many questions, too many scenarios running through her mind to settle on any of them. For some reason, she kept skipping over her uncle, though. But really, what was the reason she couldn't fathom him being involved? Because he was family? Even though she didn't think of him as family, he still was.

She turned onto their street, then stared in shock as a car—a black SUV—squealed out of her driveway. It shot past her so fast she couldn't make out the driver. She turned sharply, intending to follow, only to have the neighbor across the street back his car out of his driveway, blocking her. She slammed on her brakes, then pounded the steering wheel in frustration—the SUV was already out of sight.

Her neighbor waved apologetically at her as he drove off and she gave him a curt nod. She pulled into her driveway but sat there a moment before opening the garage door. Who the hell was it? Or was she being paranoid? Maybe someone was simply turning around, and they happened to use her driveway. A coincidence.

She didn't think that was the case, no. She pushed the button above the rearview mirror, waiting as the garage door opened. On impulse, she pushed it closed again and backed out onto the street. She drove around the neighborhood, taking different streets, most she'd never been on before. There was no sign of a black SUV, so she returned home.

By the time she drove into her driveway for the second time, she'd convinced herself that it was definitely *not* a coincidence and that someone was either following her or looking for her.

* * *

The first thing she did when she went inside was email Boris and request a meeting. Early. Tomorrow. Then she showered and changed. By the time Sam came in carrying the bag that contained their dinner, she'd had wine poured and the table set.

Sam fell into her arms with a sigh. "These are going to be the longest weeks of my life. It's like they've taken everything away from me. I have nothing to do. And I mean *nothing*."

"You've got vacation time. Take it."

"I know. But they'll pay me for what I don't take, and it'll be a nice chunk."

Tori kissed her. "We don't need the money. Your sanity is worth it."

Sam touched her cheek before pulling away. "Are you concerned with my sanity for your sake or mine?" she teased.

Tori laughed. "Mostly mine."

"Well, I don't want to take vacation time just to be stuck here at home without you. I might as well be stuck there and get paid for it." Sam picked up one of the wineglasses and took a sip. "How was your day?"

Tori took the wineglass from her and set it back down. "We'll talk over dinner. Go change."

"I'm going to grab a shower too. Can you keep it warm?"

"Of course."

Sam turned to go, then turned back to her and kissed her. "You look stressed. Did something happen?"

"No. I'm fine. Tired."

"Okay. Then let's plan a short night and head to bed early." Sam squeezed her arm. "I'll even toss in another backrub."

Tori smiled at her. "I accept."

As soon as Sam left, Tori took out her phone and checked email. There was a reply from Boris. "I have the goods. Meet early. Same place."

The *goods*? What the hell did that mean? Then she tilted her head. Burner phones maybe. And early? What was early on a Saturday?

CHAPTER THIRTY-FOUR

Tori parked not far from the spot the food truck normally occupied on weekdays. A quick glance at her car's touchscreen told her it was 7:07. She had no idea what early was to Simon—hopefully before eight. Sam had wanted to come with her, but she'd talked her out of it.

"I'll only be a few minutes," she'd told her. "I'll pick up something for breakfast on my way back."

Sam's green eyes had captured hers, and Tori knew that she'd been trying to read them, trying to decide if there was something Tori wasn't telling her. Was there? She hadn't learned anything earth-shattering, no. It was mostly speculation—and suspicion—on her part. Sam had finally nodded, although Tori could tell she was upset.

Tori shook her head. No. Not upset. Sam didn't get upset. Sam was feeling left out, that was all. And yes, maybe so. She hadn't shared much with her. Not even about Staley.

She saw Simon at 7:18. He was wearing the same ball cap and sunglasses as the first time. He acknowledged her with a brief nod in her direction, then went on into the park. At this early hour, it was nearly empty except for a few joggers that were seen along the trail. She got out of her car and followed him, pausing to look around, making sure no one was watching. She'd been just paranoid enough on her way over to practically drive in circles before heading this way. She saw no one tailing her.

"Good morning," she said as she leaned against the tree he was standing by.

"Good morning, Tori," he said cheerfully. Then he grinned. "I was hoping you'd contact me." From each front pocket, he pulled out a phone. "Because I got burners for us. I've already programmed my number into yours and vice versa." He handed her one. "Now we can talk."

She took the cell, nodding. "And you're sure it's safe?"

"Oh, yeah. We'll only use it to call each other. No one will know the numbers. Just us."

"Okay." She looked around them again. "It looks like Staley was killed by the same guys who took out Charles Griffin. Those guys were fished out of the Trinity River yesterday morning. Shot. Still in the car. Matches our silver Chevy."

"So who killed them?"

"Probably whoever hired them. And I interviewed Cunningham yesterday too. He was the only one on the list not mentioned in my father's notes. He said that Staley was going to confess." She shrugged. "Too much to go into but let's just say that, yeah, they were dirty cops. Cunningham said Staley mentioned murders, as in he was going to confess about some. Cunningham said he was way down in the pecking order, though, and didn't know anything about murders."

"You believe him?"

"Yeah, I do. So I tried to meet with Bexley. He wasn't home and didn't answer his cell. Then I went by McMillan's place. He wouldn't talk. Practically slammed the door in my face."

"Why do you think Cunningham talked to you?"

"Staley warned him that he was going to confess. Told him to be prepared to answer questions." Tori looked up as a jogger approached and she waited until he passed by before continuing. "Cunningham did nothing more than snatch drug money thirty years ago. I don't think he's worried about any repercussions. But if Staley warned him that he was going to confess to more—like murder—then he probably warned the others too."

"And you think that's what got him killed?"

"Yes. One of the people he warned didn't want it to get out. McMillan was very nervous, I could tell. So he either knew about Staley—meaning his death—or he didn't want me poking around. Based on my father's notes, he assumed they knew he was investigating them. And here I come around—his daughter—asking questions about it all. Hell, maybe my uncle called McMillan and told him I'd been over asking about the Blue Dragons."

"Okay. Well, get this. Harken—there was no official cause of death. There was an autopsy, but nothing's been filed yet."

"He was over eighty. Why an autopsy?"

"Because he died in the hospital." Simon leaned closer, his voice quiet. "Car accident. Brakes failed. He survived. Broken leg that needed surgery. Everything went well. He was about to get discharged the next day."

"Heart attack?"

"No. From what I was able to find at the ME's office, they've ruled out cardiac arrest."

Tori arched an eyebrow. "You hacked their files?"

Simon smiled. "I did. And people don't just stop breathing and die for no reason, even in their eighties."

"What are you suggesting?"

Simon's voice lowered even more. "I'm suggesting that like Brewster, the car accident is suspicious. Brewster died but Harken survived. So they found some other way to kill him."

"They? The Blue Dragons?" Tori shook her head. "Hospitals have too much security. Besides, if you're a patient, you have monitors on you and stuff, right?"

"Yeah, I guess. Maybe he was drugged. Someone came in, slipped something in his water maybe. Maybe they smothered him."

"I take it you're pretty much convinced it wasn't natural causes."

"They're doing a full tox. If he was drugged, they'll find it. But it's suspicious, don't you think?"

Tori nodded. "Yeah. But as it stands, his death *could* be natural causes. Let's don't jump to conclusions, even though, yeah, I agree it looks suspicious." She ran a hand through her hair. "I have enough going on with Staley. I hope Harken is not going to be one more to look into."

"So what do you want me to do?"

"There was a black SUV. Looked to be a newer model. I didn't get the make. But it was speeding out of my driveway yesterday when I got home."

Simon smiled. "I'm good, Hunter, but I'm not that good. That's not much to go on. You're going to have to give me a little more than that."

"Can you look at the names on our list and see if any of them own a black SUV?"

"Oh, sure. I can do that. I'm also going to try to find out who visited Harken in the hospital."

"Okay, good." She glanced at her watch. "I need to get going." She looked back at him. "You got plans today?"

"I'll probably play around with this stuff, do some snooping. You?"

Tori sighed and shook her head. "Not really, no. I'll probably try to see if I can catch up with some of these guys."

"If you need me for anything, use the new phone. I'll keep it with me."

"Okay. Thanks, Simon. For all your help with this, you know. It means a lot to me."

"No problem. I like doing this kind of stuff."

She tapped his arm as she walked past. "I'll be in touch."

CHAPTER THIRTY-FIVE

Just as Tori had pulled into the drive-thru at a local taco joint Sam liked, she got a text from her. *Change of plans. We're doing brunch instead.* Tori stared at the text for a second. *Why?* Sam's reply was quick. *Family intervention. Because we love you.*

She blew out her breath, then got out of line, heading back home. Family intervention meant Casey and Leslie would be joining them. It was probably just as well. She needed a sounding board. She needed to talk it out, sort through it. Who better than her best friends? Because, with Simon's help, she felt like she was getting close. Maybe too close.

As expected, Casey's truck was parked in their driveway. She wondered if Sam had called Casey the minute she'd left the house. Most likely. She found them in the kitchen, sitting at the bar drinking coffee.

"Family intervention, huh?"

"My doing," Sam admitted.

"You're worried about me?"

"I am."

Tori shoved her hands into her pockets of her jeans. "I'm sorry. I was trying to keep you all out of it. I was—"

"Well, let's stop with all that bullshit then," Casey said bluntly. "We're here. All of us. Let's talk this out. We're all goddamn cops, Hunter. I know you want to go all cowboy on us and handle this yourself, but it's going to come back and bite you in the ass," she said, her voice getting louder with each word.

Tori stared at her. "And like Sam, you think I should go to Malone?"

Casey held her gaze. "Yes, I do."

Tori shook her head. "He'll hand it over to CIU. He'll—"

"I think if we talk to him, explain it all, he'll let us run with it. He'll—"

"Oh, hell, O'Connor, you're living in a goddamn dream world," Tori said loudly. "He won't let us run with it. He can't. He'll have to—"

"Stop." Sam stepped between them, holding her hands up. "This is not how we do things. Not in this family." Sam turned to her. "We're going to talk about it, Tori. Tell us what you know. Tell us what you're thinking. And more importantly, tell us your plan." Sam's expression softened as she touched Tori's arm. "Please?"

Tori acknowledged Sam's gentle touch on her, the love in her eyes. She'd told herself she was trying to protect them. Of course she was. But was that *really* it? Not completely. Because of this. Because she knew they'd intervene. Knew they'd try to talk some sense into her.

She looked out the kitchen window, seeing the blue skies, the bright sunshine. She knew how perfect of a morning it was—she'd been out in it. She suddenly wished they were out on the boat. Right now. All of them. She could imagine the water, the wind barely making a ripple on the lake's surface. And if she wasn't obsessed with finding her family's killer, she would have thought it a nearly perfect spring day.

But she was obsessed, wasn't she? So much so that she'd withdrawn from Sam, withdrawn from Casey. She looked at them now. First Sam, then Casey and Les. Sam was her whole life, her reason for living. Sam loved her without question. Even though she'd been distant—emotionally, at least—Sam was still here for her. Because Sam understood. Tori didn't have to tell her everything she was feeling, thinking, because Sam already knew. Sam knew her better than she knew herself.

And Casey? Casey was her rock. Casey kept her out of trouble. And like Sam, Casey loved her without question. These were her *people*. Leslie, too. She could count on them. She could trust them.

She finally blew out her breath. "Okay. Let's talk."

While Sam poured coffee for her, Tori went into the office to get the folder—the folder with her father's notes, Simon's stuff and Charles Griffin's confession letter. She supposed she'd let Casey and Les read all of it. Sam already had.

"You both know the gist of what's been going on. I'll go into what I've learned in a little more detail." She stood at the corner of the bar and placed the folder in front of her. She glanced at Casey. "I showed you some of this, the notes and the list of names. My father had been investigating the Blue Dragons at the request of his captain, Captain Brewster. The notes were hidden, stuck in a file with old tax returns. All these years they were in my possession, and I had no clue. Why he hid them there, I don't know. The fact that I hadn't gone through all that stuff and thrown it away is a damn miracle." She met Sam's eyes. "I guess holding on to grief like I did was a blessing."

Sam gave her a quick nod but said nothing.

"Anyway, there was a list of names and some notes he'd made," she said, glancing at Leslie. She wasn't sure how much Casey had relayed to her. "Surveillance notes, really. Then there were some notes that were written in code. They looked like jumbled letters. I had them…well, decrypted. The guy who did it—I'll call him Boris."

"Yeah, your Russian friend," Casey said with a smile.

"By not telling you who he is, I'm protecting him as well as you." She took out the spreadsheet. "These were the names my father had written down. Sawyer. Jenson. Hamilton. Jaworski. Douglas. Bexley. Casper. Dewberry. Cunningham. Harken. Staley. McMillan." She paused. "And Hunter." She looked at them all. "My uncle. My dad's brother. The last four were all lieutenants at the time."

She handed the spreadsheet to Casey. "Casper is deceased, so out of the equation. I learned from the notes that were decrypted that Dewberry wasn't involved. Besides, I'd already interviewed him. He's clean. I trust him. The rest are still in play, other than Lieutenant Staley, who was killed in his home the same day as Griffin."

"*What*? You're kidding," Sam said, obviously shocked by the news.

"No. And Lieutenant Harken died the week before. Cause of death is unknown. There was a car accident. Boris thinks it was suspicious. Harken was in the hospital, about to be released. Died the night before release."

"This can't all be a coincidence," Casey stated.

"No." She took out the notes that were in her father's handwriting. "These notes were not encrypted, for whatever reason." She handed them to Casey, knowing she'd read them the other day. "Surveillance. It appears he started writing them in code when he felt like he was being followed."

"Followed? By whom?" Leslie asked.

"The notes will explain." She took the ones Simon had printed out for her. "These are all in order. Read them as such."

She sipped her coffee while Casey read through the notes, handing each page to Les when she finished. Sam came closer, leaning into her, their shoulders touching.

"Are you mad at me?" Sam whispered.

Tori looked into her eyes and shook her head. "No."

She felt Sam's hand on her back, felt her rub softly against her, but Sam said nothing else.

"Wow. This is telling," Casey said. "And what about Brewster?"

"Simon thinks his death is suspicious." *Shit.* "Boris," she corrected. "No way to go back to it now, though. I think my dad inferred it was suspicious too."

"That's what I took from it." Casey handed Leslie the last page. "And your uncle? These notes indicate that he was involved."

"Yeah. I spoke with him the other day. Thursday. He said his only knowledge of the Blue Dragons was from the old days. I think he was lying to me. Well, I guess I now *know* he was lying," Tori corrected herself. "But with everything my father witnessed, it still doesn't implicate these guys in murder."

"Your father thought someone was following him," Casey said. "These guys, right?"

Tori shrugged. "I guess. He pegged Jenson for sure."

"At the pharmacy," Leslie added as she read.

"Whatever other evidence he had on them, he'd already given to Brewster. And we now know that he never got the chance to meet with the chief. So, all this died with Brewster and my dad. As far as the Blue Dragons were concerned, it was end of story."

"Until Charles Griffin left you that letter," Sam said.

"I think it all started with Staley, not Griffin. His wife had a stroke, clinging to life, I'm told. He freaks out, falls to his knees, begs forgiveness from God to save his wife." Tori shrugged. "Don't know about you, but if all I did was take some drug money, I don't think that begs for forgiveness. But murder? More than one?" She nodded. "Yeah. That might have me begging."

"Go on," Sam said. "What are your thoughts?"

"Staley was going to confess to what all happened back then. I learned that from Cunningham. Staley asked to meet with him. Had drinks. Wanted to warn him that he was going to the authorities. Cunningham found out that they were involved in a lot of things other than just grabbing drug money. They planted evidence. They removed evidence. They took bribes. They let suspects walk. But Staley's main concern was the murders. Cunningham said he had no knowledge of any murders."

"You believe that?" Casey asked.

"I do. He didn't appear to be hiding anything. As he told me, he was low man on the totem pole, and I believe that. For one reason, he was never mentioned in my father's surveillance notes. All the others were." She pointed to the papers on the bar. "Well, at least the notes that I have."

"Do you still plan to interview all these guys?"

"I don't know what I'm going to do. Staley put it in motion. His threats to confess got someone very worried. So they called Griffin, thinking they still owned him, and tried to get him to off Staley."

"You think Staley was the target Griffin mentioned in his letter?" Casey asked.

"Yeah, I do. But Griffin wouldn't do it. Griffin threatened to go to the cops too. Now you've got both Staley and Griffin threatening. What do you do?"

Casey shook her head. "I don't know, Tori. That's taking a chance. I mean, these guys are old now, retired. Are they going to have the balls to pay some hired gun to take out these two guys?" She held up her hand. "And I know at the beginning we thought that there really wasn't a target. We thought they just wanted to eliminate Griffin because he knew too much, and his sister had died, and they had nothing on him anymore."

"Right. But I now think there really *was* a target. Staley. Hell, maybe even Harken too. They probably didn't know that Griffin no longer had family—immediate family. They may have not even kept up with him all these years. And yes, these guys are older. Some more than others. Late seventies, most. Like my uncle. Pete Dewberry is only seventy-two. And Cunningham is in his sixties." She grabbed the spreadsheet. "Bexley is sixty-eight. Jaworski and Hamilton, both mid-seventies. Harken was eighty-one."

"Like I said, they're old guys. They've been off the force and out of touch for years now."

"Not so out of touch that they didn't hire two guys to kill for them," she reminded Casey.

"But you can't prove anything," Sam said. "That's the problem with going back over thirty years."

"And without Staley's confession, we got nothing," Casey said.

"But he did confess," Tori said. "He confessed to Cunningham."

"I think you're overlooking a big piece of the puzzle here," Leslie interjected. "If you think one of these guys hired two hitmen and those hitmen killed Staley and Griffin, why not go with that angle?"

"Because those two guys are now dead," Casey said.

"Right. You told me that. But ID the guys, find out who hired them. See if phone records lead to one of the guys on the list."

"Fort Worth PD has the case, and they did ID one of them," Casey said. "Jeffrey Scarsdale. He's from Phoenix. Was arrested here in Dallas eight years ago. Felony weapons charge, possession. Got basically a slap on the wrist for his trouble."

"What are you talking about?" Sam asked with a frown.

"I'm sorry," Tori said. "Too much was happening at once and I didn't get a chance to tell you."

"Our Chevy Impala was caught on camera leaving the Staley residence," Casey explained. "Fort Worth PD pulled the car from the Trinity. Two bodies inside. Shot in the head. Found a gun in there too. Waiting on ballistics, but it was a 9-mil in the car. And a 9-mil was used in the murders of Griffin and Staley. We're thinking—hoping—it's a match."

"Wow. I don't get it then. You hire a hitman, why the hell kill him after he's done the job?" Sam asked. "That makes no sense. Now you're really calling attention to it all."

"I don't know the reason," Tori said. "Maybe they overheard something. Maybe they knew too much. Hell, maybe they weren't real hired killers. Maybe they were just a couple of thugs."

"Still, why kill them?"

"Maybe the thugs turned the tables on them," Leslie suggested. "Wanted more money or something."

Casey nodded. "Yeah, that could be. Or it could be any number of reasons."

"They panicked," Sam said. "Like you said, they're older now. Maybe the stress of it all was too much. Get rid of the evidence—the guys who did the killing for them."

"Which, of course, only leads to more evidence." Tori gathered up the papers, knowing that they were only speculating now. There were no answers. No concrete answers anyway.

Casey stilled her hand. "You need to go to Malone with all this, Tori. You know you do."

"Honey, I think there's enough here—especially with the murders of Staley and Griffin—to go forward with this," Sam said to her.

"Who's going to go forward, Sam? CIU? Another team?" She tapped her chest. "It won't be me. And I need it to be me. I don't trust anyone else with this."

Sam held her gaze. "I think you're underestimating Stan. I truly think he would let you continue this, Tori."

Tori looked at Casey instead. "You said this would come back to bite me in the ass. Well, if Malone lets us run with this, as you said, then it will surely come back to bite *him* in the ass. I don't think he takes that chance. The captain already booted me from the case."

"You should still—"

"No. You tell him what you need to as far as Griffin is concerned. But for me? No. I want to know who killed my goddamn family. That's all I'm concerned with."

CHAPTER THIRTY-SIX

Their brunch turned into lunch. Although it was the kind of lunch she and Casey most enjoyed—pizza and beer. Too bad it wasn't football season. They could relax and catch a college game then.

"We eat entirely too much pizza," Leslie said as she bit into her slice.

"Not my fault," Tori said as she reached across Casey for another piece. "I started off the morning planning to pick up tacos for breakfast." She looked at Sam. "How soon after I left did you call them?"

Sam smiled at her. "You weren't even out of the garage."

"So what did you learn from Boris?" Casey asked. "Or should we call him Simon?"

"Look, let's just stick with Boris, okay? He's a nice guy. I'd hate to see him get into trouble. Because he's hacking into all sorts of things he shouldn't be. For one thing, he got into the ME's records for Harken. There's no COD yet. There was a car accident, brakes failed. Eerily similar to Brewster. Boris said

Harken had surgery for a broken leg and was doing well. Was about to be discharged. Died during the night."

"He suspects foul play?"

Tori smiled. "Boris has watched too many movies. I think he's going with someone smothered him or slipped something into his water. Regardless, they're doing a full tox on him. Had he died at home, they probably wouldn't have thought twice about COD because of his age. But because he died in the hospital, supposedly in good health, they're doing a full workup."

"Lawsuits," Sam said.

"Right."

A cell phone ringing broke up their discussion, and everyone reached for theirs at once. The phone continued to ring. Damn. The burner. She'd placed it by the coffeepot earlier.

"Yeah," she answered as she snatched it up.

"It's me. Simon."

She smiled at that. "Good. I was hoping your phone hadn't been stolen already."

He laughed quietly. "Sorry, yeah. But I found something. It's about Harken. I went through the hospital security cameras while he was there. I ran a face recognition program. Staley went to see him two days before he died."

"Before Harken died or two days before Staley died?"

"Right, before Harken died. And that's not all. I put in all the photos of the guys on your list. Wasn't only Staley who visited. McMillan showed up too. The afternoon before he died."

"Are you going with the theory that McMillan slipped something in his water?"

"Staley visits Harken. Two days later, Harken is dead."

"Staley was the one who was going to confess. I can see them wanting him out of the way, but why would they kill Harken too?" Tori glanced at the others, who were all blatantly listening to her side of the conversation.

"More importantly, who is 'they?'" Simon asked. "So I dumped all the cell phone records. You won't believe this, Hunter. I went back a year. Some carriers keep records longer than that, but I thought a year was enough. There was absolutely no activity between any of these guys on your list. None whatsoever. Except for two of them. James Hunter and Thomas Bexley had two calls between them during that year. That is, until sixteen days before Harken died. On that day, Staley called three people. McMillan, Bexley, and your uncle. The next day, he called Cunningham and Harken. Over the next few days, he called everyone on your list except Pete Dewberry." Simon paused. "Well, obviously not Casper, since he's deceased."

"You never mentioned his COD. It wasn't recently too, was it?"

"No, no. His is legit. Cancer. Years ago."

"Okay. Go on."

"Yeah, so since Staley's first calls, the others have been calling each other. But not all of them. Cunningham got no calls from anyone except Staley, Bexley, and Douglas. Three from Staley, two from Bexley, and a brief one from Douglas."

"Right. Staley was making plans to meet up with him. Bexley used to be his partner. Bexley introduced him to the Blue Dragons."

"I show McMillan, Harken, Hamilton, Jaworski, Jenson, Sawyer, Douglas, and your uncle with several calls between them over the course of that week. Your uncle made the first call—to McMillan. Bexley is mixed in there a couple of times too but not as much as all the others. Then complete silence for four days leading up to Harken's accident. The day of the accident, calls start up again." He paused. "On the timeline that I've got, your uncle made the first call again. And again, it was to McMillan."

Tori felt her hand squeeze tightly on the phone. "Are you sure?"

"Yes. I've dumped all the records. I've got them on a spreadsheet for you and cross-referenced the calls and times. I've got calls up to Thursday. Nothing yesterday. I haven't checked today."

She felt her jaw clench tightly and she had to make herself relax. Her uncle made the first call? Her *uncle*?

"Can Boris email that to me?" she asked a bit tersely.

"Of course. But there's more."

Before he could continue, her real cell rang. She felt it vibrating in her jeans pocket. "Hold on, Simon." She met Sam's eyes as she took her phone out. It was the marina.

"Hello. This is Hunter."

"Hello, Tori. It's Jimmy from down at the marina."

"Yeah, Jimmy. What's up?"

"Well, the police are here. I thought I should give you a heads-up before they called you."

She met Sam's eyes again. "What's going on, Jimmy?"

"Some people saw a lot of blood on the pier or something. Went to investigate, saw blood on your boat, called security here. There's a body on your boat. Dead. I don't know much else. The police kinda ran me off after that."

"Christ," she murmured, her eyes still locked with Sam. "I'm on my way. Thanks for calling, Jimmy." She put the burner phone to her ear again. "Simon, I've got to go. I'll be in touch."

"Okay, Tori. I've already emailed that to you."

"Thanks." She disconnected the call, then turned, finding the three of them staring at her.

"Well? What's going on?" Casey demanded. "You turned white as a ghost."

"What is it?" Sam asked.

"There's a goddamn body on our boat."

"Then let's get out there."

But Tori shook her head. "No, Sam. You and Les stay here. Casey—"

"We can all go."

"No. Casey and I can handle it."

She went over and pulled her into a hug, then gave her a quick kiss. "Be right back."

The look in Sam's eyes told her she wasn't happy, but she didn't argue.

CHAPTER THIRTY-SEVEN

"Why do you have two phones?"

"Because Simon watches too many movies," she said as she sped down I-30 toward Fort Worth.

"A burner?"

"Yeah. He got us both one so we could talk freely without having to have secret meetings," she said.

"What all did he say?"

"Not a lot," she lied.

"Bullshit, Hunter. I can read you as well as Sam can. Your jaw did the clench thing and your eyes turned nearly black. So spill it."

"He pulled phone records. He's got a timeline as to when the calls started. Staley made the first calls to let everyone know he was going to go in and confess. My uncle made the first call to the others."

"Holy shit. You don't think…"

"I don't know what to think." She hit the steering wheel hard. "No, I *do* know what to think, I just don't want to think it. And now, Jesus, there's a fucking body on my goddamn boat!"

"It can't be related. There's no way in hell they'd kill someone and dump the body on your boat. For what purpose?"

"Hell, I don't know. What purpose was it to hire a hitman and then kill the goddamn hitman." She ran a hand through her hair. "Logically, it shouldn't be related. But my gut tells me it is."

By the time they made it through Fort Worth traffic and out to the marina on Eagle Mountain Lake, the ME was already at the scene. Even though this was way out of their jurisdiction, they both held up their shields as they walked up.

"Detectives Hunter and O'Connor, Dallas PD," she explained. "That's my boat."

"Okay, sure, Detectives. Go on in."

It was a small marina, not far from where they used to keep the boat. She and Sam had bought this boat just last summer. It was a thirty-five-footer, like the old one, but a little newer. Ten years newer, in fact. They'd kept the name—*Hunter's Way*. She had wanted to name her something different, something that reflected both of them, but Sam wouldn't hear of it.

A large community deck was built off the piers, each slip owner having access to a portion of it. This part was covered. She and Sam had put a small table and chairs on their section. When they all came at once, Sikes included, the boat was too crowded to comfortably sit them all, so they'd use the deck instead.

The familiar yellow crime scene tape had already been stretched across the walkway that led past their table and chairs to the boat. She and Casey ducked under it. Judging by the blood on the pier, she would guess the guy had been killed right there.

"Hang on, ma'am. You can't be back here."

Tori narrowed her eyes at the officer who blocked her path. "Tori Hunter. It's my boat."

He held both hands up, stopping them. "Sorry, ma'am. You can't go on that thing. Now get back behind the tape. This is a crime scene."

"I can board my own goddamn boat." She held her shield up. "Now get out of my way." She moved his hand aside. "Idiot," she murmured under her breath as she went to the gangway.

She stopped up short, though, when she saw the body lying facedown on the deck. A large man. Forty- or fifty-pounds overweight. *Oh, Christ. Was it him?*

"Got ID?" she asked to no one in particular.

"Nothing on him," someone answered without turning around. The ME or a forensic tech, she guessed. There were three people and the body on board. She and Casey made five. There was hardly room to stand on the small back deck.

She stepped closer. "If you'll flip him over…"

The man turned then, eyeing her. "You are?"

"Detective Hunter, Dallas PD."

"A little out of your range, aren't you?"

"It's my boat."

"Ah." The man nodded. "I see. Sure. We can turn him over. I've got everything I need." He turned to another man. "Doc? Okay to turn him?"

"Sure, sure."

Tori stared at the face of Darrell Cunningham, his blank eyes opened and seemingly staring accusingly up at her. She swallowed and turned to Casey.

"Cunningham," she said quietly.

Casey nodded. "Not logical, no, but I guess we should always trust your gut."

Tori turned abruptly and jumped back on the pier, her force rocking the boat a little as she stepped over the gangway.

"Where are you going?"

"You stay here. Handle it, O'Connor."

"Hunter, where the hell are you going?"

Tori ignored her as she nearly broke out into a sprint. *That son of a bitch. That goddamn son of a bitch.*

CHAPTER THIRTY-EIGHT

Even though she'd taken off with a squeal of her tires from the marina, she'd calmed down some as she headed back to Dallas. She ignored the calls from Casey. And she ignored Sam's calls. She couldn't talk to either of them right now. She needed some answers first. She needed to see him, look into his eyes. She pounded her fist on the wheel. Yes, she needed some goddamn answers.

She was driving ten miles over the speed limit, and she made herself slow down. Why the hell kill Cunningham? Because he'd talked to her? What good would that do if he'd already spilled his guts to her? And if they were willing to kill Cunningham, again, why the hell hire somebody in the first place? It made no goddamn sense.

She took her phone out, calling Pete Dewberry. He answered on the third ring.

"Hey, Tori. Got something new?"

"Pete, listen to me. Don't answer your door for anyone. You be alert. Get your gun. Keep it with you."

"What the hell's got you all shook up? I'm out on my deck having my beer with the missus. What's going on?"

"Darrell Cunningham was killed. They goddamn left him on my boat."

"Whoa now. What boat?"

"That doesn't matter, Pete. I just need you to be careful. If they know I talked to Cunningham, then they know I talked to you."

"Okay, Tori. I'll heed your warning." She heard his back door open. "I'll lock myself inside. Now. Where are you going? I hear road noise."

She took a deep breath. "I'm going to see my uncle."

* * *

She rang the doorbell three or four times, then pounded her fist on the door. It wasn't Aunt Judith who answered it this time. It was her uncle. His eyes widened in surprise when he saw her. She pushed her way inside, closing the door forcibly behind her.

"What the hell are you doing?"

"Where's Aunt Judith?" she asked, her voice sounding much calmer than she felt.

"She's out shopping with the girls. Why?"

She slowly pulled her weapon from the holster at her hip. "Because I don't want an audience, that's why."

He took several steps back, his face turning pale. "What the *hell* are you doing?"

"Don't act stupid with me. You know what the hell I'm doing." She grabbed his arm roughly and shoved him down into one of the pristine white chairs in the formal living room. A room reserved for family Christmas parties only. She pointed her gun at him.

"Why did you lie to me?"

He held his hands up as if in self-defense. "I don't know what you're talking about."

"The goddamn Blue Dragons," she nearly yelled. "You said it didn't exist. You said it was only rumors, yet you were involved in it the whole goddamn time!"

"I don't know what you're talking about," he said again.

She took a step away from him, trying to gather her thoughts. "My dad had some notes on a case he was working on. You know the case, don't you? The one Brewster had him working on. Investigating the Blue Dragons. He handed all his notes over to Brewster. But you guys thought all that had burned up with him in the car crash, didn't you?"

He shook his head. "I don't know anything about that."

"Bullshit! You know exactly what I'm talking about." She paced in front of him. "I can understand why you'd kill Staley. He was about to talk. But why Harken? Why Cunningham?"

"You got it all wrong, Tori."

"Do I?" She went to him, the gun held to his head. "How could you? That was your goddamn brother!" she yelled. "My family." She tapped her chest. "That was *my* family. How could you kill them like that as if they were nothing?"

"I swear, it wasn't me. I swear," he said, his lips quivering.

"My *family*! My mother. My brothers. For god's sake, Emily was only ten years old. How could you do that to them?"

"It wasn't me," he said again, his voice was hoarse with desperation.

Tori met his eyes. "I want to put a bullet in your goddamn head so bad." She held the gun closer, nearly touching him. Her words were slow now, to the point. "I want to avenge their deaths. Do you understand me?" She felt tears in her eyes, and she blinked them away impatiently. "I've lived with this for so many years. This hatred that I had. Hatred that wasn't directed at anyone because I didn't know who was responsible." She touched his forehead with the barrel of her gun. "I know now, don't I?"

"I beg you, Tori. It wasn't me."

"You *beg* me? Do you think my family begged for their lives?"

"It wasn't me," he whispered.

"It *was* you!" she countered, her voice loud. "I have phone records. You made the first call. *You!* After Staley was going to confess, you made the first call."

"No! Someone came to see me. They—"

"I don't believe you!"

"I'm telling you the truth. I swear."

"Who was it?"

He shook his head. "I...I can't say, Tori. He...he's lost his mind. He's threatened all of us. He's threatened our families."

"Why kill Cunningham? Why him?"

"Because he talked to you. He was afraid of how much he told you."

"Then why dump his body on my goddamn boat?"

"I told you, he's lost his mind. He came here talking crazy stuff."

She again touched his forehead with her gun. "Who is it?" she asked again slowly.

"He'll...he'll kill me," he said weakly. "He'll kill Judy. Just like he killed Cunningham, he'll kill me. He said as much."

"*He'll* kill you? I'm the one with a goddamn gun to your head! If it wasn't you, then who the fuck was it?"

She felt a presence behind her a second before she saw movement. Her uncle's eyes darted in that direction, but she didn't move. She knew who it was.

"Get out of here, O'Connor," she said without looking.

"Tori, you do not want to do this," Casey said, her voice almost calm.

"Get out of here, O'Connor," she said again. "This is my deal, not yours."

"Tori, Sam loves you. I love you. This isn't going to bring them back. This isn't going to do anything for you. Put the gun down, Tori. You're not this person."

"I *am* this person."

"No, you're not. The Tori I know would never do this."

"That was my goddamn family," she said, her voice weak now. "And he...he was a part of it. He—"

"Sam is your family now. We're your family. And you're going to throw that away for *this*? For revenge? Then what will you have? Spend your life in prison? Will that be worth it? Are you willing to lose everything you have for *this*?"

She let Casey's words wash over her as she stared into the frightened eyes of her uncle. Was she this person? Yes. She wanted revenge. It ate at her. It had always eaten at her. She'd never been able to do anything about it, though. It just festered inside. Then one day a man named Charles Griffin decided to write her a letter. He put things in motion.

That letter brought everything flying back in candid color. Thoughts of revenge—thoughts that she'd tucked into the dark recesses of her heart, her soul—peeked out. Thoughts that she'd kept hidden from Sam. These last few years, hidden from herself even. Those thoughts—those dark, dark thoughts of revenge—were the ones in control now. The ones that had been dictating her actions for the last week.

She could have that revenge right now. Pull the trigger. It would be *so* easy. It would be over with then. But no, it wouldn't. There were still others. Her uncle wasn't the only player. Not the one in charge. Was she going to hunt them all down?

Casey was right, of course. It wasn't worth it. She'd lose Sam. She'd lose this life she'd built. This life that had only a few very close-knit friends—her family now. She'd lose it just to watch her uncle's blood spill from his head, much like her father's had all those years ago.

Sam loves you. I love you.

No. She didn't want to be that person. She *wasn't* that person. She lowered her gun.

CHAPTER THIRTY-NINE

Sam didn't want to push. She could sense how fragile Tori was right now. Tori had shown her vulnerable side before but never like this. The first time she'd seen Tori cry, it had been after Sam had been assaulted—raped. They hadn't been lovers yet. Not quite. And Sam had finally been able to talk about it, to get it out, to cry. Her tears had brought on Tori's. And she had cried again when Sam had first told her that she was in love with her. Tori hadn't been able to say the words back to her, but Sam knew she loved her too. Like she knew it still today. Tori had been such a force back then. To say she'd mellowed over the years was an understatement. She'd fallen in love with Tori as she'd been back then, and Tori was certainly still as passionate about things. She simply went about it in a more subtle manner now. Tori wasn't quite as hard around the edges as she'd been when they met, but she loved her just as fiercely.

Today, Tori's eyes were filled with tears, and she'd said she didn't want to talk. Casey had given her a quick rundown on what had happened. Tori's uncle had been shaken, no doubt, but he wouldn't report Tori. He couldn't. Tori had evidence. Tori had notes and surveillance. Tori now had phone records.

"She's got to go to Malone," Casey had said. "You've got to make her, Sam."

Could she make her? She wasn't sure. She only knew she couldn't stand to see Tori like this. Tori was at the sliding door, looking out on the patio. Sam wondered if she was seeing anything or if she was simply lost in her own mind. Well, she'd given her enough time. Tori saying she didn't want to talk was an excuse to gather her thoughts before they actually *did* talk.

She took a deep breath, then moved to her. Tori jumped when she slid her arms around her waist from behind. Sam ignored the stiffness she felt. Instead, she squeezed her tighter and rested her cheek against Tori's back. She just held her, saying nothing. After what felt like minutes—and it probably was—she felt Tori relax. Sam relaxed too.

"Talk to me," she requested quietly. "Please? Don't shut me out."

She felt Tori tremble in her arms, and it nearly broke her heart.

"I'm not sure what to say, Sam. I...I lost it. I completely lost it. If O'Connor hadn't shown up, who the hell knows what might have happened."

"But it didn't happen."

Tori turned around then, pulling out of her arms. "I had my goddamn gun held to his head!" she said loudly. "I wanted to pull the trigger, Sam. I did. I came so close to pulling that fucking trigger."

Sam met her eyes, only barely resisting the urge to reach out and wipe Tori's tears away. "Why didn't you?" she asked instead.

Their eyes locked together, both swimming in tears now. "Because of you. I couldn't do that to you. I couldn't ruin this, ruin you." Tori finally brushed at her own cheek. "Ruin *us*. And now I goddamn feel like a coward. Like I let them down. All these years, I'd dreamed of finding the bastard who killed them. Finding him and exacting revenge. I *promised* them, Sam. And I failed. I—"

"Oh, sweetheart, no. You haven't failed. If you'd shot—killed—your uncle, if you thought that was going to be your revenge, *then* you would have failed. You would have failed me, yes. But more importantly, you would have failed yourself." She took both of Tori's hands. "You are the most sincere, trustworthy person I know. You have integrity, honor. You may not always follow the rules, Tori, but you *always* do the right thing. You may think you stopped for me...for us. But I think you stopped because you knew it was the *wrong* thing you were doing."

Their eyes held for a long moment, and she knew Tori was trying to absorb her words, trying to fit them into her jumbled mind. Tori looked away then and covered her face with her hands, rubbing vigorously against it.

"I'm a goddamn idiot," Tori mumbled behind her fingers.

Sam smiled at that, knowing that Tori was back. She didn't reply, though. She let Tori sift through her thoughts alone. Tori dropped her hands then, her eyes still red and teary.

"Did Casey tell you about the phone records?"

"She mentioned it, yes."

"Simon sent me a spreadsheet. I haven't looked at it yet."

Sam chewed on her lower lip. "Honey, don't you think you should take all of this to Malone?"

Tori shook her head. "No. Not directly."

"What does that mean?"

"Casey is working Griffin's murder. It's going to tie to Staley's murder. I think she should do what Leslie suggested—work it from the hitman angle. Find out who the hell hired them." She paused, meeting Sam's gaze. "And depending on what happens, I'll go from there."

She nodded slowly, knowing Tori had to do this on her own, in her own way. "Okay," she said simply.

Tori reached out and touched her face. "I can't go to Malone with all of this, Sam. Most of the evidence I got from a hacker. Nothing is admissible. And the phone records? Malone would have my ass."

Sam gave a quick smile. "You're right. He would have your ass."

Tori's expression turned serious. "I'm sorry, Sam. What I did today...I'm sorry. I know I disappointed you. I—"

"I love you. You could never disappoint me. I know how passionate you are, Tori. About everything. So you didn't disappoint me."

Tori gave her a sad smile. "Thank you for saying that, Sam, but I—I snapped. I—"

Sam put a finger to Tori's lips. "No. Don't beat yourself up. It's over with. You need to focus on tomorrow. Get a fresh start." She removed her finger and replaced it with her mouth. "Let's relax for the rest of today, huh? I could use a little us time."

Their eyes met and she could tell Tori was warring with herself, no doubt thinking she had countless things to do on this late Saturday afternoon. Then Tori nodded and pulled her close, giving her such a slow, drawn-out kiss, it nearly made her toes curl. Those old familiar feelings—the ones that made her feel like a teenager in love—hit and she pressed her body against Tori's. After all these years, Tori could still make the butterflies in her stomach take flight.

It had been a while since they'd made love on a Saturday afternoon. She felt almost shy as she led Tori into their bedroom.

CHAPTER FORTY

"Damn, Mac is dedicated."

Casey was sitting at Sam's desk in their home office, and she tossed her phone down. "On the job in the lab on a Sunday. Gotta love him."

"That's probably why he's divorced. He works every day."

Casey looked at her. "He's divorced? But he's got all those pictures on his desk."

Tori nodded. "Grandkids and stuff." She waved her hand at Casey. "What did he say?"

"Yeah, the two guys in the Chevy were killed with a .45, point-blank, even had powder burns on their skulls."

"And the 9-mil they found?"

Casey grinned. "Yeah, that's a match to Griffin and Staley. And there's more. The slug they pulled from Cunningham—it's a .45. He's been in touch with the lab in Fort Worth. They haven't done ballistics yet, but the lab tech there said they were going to run it today, thinking it's a match with the two guys in the car."

"That's great. You can tie Griffin and Staley. You can tie Cunningham to the two dead guys. What about an ID on the second guy in the car?"

Casey shook her head. "Mac didn't know. And I called the detective on the scene, but he's not answering, and I don't have his cell."

Tori shrugged. "It's Sunday. Not everyone's working, you know." She drummed her desk a few times with her fingers. "Listen, I need to apologize...or thank you." She met Casey's gaze. "Or both, I guess."

Casey gave her a smirk. "Apologize for leaving my ass at the boat? Or thank me for keeping you out of jail?"

Tori smiled at her. "Like I said—both."

"No need to thank me, Hunter. It was totally selfish on my part. If you're in prison, then I'd feel obligated to visit you at least once a week. That would surely cut into my time. Not to mention, I'd lose my fishing buddy."

"How did you get there so fast?"

"Got one of the Fort Worth officers to drive me. Sirens and everything. That was pretty cool. They're going to want to interview you, by the way." Then Casey's expression turned serious. "Were you really going to shoot him?"

"I honestly don't know. Maybe."

"Did you believe him? When he said he wasn't the one?"

Tori shrugged. "I don't know. You'll say a lot of things when there's a gun held to your head."

Casey nodded. "Okay. So now what?"

Tori pointed at the wall of the office. "We'll use our whiteboard. Let's try to make some sense of these phone records that Simon—*Boris*—gave me." Tori stood and tossed the folder to where Casey was sitting. "And I think you should do an official request for phone records for Staley and Cunningham. We know that neither of them was the one who contracted with a hired gun, but they'll link to these others. Then you can run something like Simon did." She pointed at the folder. "In the meantime, we'll get a head start."

"Neither Staley nor Cunningham is in our jurisdiction. Malone won't go for that. And you keep saying *you*, Tori. Does that mean you're not ready to come back?"

"Come back for what? Malone pulled me from the case, remember? And both Staley and Cunningham are retired cops from Dallas. There's your angle."

"I still don't think he'll go for it. And you pulled yourself from the case, not him."

"Semantics," she said absently as she sorted through the colored markers. "He was about to pull me."

She took a blue one and drew a box in the center of the whiteboard. Inside the box she wrote STALEY. Then she drew boxes in a circle around that one, adding names to each box from her list.

"Okay. Staley made the first call." She picked up a red marker. "To McMillan, right?"

Casey stared at the spreadsheet. "What about these first two? Bexley and your uncle?"

"Neither were recent. Months ago. Let's start when Staley makes the first call."

"Right. Okay, Staley called McMillan. The call lasted six minutes. Then he called Bexley. This call lasted eleven minutes. Then his next call was to your uncle, but it was nearly two hours later. It was quick. Three minutes."

Tori drew a red line with an arrow from Staley to all three, marking each as one, two, and three. "That was all on Day One?"

"Yes, that was all from Staley on that day. But the same day, later that night—11:08 to be exact—your uncle called McMillan. The call lasted eight minutes."

Tori chose a yellow marker this time, drawing a line from her uncle's box to McMillan, again with an arrow. "So Staley tells McMillan, Bexley, and my uncle that he's going to confess. The other two don't make any calls, yet late that night my uncle does."

"Right."

"Okay, what's next?"

"Next morning, your uncle called Bexley. Fifteen minutes. As soon as that ended, your uncle called McMillan again."

Still using the yellow marker, she added lines to Bexley and another to McMillan, waiting for Casey to continue.

"Okay, then Staley's first call that day went to Cunningham. They talked for four minutes. Then Staley called Harken. Eleven minutes."

Tori used the red marker to draw lines from Staley to each of them, marking them four and five. "Then what?"

"Okay, this is where it gets jumbled," Casey said. "We've got all of these guys calling each other. It's like they hang up with one and call the other. All of them." She was using her index finger, going over the spreadsheet. "No, wait. Cunningham is out of the loop. No one called him except Bexley a couple of times. Oh, and Douglas."

Tori tapped the board. "Staley called Cunningham here."

"Well, I meant besides Staley. Why do you think that was?"

Tori stared at her names. "Cunningham was probably the last to join the group. He was also the one who didn't participate in anything other than drug money. Maybe the others didn't trust him. Or hell, maybe they just didn't know him that well. He and Bexley were partners and rode together. That's probably why Bexley called him."

"Okay, but what's weird is that after Staley made his initial calls to everyone, he did not call any of them back a second time *except* for Cunningham. He called him…one, two…three times," she said as she studied the spreadsheet. "Don't you think that's odd?"

"Cunningham had been out of the loop and didn't really know what all had gone on. I think Staley wanted to confess, wanted to say it all out loud to someone. Cunningham was the only one who didn't already know."

"Something Cunningham told you or are you just guessing?"

"Mostly guessing," she admitted. "Okay, what's next? We've got a jumble of calls. Simon said something about there being a lull."

"Right. The calls went on for over a week. Staley didn't call any of the other ones except Jenson. McMillan called Hamilton and Jaworski. Your uncle called Sawyer and Douglas. Then there are calls between Jenson and Sawyer. Again, all at once. It's like they end one call and start another. Then they stop." Casey tapped the spreadsheet. "Four days. Nothing. There's your lull."

"That was leading up to Harken's accident. Simon said they started up again the day of."

"The first call was from your uncle to McMillan. A long call. Thirty-three minutes."

Tori walked over to Casey. "What about Staley? Was anyone calling him?"

Casey ran her finger down the spreadsheet and nodded. "One. There was a call from your uncle two days later."

Tori opened up her folder, pulling out the notes she'd made. "Harken died on Thursday. The following Monday, Staley is gunned down. And Griffin."

Casey looked at Simon's timeline. "When did you visit your uncle the first time?"

"It was…Thursday. This past Thursday."

"Okay, so it had been a week after Harken died and three days after Staley. No calls before then, but on Thursday evening—after your visit—your uncle called Bexley. Six minutes."

"So on the day that Staley was killed, there were no calls? None? Radio silence?"

"No calls. The first call was Thursday after your visit—your uncle to Bexley. Then he called McMillan. Eleven minutes."

Tori stared at the boxes on the board. "Seems like Hunter and McMillan did an awful lot of talking throughout all this, doesn't it?"

"Still doesn't prove anything."

"No, it doesn't prove a damn thing." She tossed the marker down. "Are we wasting time doing this?"

"It gives a clearer picture, at least."

"Maybe." Tori blew out her breath. "Let's call it a day. It's Sunday. Go home. We don't want to end up divorced like Mac."

Casey laughed. "Yeah. I'll tell Sam it's safe to come back home. But knowing them, they're in the middle of a good movie." She put the spreadsheet back inside the folder. "The weather is great today. If there wasn't crime scene tape up on your boat, we could maybe sneak away for a little fishing."

"Blood on the deck does put a damper on things." She paused. "I asked my uncle why Cunningham was killed. He said because he'd talked to me. I can't help but feel responsible, you know. I—"

"No." Casey shook her head. "You can't blame yourself for that, Tori."

"What if I'd picked someone else? Like Jenson? Or Sawyer? Would Cunningham still be alive?"

"Why did you pick Cunningham?"

"Because he was the only one who wasn't mentioned in my father's surveillance notes."

"What about this other guy you've spoken to? Dewberry?"

"Pete? I picked him at random."

"Do you think he's in danger?"

"I sure as hell hope not."

CHAPTER FORTY-ONE

Casey tossed her phone and keys onto her desk the next morning, eyeing Tori's empty chair. So, she really wasn't coming in. That would leave her to explain things to Malone. With a sigh, she went to get coffee, wishing she'd stopped on the way in. But she'd been running late as it was. Les had gotten a call at four that morning. There'd been another shooting at the same apartment complex, and after she'd left, Casey had drifted off to sleep again.

She took her coffee back to her desk. Malone was in his office, on the phone. He appeared agitated. *Great.* Before she even took a sip of coffee, though, she heard Malone slam his phone down.

"Okay, gonna guess he was talking to Hunter," she murmured. She didn't have long to wait before Malone's voice bellowed from his office.

"O'Connor? Get in here. Now."

Great. She left the coffee on her desk and walked slowly to his office. "Yes, sir?" she said weakly. "You want to see me?"

"Close the door."

She did as instructed and took her usual seat against the wall. He was rummaging in his desk drawer, and she wasn't surprised to see him pull out his bottle of antacids. Yeah, he'd talked to Tori.

"Heard you got a positive match on the 9-mil."

"Yes, sir."

"Good. You close the case?"

"Close it?"

"You found the killer right?"

"Well…" Casey fidgeted as Malone stared at her, waiting. "I don't think we should close the case, Lieutenant."

"What's the problem?" he asked. "Griffin was gunned down at his house. You've got two guys in possession of the gun that killed him. The car they were in matches our description. Case closed."

"But why did they kill him?"

"Why do we care about motive now?" he asked. "They're dead."

"Right. So who killed *them*?"

"Do we care? It's not our case, O'Connor. It's Fort Worth's case."

"Yeah, but the guys also killed Staley," Casey said.

"In Denton. That's not our case either."

"It matches Griffin. It was a hit, Lieutenant. Just like Griffin."

"Was it? You know this how?"

Casey stood up, pacing. "Well, there was the letter that Griffin left Tori."

Malone nodded. "Right. A letter that we have not logged as evidence and won't. So how do you know it was a hit?"

"Well, what about Cunningham?"

"Who the hell is Cunningham?"

Casey sat back down. "His body was found on Tori's boat on Saturday."

Malone sat up straighter, eyebrows raised. "Someone was killed on her boat?"

She nodded. "Darrell Cunningham. He was a retired Dallas cop too. Like Staley."

Malone frowned. "What the hell is going on? Was this someone she knew?"

Casey blinked at him. "No." Was that a lie? Technically, no, Tori didn't *know* the man. "But they're obviously linked. Don't you think?"

Malone ran a hand across his smooth head. "The boat is at Eagle Mountain Lake still, right? Who's got jurisdiction out there? Fort Worth?"

"Yes, sir."

"So that one belongs to them too. Just like the two guys in the Chevy. Again, not our case. Griffin is the only one we care about. The others have nothing to do with us. Out of our jurisdiction, O'Connor."

Casey stood up again. "It's all linked, Lieutenant. Griffin. Staley. Cunningham. The two guys. They're all linked. Griffin was the target of a hit. Who hired the hitman?"

Malone eyed her. "Why was a body left on her boat?"

Casey looked away from him. "I don't know."

Malone stared at her for the longest time, his hand unconsciously rubbing his head. "Take a guess, O'Connor."

"They are all linked," she said again.

"All linked to Griffin?"

She held his gaze. "All linked to Tori's father."

Malone pointed at the chair, and she obediently sat down again. God, Tori was going to kill her. She waited as he opened the bottle of antacids.

Before he popped two into his mouth, he held the bottle up.

"I wonder how many of these things I've been through over the years." He surprised her by smiling. "Most of them had Hunter's name on it."

"Yes, sir."

He cocked his head, looking at her thoughtfully. "Back before Sam came around, Tori used to get into so much trouble."

"I can imagine."

"The very first day she got here, I knew she was going to be a handful. I also knew she would be my best detective. She would always bend the rules as far as they would go. And break them more often than not."

Casey simply nodded.

"Yeah, I don't guess I have to tell you that. Sam used to keep her in line. Now I rely on you for that."

Casey smiled at that. "Tori doesn't always listen to me."

"No, I don't imagine she does." He finally chewed the tablets, then put the bottle back in his drawer. "You want to tell me what's going on, O'Connor?"

Casey swallowed. "Not really, no."

He gave her a quick, humorless smile. "I talked to her. I told her to get her ass in here this morning and she said no, said she needed a few more days." He folded his hands together. "A few more days for what, O'Connor?"

"I don't know."

"Bullshit!" He slammed a fist onto his desk. "I want to know what the hell is going on."

"Oh, man. She'll kill me."

His eyes narrowed. "You want to deal with me, O'Connor, or do you want to deal with her? Pick your poison."

"Well, if I had to choose, I—"

"Oh, for god's sake, O'Connor. I'm not stupid. I know her far too well. One thing that has never changed is her conviction for doing the job. There's no way in hell she'd take time off—vacation—when she was in the middle of a case. Especially a case that had connections to her family. No way."

"But she said you pulled her from the case. That the captain had told you to get her off."

"Right. Because she has no goddamn business working a case that might be linked to her family. And because I know her as well as I do, she's been working it behind the scenes. Behind my back, essentially. So I want to know what she dug up. Because I know she found something." He hit his desk again with his hand. "Yes, O'Connor. All these cases are linked. Of course they are. Now someone dumped a body on her boat? Another retired cop? It's no goddamn coincidence. I want to know what in the hell is going on and I want to know right now!"

His loud voice nearly shook the windows, and she knew she couldn't keep this from him any longer. But yeah, Tori would so kill her.

"She...she found some stuff that her father had left. Some surveillance notes and stuff. Something her father was investigating when he was killed. The Blue Dragons."

Malone frowned. "Blue Dragons? That's like an old fable or something from way back in the day. Just wild stories."

Casey nodded. "Yeah. They apparently started it up again. Tori's father was secretly investigating them, under orders of a Captain Brewster. Brewster was killed in a fiery car crash about two weeks before Tori's family was killed."

"And she thinks the Blue Dragons are responsible?"

"Yes, sir." She paused. "Her uncle was a member of this group."

Malone leaned back in his chair. "What evidence does she have?"

Casey nervously chewed on her lower lip. "Well, besides all the surveillance notes, she's got a hacker. Boris. From Russia."

Malone's eyes nearly popped out of his head. "A goddamn hacker from *Russia*? Has she lost her fucking mind?"

Casey smiled. "I can pretty much say for certain that he's not really from Russia, but that's what she's telling me."

"What kind of hacking?"

"Background on all the guys on her list. And then—"

"What list?"

"The list of names that her father was investigating. And phone records. He pulled some phone records for her."

"Christ." He rubbed his bald head vigorously. "Is she keeping you in the loop?"

"Well, not really. Not until Saturday. Sam did a family intervention and we all talked it out. And I went with her to her boat." She paused, wondering how much to tell him. "She kinda confronted her uncle, but he claimed he had nothing to do with it. Said one of the guys was pretty much threatening them all if they told. He wouldn't give up a name."

"He claimed he had nothing to do with what?"

"Her family's murder."

Malone reached into his drawer again, this time for ibuprofen. "What does she plan to do with all this information that she's gathering?"

"I think we both know, sir."

"Why didn't she come to me with it?"

Casey spread her hands out. "It's a thirty-something-year-old cold case, Lieutenant. Her family. Without having Boris involved, she wouldn't know half of what's going on. If she'd brought this to you, what would you have done?"

"Well, I sure as hell wouldn't have let her work her own family's murder, that's for sure," he said loudly.

"Exactly. That's why she didn't come to you."

"So, she's not actually trying to solve the case then. Because whatever evidence she has is not admissible. That tells me she's simply out for revenge."

Casey met his gaze. "I think she wants to kill whoever is responsible. Yes. That kind of revenge."

Malone nodded slowly, still holding her gaze. "We're not going to let her do that, are we?"

"No, sir."

"Good. But short of hauling her in and locking her up, what do you suggest?"

"I've been kinda trying to follow her around." She smiled. "Of course, she made me the first day."

"Take an unmarked car. Follow her." He pointed his finger at her. "But you keep me in the goddamn loop, O'Connor. And you keep her out of trouble."

"Yes, sir." She stood. "Does this mean you're not going to the captain with all this?"

"No. As far as he is concerned, Hunter is taking some time off. We'll deal with the fallout when it happens."

"And Griffin? You want me to close it?"

"No. You're right. Someone hired those two guys to kill him. Let's find out who."

CHAPTER FORTY-TWO

Casey walked the few blocks to the building where the lab was housed. She glanced to the sky. It was a damp and dreary overcast morning, and she wondered if they'd get rain later. Mac was waiting for her and motioned her into his office.

"Got all kinds of stuff for you," he said as he pulled his laptop closer to him. "I printed this out, but we'll go over it."

"You got a match?" she asked as she read over the paper.

"Oh, yeah, got a lot of matches. The 9-mil found in the car was the same gun used to kill Charles Griffin and Adam Staley. The two guys in the Chevy were Jeffrey Scarsdale, age forty-two, and Ronald Marburger, age twenty-four."

"Scarsdale was from Phoenix, right?"

"Last known address, yes. He's got quite a record, both here and in Arizona. Marburger is ex-military, dishonorable discharge two years ago. He's from Indiana. No ties to here."

"Strange partnership then."

"As I told you yesterday, they were both shot with a .45. The Fort Worth lab confirmed that the slug pulled from

Cunningham matches, as you were hoping. Here's where it gets interesting. We got ballistics matches on a .45 that killed Ester Wilkes in 2004 and Juan Cuero in 2001 and Hector Velaquez way back in 1992."

"Cold cases?"

"Yes. Cuero and Velaquez are ours. Fort Worth has Ester Wilkes. She was in the middle of divorce proceedings against Walter Wilkes." He raised his eyebrows. "Ring a bell?"

She shook her head. "No."

"Walter Wilkes is the son of Willard Wilkes. High society, old money. The divorce was quite the talk of the town back then. Seems she caught him with another woman and was divorcing him."

"For a lot of money, no doubt."

"I can't believe you don't remember this. After she was murdered, speculation was that Walter—or the old man—put a hit out on her."

"That was a long time ago. I was just a pup."

"Well, I remember the story, but then again, I am quite a bit older than you. Anyway, there was no evidence found and they couldn't prove anything, so Mr. Wilkes was able to keep his fortune." Mac smiled. "I was in the camp that thought he did it. But I don't have anything quite as exciting on Mr. Cuero or Velaquez. Both were known drug dealers. Cuero was shot in a back alley. Velaquez was shot outside of a bar. I just think it's odd that the same gun killed a socialite and a couple of drug dealers. What would be the connection?"

Casey frowned, knowing her brow was furrowed. "Wait a minute. This Velaquez. Where was he killed?"

"Oh, I don't remember," Mac said, shuffling through some papers. "I've got it here somewhere."

"How did you get a hit from 1992?" she asked. "They have all those old files in the system now?"

"Ballistics, DNA evidence, prints, that's all in. The original files, no." He held up a paper. "Here it is. It's not much. Just a quick caption when they logged in the bullet." He scanned it quickly. "Breaker's Night Club. I never heard of it."

Casey remembered the bar from Tori's father's notes. She couldn't for sure recall the name of the drug dealer, though. "I think it used to be in Deep Ellum."

"Anyway, that's about all I got. They're trying to get some usable prints off the gun," Mac said. "Prints will usually hold even if they've been submerged a few days. The lab over there will let me know if they find anything."

Casey stood, anxious to call Tori with what she had heard. "Okay, thanks, Mac. I guess I'll be in touch with Fort Worth PD then."

Mac closed his laptop. "If I hear anything else, I'll call you. Their lab has been keeping me in the loop."

"Great. Thanks."

She walked quickly from his office and through the building, hurrying outside. She pulled her phone out immediately.

"O'Connor, you checking on me?"

"Do I need to?"

"No."

"Well, I'm not. Got some news from Mac. Ballistics all match like we thought they would. But get this, the .45 was used in three other cold cases. But one of them was a Hector Velaquez, killed outside of a nightclub called—"

"Breakers," Tori supplied. "It was in my father's notes."

"Yeah, okay. I couldn't remember the guy's name. There's another drug dealer too. Juan something. Hang on." She pulled the paper that Mac had given her from her pocket. "Juan Cuero. Killed in an alley. And get this. The same .45 was used to kill a socialite in 2004. Also a cold case, but that one's in Fort Worth."

"Are you thinking what I'm thinking, O'Connor?"

"Well, I don't know, Hunter. Are you thinking that the Blue Dragons might have carried out these murders? The socialite might even have been a murder for hire."

"Yeah. And they still have the gun and are still using it."

"Right. But which one of them?"

"Listen, go pull those two cases. Find out who the detectives were. My guess is that Hamilton and Jaworski had them both."

"Okay, I can do that. And Malone gave me permission to run with the hitman angle. Going to find out what I can on those two guys."

"I'd offer to have Simon do that for you but…"

"Yeah, we probably want to do it by the book if we're looking for admissible evidence." She stopped walking. "Where are you anyway?"

"I'm staking out McMillan's house."

"Why?"

"Because he won't answer his door or his phone."

"Maybe he's not home."

"Car is in the driveway. I'm just gonna hang out for a while."

"Okay. I'll let you know what I find."

* * *

Juan Cuero's file was in the system. And yes, Hamilton and Jaworski had had the case. She shook her head as she glanced though it. A couple of witnesses with very short statements was about all that was to it. For Hector Velaquez, though, she had to go to the dungeon.

It was dark and dusty and way too hot to be comfortable. The officer leading the way was taking his sweet time too.

"Kinda in a hurry here," she finally said.

"Isn't everyone?" he asked without much enthusiasm.

She sighed rather loudly, but he didn't speed up.

"Over here. Row twelve."

The box was right where it was supposed to be, evidence that it had not been looked at or moved in decades. He pulled it off the shelf and a cloud of dust wafted up when he set it on the table.

"You going to sign for this and take it back with you or you gonna look through it here?"

"I'll do it here."

"Sure. I'll cut the seal."

He did, then stepped away, giving her some privacy. She took the lid off, peering inside.

Not much to it, she thought. One witness statement, that was all. Alex Jones. Said he saw two guys arguing after what he assumed was drugs and money being exchanged. One guy shot the other and took off. It was too dark to describe the shooter.

"Convenient," she murmured.

"What?"

"Nothing. Talking to myself."

She searched through the notes. No shell casings found. No other witnesses. No surveillance cameras. Nothing. She glanced at the sign-in sheet, nodding. Hamilton and Jaworski were the leads.

She looked at the printout of the guy's record. He had quite a rap sheet and was certainly no choirboy. She put everything back inside the box and closed the lid.

"Thanks, man. I'm done with it."

"Sure thing. Let me seal it and I'll escort you back out."

CHAPTER FORTY-THREE

Tori drummed her fingers on the steering wheel, glancing once again at her watch. She'd been there nearly three hours, and her stomach was starting to rumble. She'd only eaten half of the muffin Sam had given her that morning. She'd been poring over the phone records, rereading her father's notes again, trying to find any clue as to who the leader had been. Based on the phone records, her uncle and McMillan were the most active, so that's why she was here, parked a half a block down from McMillan's house.

A knock on the glass of her window made her jump, her hand automatically reaching for her weapon. Casey stood there, smiling, holding up a white bag. She pushed the button on her door, lowering the window.

"What the hell are you doing here, O'Connor?"

"I brought lunch. Open up."

"No."

"Come on. I know you're hungry." She waved the bag at her. "Got burgers from Dairy Cone. Freshly ground beef, cooked on demand." Casey wiggled her eyebrows. "Extra cheese."

Tori's stomach growled loudly. "Steak fries?"

"Big, fat, greasy steak fries."

"Okay. Get in."

She unwrapped the burger Casey handed her but not before shoving two steak fries into her mouth. "Thanks."

"Yeah, well, you're one of those crazy-ass people who forget to eat. It ain't normal."

The old Dairy Cone was in a dilapidated building that she was surprised passed code, but they still made the best burgers. She bit into it now, moaning at the taste.

"I knew you'd be starving." Casey nudged her arm. "Veronica was working today so she gave us extra fries."

"Veronica is old enough to be your mother. Why do you continue to flirt with her?"

"Just having some fun, Hunter." She motioned out the windshield. "What's happening here?"

"Nothing. No sign of him. What about you?"

Casey wiped her mouth first, then grabbed a fry. She bit it in half before speaking. "You were right. Hamilton and Jaworski had both cases. And both looked like they'd hardly been worked. The witness statement on Velaquez sounded staged. And that was the only witness. The other one, Cuero, had two witnesses, but there wasn't much to either of them."

"It looks like McMillan suppressed the investigation on them, doesn't it?"

"Well, we're assuming he did. Maybe Hamilton and Jaworski did it on their own."

Tori shook her head. "No, I don't think so. Not without orders." She was about to take another bite of her burger, then stopped. "Wait a minute. What are you even doing here?"

"I brought you lunch. What else?"

"I thought you said Malone gave you the okay to work the hitman angle."

"Yeah, he did."

"And?"

"And what? I got a guy in IT working with me. Found the two guys' cell numbers. He's pulling phone records. Chances are they used burners, though."

"Not the initial call." She dipped a fry into Casey's ketchup. "Maybe subsequent calls, but the initial call would have been on their real phone."

"How would our guys even know their numbers to begin with?"

Tori stared out the windshield, seeing movement on McMillan's porch. "You said they'd been arrested before. Pull their files. Most likely one of our guys was the arresting officer." She put her burger down. "Get out."

"What?"

"I think he's on the move. Get out."

"No way."

"O'Connor, get the hell out," she said forcefully.

"I'm going with you. I haven't finished my lunch."

McMillan's car backed out of the driveway, then headed in the opposite direction from them. "You piss me off sometimes," she muttered as she pulled away from the curb.

"Yeah, but you still love me."

McMillan lived in Far North Dallas, and he was now heading south on Hillcrest. She stayed several cars behind him, then glanced in her mirror, noticing a black SUV two cars behind her.

"He's turning on Belt Line," Casey said.

Tori slowed and changed lanes, still keeping an eye on the SUV behind her. It, too, changed lanes.

"He turned already. To the left. Dartbrook."

Tori turned too. "We've got someone following us. Black SUV. Looks to be the same one that was at our house the other day."

She'd no sooner said that when the SUV sped up beside them. She slammed on her brakes, causing Casey to brace herself against the dash.

"What the hell?"

"Gun!"

Casey jerked her head around, finding the black SUV within a foot of them. The man driving was wearing a ski mask and his gun was pointing at them. Tori sped up again, her tires squealing. The black SUV did the same, his front bumper clipping her rear.

Casey pulled her weapon. "Jesus Christ! Can you believe this shit?"

"Hang on." She swerved to the right, bumping him, hearing the scraping of metal as they brushed.

"Keep going," Casey said, motioning. "I got this bastard!"

Casey pushed the button at the door, lowering the window. The guy swerved into their lane, jarring them as he pushed against her car. Casey was thrown back.

"That son of a bitch!" Tori jerked her car toward him, hearing the grating of metal as she dented his door. A shot rang out, and she instinctively ducked. The bullet hit her side window. Casey returned fire, but the SUV sped away, cutting off traffic in the right-hand lane with a squeal of his tires. Two other cars crashed together, and Tori was hit from behind, causing the airbags to deploy. She pounded against them in frustration.

"Holy shit, Hunter, but did that just happen?"

"Yeah, O'Connor. Just like the goddamn movies," she said as she unbuckled her seat belt.

Casey shoved against her door without success. "Stuck."

Tori got out and Casey climbed across the seats and console, following her. They went over to where the two cars had crashed. Both drivers were out and talking, pointing in all directions, it seemed. Casey went over, holding up her shield.

"Everyone okay here?"

"I don't even know what happened," the woman said, clearly shaken.

"Do either of you need medical attention?"

They both shook their heads. Tori was about to call it in when she heard sirens. She put her phone back in her pocket, looking down the street where McMillan had fled. She turned then, inspecting her car. It was pretty much beat to hell. The front fender was twisted against the wheel and the door was smashed in. She only glanced at the crumpled rear bumper. *That goddamn bastard*, she thought.

"You were saying just the other week how you were wanting to trade this in for a new truck." Casey nudged her shoulder. "I'm thinking now's a good time, huh?"

Tori looked at her, managing a small smile at Casey's attempt at humor.

"Right."

"Wonder who the hell that was?"

"Somebody on our list, I guess. You get a look at the plates?"

"Oh, hell no. But that was kinda fun."

"Fun, O'Connor? My car is ready for the scrap heap, and we got shot at."

"Yeah, well, besides that."

A roll of thunder sounded overhead and soon raindrops began to fall. Tori met her gaze, then smiled. "It's raining, O'Connor. How about that?"

Casey laughed. "Yeah, we got all the luck today, don't we?"

CHAPTER FORTY-FOUR

After clearing the accident and having her car towed away, they got one of the patrol officers to take them back to McMillan's house, where Casey's unmarked car was still parked. The rain had subsided to a cloudy mist.

"What are we going to tell Malone?"

"That we got into a little traffic accident," Tori said.

Casey put her hands on her hips. "Besides the bullet hole in your window, I fired my weapon, and we already gave a statement. I don't think a little traffic accident is going to fly."

Before she could answer, her phone rang. She pulled each from her pocket. It was her burner. "I hate having two phones," she murmured to Casey as she answered. "Hunter."

"Yeah, Tori. I got some information for you. A bit much for the phone, but I think I know who the black SUV belongs to."

"I hope so because they just tried to run us off the road. Who was the bastard?"

"It's detailed. Let's meet. Can you come over?"

"Are you at your apartment?"

"Yeah. I took some vacation time."

"Simon, please don't get fired. There's not enough scotch in the world to make up for that."

"I've got lots of vacation time built up. It's no problem. Come by when you can."

"We're way the hell in Far North Dallas. Be half hour or more before we get there."

Simon paused. "We?"

"Yeah, my partner." Tori met Casey's gaze. "She's cool."

"Okay. If you trust her, I'm fine with it. Call me when you get to the gate. I can open it remotely."

She nodded. "Will do. Thanks, Simon."

"Well?" Casey asked as soon as she disconnected.

"He's got something. Says he knows who the SUV belongs to."

"All right. Then let's go."

Tori got into the passenger's seat and buckled her seat belt. "You know, I'm supposed to be doing this on my own."

"I never did like that plan, Hunter." Casey sped away. "Where to?"

"Head south. He lives in an apartment in the Turtle Creek area."

Casey grinned at her. "Can you believe we were in a car chase and some asshole shot at us?"

"You want to call that a car chase? We got our ass run off the road."

"I told you not to buy a car. Remember? I told you to get something bigger."

Tori leaned her head back and closed her eyes. Yeah, Casey had told her to get a truck like she had. Now she supposed she would. She opened her eyes and sighed.

"You ever think about retiring, O'Connor?"

"Retiring? Shit, Hunter, we got a good ten years left in us, don't you think?"

"Do we?"

"Well, I'd like to think so. I've got a couple more years yet before I hit my twenty. Even then, is the pension enough? Don't think so. Hell, I'll end up as some goddamn security guard or something."

Tori laughed. "Yeah. Guarding a bank. Like Pete Dewberry told me, he prayed someone would come in and try to rob the place."

Casey glanced at her quickly, then turned her attention back to the road. "You thinking about it, Tori? Retiring?"

Tori sucked in a long, heavy breath. "I'm just tired, I guess. It's been an emotional week."

Casey reached over and touched her arm. "Your sole purpose of joining the force back then was to solve your family's murder. You're close now. Do you think your job is finished?"

Is that what she thought? She was a damn good cop, she knew that. But what was her driving force? What made her do what she did? In her early years, she took risks she had no business taking. There was a time when she didn't really care whether she lived or died. Yeah, those early years. Not now, no. Not in a long time. There was Sam. They had a good life. A happy life. Before she met Sam, she didn't remember what being happy felt like. Most all of the joy left her life when she was twelve years old. Sam changed all that.

But now? If she got through this, if she found out who killed her family, would that be enough? Would her purpose in life—her quest to find the killer—be no more? Was that it?

"You're the best cop I've ever known, Tori. You care. You care about people. You sometimes don't want to, or you don't want others to think you do, but you damn well care. That's a good cop right there."

"Thanks, O'Connor. Like I said, I'm just tired. This will pass." She motioned up ahead. "Exit on Blackburn."

"Maybe when this is over with, you really do need to take some vacation time. Relax out on your boat or something."

"Yeah, I called the marina this morning. Jimmy is going to hire someone to clean her for me." She shook her head. "Still can't believe they killed Cunningham. I feel like I should go apologize to his wife or something." She held her hand up. "You can say what you want, but if I hadn't gone to interview him, he'd probably still be alive."

"No way to know, I guess."

"Up there. Emerald Ridge Apartments." She took out her burner phone when Casey pulled in at the gate. "Yeah, Simon. We're here."

"Okay. Come on up."

The gate opened and Casey drove through. "Park on the back row," Tori told her. "Simon said they only check for parking passes at night."

"Oh, great. You know how our luck has been running today."

"We won't be here long enough to get towed. Come on."

Simon was waiting with the door open. He eyed Casey suspiciously. "Are you sure we can trust her?"

"I trust her with my life."

"Oh, thanks, Hunter. That's sweet of you," Casey drawled. "I'll try not to let you down." Then she stuck her hand out to Simon. "Casey O'Connor. Me and the old girl here are not only partners but best friends. So whatever secrets you got going on here, I'm good with it."

Simon shook her hand. "Okay, then. Come in." He went directly to his desk. "I think I know who the black SUV belongs to." He pulled up an image on his screen. "Pulled this from an ATM camera."

She and Casey leaned over his shoulders. "How do you know it's our guy?" Tori asked.

"It's Vance Bexley."

"Bexley? The guy on our list is Thomas, not Vance."

"Right. Vance is his nephew."

Tori moved away from his desk. "Okay. I'll buy it. What did you find?"

"Man, I found all kinds of stuff." He picked up a piece of paper. "I did bullet points because it's confusing. Look at this. Randal Bexley, Thomas Bexley's uncle, was with Dallas PD way back in the '60s. He was at first suspended, then dismissed outright."

"What for?" Casey asked.

"Blue Dragons?" Tori guessed.

"Yep. And Randal's brother—Patrick—was a car mechanic and owned a shop. Randal went to work for him when he lost his job."

Casey held her hand up. "What's all that got to do with our case?"

"Patrick—Randal's brother—is Thomas Bexley's father." Simon handed her the paper. "Thomas Bexley's father and uncle ran this auto shop. Thomas went into law enforcement and became a cop. Thomas' brother, Matt, went into the family business instead and now so did his son. And that son is Vance Bexley, who happens to own this SUV."

"The fact that he owns a black SUV doesn't mean he's our guy," Casey said. "Circumstantial."

"Patrick and Randall are both retired now, long out of the business. But Matt and his son Vance have kept up the shop. Whiz mechanics, if you believe the reviews." He met her gaze. "Good with cars."

Tori nodded. "Harken's accident."

"And back in the early '90s, Brewster's accident," he continued.

Tori ran a hand through her hair several times. "Still circumstantial."

Casey held her hand up. "Okay, I'm not following anything with this line of thinking. Are you?" she asked Tori.

Tori nodded. "He's suggesting that Thomas Bexley got his brother to jack with Brewster's car enough to cause an accident and kill the man. And now Bexley got his brother and nephew to do the same to Harken's car."

"Only Harken didn't die," Simon added. "Well, not in the car anyway."

Casey stared at her. "And then he got his nephew to try to run us off the road?"

"Yeah."

"We can't prove it, though," Casey said.

"We find the SUV," Tori said. "It'll be damaged, dented on the driver's side for sure."

Simon started typing again. "I've got the address for the shop. Let me get you their home addresses too."

"Say we find the SUV. Then what?" Casey asked. "We still can't prove anything."

"Who got Bexley to get his family involved?" Tori asked. "He wouldn't have done it on his own. I'm talking about Brewster's accident back then."

No, Bexley was just a name on her list like all the other middle guys. Sawyer. Casper. Douglas. He hadn't even registered on her radar. He was a patrol officer. What had Cunningham said about Bexley? Nothing really. They rode together for a while. Bexley was the one who got him involved.

She now paced behind Simon's desk, her thoughts racing. If Bexley was only a middle guy, would he have been able to recruit someone else into the Blue Dragons? Would he have dared bring in someone new—Cunningham—without clearing it with the others? No, she didn't think so. What they were doing was too controversial. Too secretive. If he was one of the bit players, there's no way he would be allowed to bring someone else into the fold.

"Christ," she murmured.

"What are you thinking?" Casey asked.

"He was a patrol officer. Bexley. He was a patrol officer. Yet the Blue Dragons had four lieutenants involved and two detectives."

"Yeah. And?"

"Bexley recruited Cunningham into the group, so he had to have some sort of power to do that. It wasn't one of the lieutenants who brought Cunningham in. It was Bexley."

"You think Bexley, a patrol officer, had gained control over the Blue Dragons?"

Tori met her gaze. "But what if he didn't *gain* control? The Blue Dragons were no longer in existence, remember?"

"What are you saying?"

"Maybe he was the one who started them up again in the first place."

Casey nodded quickly. "Yeah. Okay. Like he heard stories from his uncle about the old days or something."

"Right. Only this time, his uncle told him to keep it small, keep it quiet."

"But how could he add four lieutenants to the group?"

"Money," Simon said.

Tori nodded. "Imagine doing a drug bust, only you wait until after money has exchanged hands. You grab the money and leave."

"Meaning no legitimate bust?" Casey asked.

"Right. Take the money, let the bad guys go. You might even get to bust them again down the road."

"That's taking a chance, Hunter. Now you've got drug dealers knowing there are dirty cops."

"So? You think the drug dealers are going to turn them in? Like call in and say, 'Yeah, some of your cops just stole my drug money and I want it back,'" she said with a grin. "Don't think so. They take their loss and go on about their business."

"And according to your father's notes, there was a dead drug dealer outside that club they went to."

"Hector Velaquez, killed with the same .45. What if it wasn't a drug deal? What if he went there to get his money back?"

Casey laughed. "God, I love speculating with you. We can come up with some shit, can't we?"

"It's all very possible."

"Yeah, it is. Can't prove a goddamn thing, though."

"We find out who arrested Scarsdale. I guarantee you it was one of these guys. Let's see which of our guys called him first." She turned to Simon. "Can you find Scarsdale's cell number? Cross it with these guys?"

"Of course."

"Wait," Casey said. "If Simon does it, it won't be admissible. Let me do it. I can call the guy in IT."

"You don't have cause to pull phone records on any of these guys on the list, other than Staley and Cunningham."

"But—"

"I don't care what's admissible, O'Connor. We just need the information. You can try to pull records later."

Casey stared at her for a long moment, then nodded. "Okay, Hunter. Your call."

"Good. And, Simon, if you'll print out those addresses for me, we'll try to find Vance Bexley and his SUV."

"That's where you want to start?" Casey asked. "Why not go straight to Thomas?"

"With what? With all of our speculations? Like you said, we can't prove any of this yet. Not until Simon finds something in the phone logs. What we *can* prove is someone tried to run us off the road this morning. Let's start there."

CHAPTER FORTY-FIVE

"I'm thinking I want Mexican food for dinner," Casey said as she drove.

"How can you think of food? You just ate."

"And a Rios Rita. Let's see if Sam and Les want to meet us there."

"Maybe."

The auto shop—officially called Bexley Auto Repairs—was in West Dallas, off Interstate 30. Casey took the Hampton exit to the right. The area was a mix of commercial warehouses and smaller businesses like Bexley's.

"Where to?"

"Turn on Commerce." Tori looked at the map on her phone. "To the left. Then the shop is on the right."

Casey slowed, letting another car go ahead of her before turning on Commerce. The shop was three buildings down on the right. It had four large bays, but the doors were closed on all of them. The misty rain was just enough for Casey to use the wipers intermittently, and she crept along the street.

"Doesn't look like they're open."

"Pull in anyway."

Casey did and parked behind the first bay. The door marked "OFFICE" was to the left. It had a window, but the blinds were pulled down, hiding the interior. Tori opened the door and got out.

"Let's take a look."

"Sign says they should be open," Casey said as she walked up beside her.

The office door was locked, so Tori knocked. "Anybody there?" she called.

Casey went over the bays, trying those doors. All were locked too. Casey put her hands on her hips. "I say we break in."

"On what grounds?"

"Oh my god, Hunter. You're a rogue cop on the run and *now* you want to ask on what grounds?"

"Rogue? On the run?"

"Yeah, with a hacker and a burner phone. So let's break in. We heard something. Thought maybe someone was in distress."

Tori tilted her head. "You're going to tell Malone this was my idea, aren't you?"

"Of course."

They both eyed the door, then looked at each other.

"Break the window or try to kick the door in?" Casey asked.

Tori tapped on it. "Solid. Dead bolt. I doubt we can kick it in." She took her gun out of her holster, but Casey stopped her with a hand on her arm.

"Jesus, Hunter, don't shoot it open. I'd kinda like to look around before someone calls the cops on us."

"I'm just using it to break the glass, O'Connor. I'm not going to shoot." She paused, waiting as a car drove past them on the street. She looked around quickly, then hammered the corner of the window. The glass only cracked, and she hit it harder. It shattered enough for her to stick her hand inside. She fumbled with the lock, finally hearing it click.

"You think they have an alarm?"

"Probably. Let's be quick."

The office was large with two desks. It smelled much as she assumed it would—of oil and gasoline. She kept her gun out, moving quickly to the inner door. It opened into the work area, but it was too dark to see anything.

"Find a light," she murmured quietly.

Casey moved to the wall, finding the panel of switches. She flipped one and the lights in the farthest bay came on.

"Well, look at that," Casey drawled. "It's a black SUV. Looks like it was in a little accident or something. Driver's side is smashed in."

The SUV was up on a hydraulic lift in bay two, six or seven feet above ground. She walked toward it, inspecting the outside. Casey went around to the back, using her phone to take a picture of the license plate.

"Why the hell would they leave it here?" Casey asked.

"Maybe they don't think we've connected the dots yet. Besides, it's probably safer hiding in here than if he was still driving it around."

Casey stared up at the vehicle, then snapped a couple of pictures of the dented side too. "Still, it makes no sense. You try to run two cops off the road, shoot at them too, the first thing you do is get rid of the evidence." She pointed to the SUV. "You don't have it up on a rack for anybody to see."

"Maybe he panicked. Brought it here and closed up the shop. Maybe he planned to wait until dark to dispose of it."

"Chop shop?"

"They've been in the car repair business a long time. I'm sure they know of some."

"Okay, so now what? We've confirmed what Simon thought. It was Vance Bexley's SUV. Now what? Go see him?"

"Yeah. Let's go see him."

They headed back into the office, and Casey bumped her shoulder. "When are we going to tell Malone?"

"About breaking the window?"

"Yeah, that too."

Tori stopped. "I can't tell him anything, O'Connor. What I'm working on has nothing to do with the Griffin murder. That's your deal."

"We broke into this place, Hunter! We can't—"

"Save your breath," she said as she walked away. "Go back to the station. Tell him what you want. I'm going after Bexley."

"Yeah? So are you going to take a cab or what?"

Tori turned to glare at her, but Casey's smile made her smile too. "Yeah. I'm going to need a ride." Tori bumped her shoulder as they walked out. "How about you let me take your truck and you keep this unit."

"My truck? I don't know, Hunter. The way you drive? The streets are wet. You might—"

They heard sirens coming down the street and bolted toward the car. Casey backed onto the street and pulled away with a squeal of her tires, turning onto the next street just as a patrol unit skidded to a halt in front of the shop.

"Malone's going to have our asses," Casey murmured. "He's probably going to kill us."

"No doubt."

CHAPTER FORTY-SIX

Tori had no luck finding Vance Bexley. His house had been dark and quiet. She'd walked around the outside, peering into the few windows that weren't covered completely by curtains. There'd been nothing to indicate that anyone was there. She drove carefully, taking extra caution with Casey's truck. She'd promised her she wouldn't put even a scratch on it.

She took out her burner and called Simon. It rang four times before he answered.

"You got anything?"

"Enough to think that Thomas Bexley is your guy. I'm still running some stuff, but Bexley called Jeffrey Scarsdale seven times. The first one was about a month before Staley and Griffin were killed. The last one on Thursday."

"And their car was found in the river on Friday." She shook her head. "But Simon, that makes no sense. Why continue to use his real phone? He must know we would trace it."

"Maybe he never intended to kill the guys. They leave town after they do their thing. Nothing to trace."

"Then why the hell did he kill them?" She shook her head. "Sorry. Thinking out loud."

"That's okay."

"All right. Thanks, Simon." She put that phone down, then picked up her real one. As with Simon, it rang four times before Casey picked up.

"This is O'Connor," she answered rather formally.

Tori smiled. "Let me guess. You're with Malone." She heard a door close, then footsteps.

"Damn, Hunter. He was grilling me. And I mean grilling. You're going to so owe me for this."

"He knows about the SUV?"

"Oh, yeah, he knows. And he knows about our break-in at the shop. And yes, I told him it was your idea."

"Whatever," she murmured.

"And Fort Worth PD called him. They want to talk to you about Cunningham. His wife said you'd been at their house."

"Great."

"Malone put them off. Told them Cunningham's name had come up in an investigation."

"Okay. Did your IT guy find anything?"

"I haven't talked to him yet."

"Well, Simon said Thomas Bexley was the one who contacted Scarsdale. He got seven hits, starting about a month before Staley and Griffin were killed. The last call was on Thursday."

"Called them on Thursday to meet, killed them, dumped them in the river," Casey said matter-of-factly. "But why?"

"We can speculate all we want to, but we'll probably never know why. And I had no luck with Vance. No one was there. Now I'm hesitant to go to these other guys. Nothing about this makes sense." She turned and slowed, going down a residential street. "Bexley was a middleman. In the notes, he's mentioned no more or no less than the others."

"That's because your father didn't know who was in charge. If he had, he would have stated as much."

"Reading between the lines, he thought Staley was in charge."

"But someone killed Staley, so it couldn't be him."

"What if it was made to seem like Staley was in charge? At least at the beginning. Bexley wouldn't have had the clout to get the Blue Dragons started up again. Not by himself." She finally pulled over toward the curb and stopped. "But Staley would. He was over narcotics. Staley would know who he could trust and who he couldn't."

"Okay, so now you think Staley started it up? Earlier you said Bexley."

Tori shook her head. "No. Everything points to Bexley. But how? How could he get it started?"

"We can guess all we want, but until we interview the guys on this list, that's all we're doing—guessing."

"With everything that's gone on, I doubt any of them would open up to me like Cunningham did. And he took a bullet for his trouble." She hesitated, drumming her fingers on the steering wheel. "I think I need to talk to my uncle again."

Casey gave a nervous laugh. "You can't be serious. Your uncle will probably shoot you on sight. Besides, we still don't know for sure what his part is in all this. Per Simon, he made all the first calls, remember."

"He swore he wasn't the one."

"You had a goddamn gun to his head! Of course he swore he wasn't the one."

Tori closed her eyes, picturing the scene at her uncle's house. "I believe him. He was scared, but he was more scared of this guy than of me."

"And you think that guy is Bexley?"

"Appears to be, right?"

She heard Casey sigh. "You're going to go see your uncle, aren't you?"

"I think so, yeah. Later this evening." She pulled away again. "Going to head home, see Sam. Get something to eat."

"Okay, so when should I meet you?"

"No, O'Connor. I'm doing this alone. I promise I won't shoot him. I just want to ask him some point-blank questions, that's all."

"He may shoot *you*. And the chances of him even talking to you are slim, Hunter. So you can promise all you want. I'm still going with you. What time?"

Tori blew out her breath. "Okay. I'll call you." Of course, she had no intention of doing so.

"Great. Talk to you later."

Casey disconnected without another word, and Tori frowned. That was too easy. Maybe someone had interrupted her. Malone? Good, she thought. She wouldn't have to spend five minutes arguing with her. She tossed her phone down beside the burner and headed home.

CHAPTER FORTY-SEVEN

Sam had gotten home early—again. She decided she would take vacation days for her last two weeks after all. Suddenly, everything going on at CIU seemed like one big secret and she wasn't allowed in on it. She couldn't imagine what they thought she might learn and take with her to the DA's office. So instead of being holed up in her office without a thing to do, she'd put in her request for time off. It was approved within seconds.

She'd stopped at the supermarket on the way home and picked up a few things. She was in the mood for a steak and a buttery baked potato. Despite the rainy afternoon, their covered patio afforded them the opportunity to grill out in any weather. She'd already opened a bottle of wine—a nice red. The steaks were seasoned, and the potatoes were in the oven. The asparagus was washed and cut and ready to steam.

She added a little more wine to her glass, then smiled when she heard the garage door open. Before long, Tori came in, a questioning look on her face.

"You beat me home."

"I did." Sam leaned closer for her kiss. "I am officially on vacation for the duration."

Tori took the wineglass from her, taking a sip before handing it back. "I thought you didn't want to."

"Well, you were right. Sanity and all." She moved to the fridge. "You want a beer?"

Tori shook her head. "I'll have wine with you. Let me grab a shower. It's been one of those days."

Sam nodded and watched her leave. Yes, Leslie had called her earlier. She wondered why Tori hadn't bothered to tell her about the accident. She took a deep breath, reminding herself that Tori was preoccupied with other things right now. Sam had to accept that she wasn't at the forefront of Tori's mind. She hadn't been for the last week.

With another sigh, she took her wineglass out to the patio. She started the gas grill, then sat down at the small table. The evening was cool and damp, and she shivered, wishing she'd put on a sweatshirt. Instead, she wrapped her arms around herself, looking out into the darkening sky. They would have heavy thunderstorms tonight, she'd heard.

She tried not to worry about Tori, about her emotional state. But she did. Because Tori hadn't been herself for the last week. Oh, she pretended to be, and she put on a good show, but she knew her presence here was only half-hearted. Her mind was on other things. She and their life together had taken a back seat to it. That, of course, was something she wasn't used to. She was used to Tori putting her first. Always.

Still, that wasn't what bothered her the most. It was what Leslie had said, passing on Casey's words—"Something's going on in that stubborn head of hers. I think she's going to really go rogue."

Stubborn? Oh, yes. Sam had known that from the moment they'd become partners all those years ago. And rogue? That had been Casey's favorite word lately. When Casey had first used it, it wasn't something Sam was really worried about. Because even in Tori's early reckless days, even when she bent the rules as far as they would bend, she still knew that there *were* rules.

And even the other night with her uncle, Tori hadn't lost sight of that. Well, at least not totally. So now, was Casey's fear warranted? Maybe. Sam still didn't know everything that had happened today. It was enough to know that Tori was driving Casey's truck.

She jumped when a hand touched her shoulder. Then a sweatshirt was placed in her lap as Tori put the platter of steaks and the bottle of wine on the table.

"Thanks. How did you know?"

Tori sat down, then topped off her wineglass before answering. "After this many years, I think I can read you pretty well."

Sam slipped the sweatshirt over her head and snuggled into it. She reached for her wine and nodded. "That goes both ways, sweetheart."

Their eyes met in the waning light, and she could tell that Tori was trying hard to keep hers guarded. Trying in vain, Sam wanted to tell her. Because yes, after this many years, she could read Tori like a book.

Tori turned away from her gaze, looking out into the night instead. Sam warred between asking questions and demanding answers or just letting it go. She wasn't sure which faction won.

"Going to tell me about it?"

Tori feigned ignorance. "Tell you what?"

Okay, so she did know which side won. She nearly slammed her wineglass down. "Let's stop playing games. I know you wrecked your car. I know you were shot at. Stop keeping me in the goddamn dark," she said sharply.

The vulnerable look in Tori's eyes brought back a memory from long ago. A time when Tori often had that look, when she was unsure of their relationship, unsure of their love. Unsure of the future. It was a look that usually crumpled her defenses.

"I'm sorry, Sam. Had a lot going on today. I didn't have time to call you."

"Didn't have time? Or didn't make time?"

Tori's expression softened. "Didn't make time. I didn't want you to worry."

"Do you think I'm worried?"

"Aren't you?" Tori got up then and moved to the edge of the patio. "I am, to be honest," she said quietly.

Sam got up too, walking behind her. She slipped her arms around Tori's waist and leaned against her back.

"You don't have to do this alone. I know you think you do, but you don't." She heard Tori sigh.

"Everything is messed up. I don't know what direction to go in. I've got evidence from thirty years ago and I have evidence from last week and most of it is inadmissible." Tori pulled away from her. "And I don't even care about that. I just need to know who did it—who ordered my family to be killed. That's all I care about."

"And when you find out? Then what?"

Tori moved back to the table and picked up her wineglass. Sam noticed that her hand was shaking as she took a sip.

"I'm afraid I'll kill them."

Sam moved closer to her. "So it's premeditated? Is that what you think you've been reduced to? A cold-blooded murderer?"

"I want to do the right thing, Sam. I do. But what is right? Should I have handed all this over to Malone at the beginning? Should I have let it go through the system, let it play out?"

"Is that what you're worried about? That you did the wrong thing, and they won't be punished?" Sam squeezed her arm. "They won't be punished unless you kill them?"

When Tori met her gaze, she knew she'd hit on the truth. Tori didn't *want* to kill them. Oh, she may think she did, and she may say she did, but deep down, Tori didn't want to have to do it. Because that's not who she is.

"I don't want to let them down," Tori said in a quiet voice. "My family. I don't want to let them down."

"It's not too late to go to Malone with it all."

"I know. But I want to be able to give him a name. All signs point to Thomas Bexley. That's where the evidence points." She shrugged. "It's just not adding up." Tori tapped her head. "In here, it doesn't make sense. So I thought, after dinner, I'd go over to my uncle's house. Try to get some answers from him."

Sam's eyes widened. "Your uncle? After the other night…"

Tori smiled. "Yeah. O'Connor is afraid he's going to shoot me on sight."

"Not only that, you said he'd been threatened. His wife too. Why would he talk to you?"

"Because I'm hoping he'll do the right thing."

Sam nodded. "So if he confirms that Thomas Bexley is the one, then what? Will you go after him? Will you go to Malone with it? What?"

"I don't know, Sam. Yeah, I guess I'll have to go to Malone. I know I'm not judge and jury, even though in this case, I want to be." Tori took a deep breath. "I want to…to see him, look at him, let him see me. I need to know the *why* of it. Why my whole family? Bexley was a nobody to me and my family. Why was it so personal for him that he had to kill *everyone*?"

"Personal?"

"There had to be a reason, Sam. Kill Brewster? Kill my father? Sure. I understand the reasoning behind that. They were investigating the Blue Dragons. Getting close, too. But what purpose did it serve to kill my mother? My brothers? Emily? What was the *purpose*?"

"And if you find the reason? The purpose? Then what?" she pushed.

"Then we'll see what happens."

Sam held her gaze. "Yes, it's a fine line between justice and revenge, isn't it?"

Even a loud clap of thunder in the distance didn't break their stare. The wind stirred, blowing cool air around them. Tori finally nodded.

"I love you more than anything in this world, Sam. You taught me what it was like to love again. You taught me it was *okay* to love again."

Sam moved closer. "Whatever happens, Tori, my love for you won't change." She let her hand slip up, touching above Tori's left breast. "I know who you are, what you are. In here," she said, tapping her chest. "I know you'll do the right thing.

I know that because I truly believe what you just said. You *do* love me more than anything in this world." She slid her hand higher, gently cupping Tori's cheek. "And I want to believe that you love me more than you'll love any revenge you think you might need."

Tori's eyes closed and Sam was shocked to see a tear escape from one. "I don't want to let them down, but I don't want to let you down either."

"You've always been my hero, Tori. I don't think you'll let me down."

Tori wiped at her tear, then seemed to gather herself. She took the steaks over to the grill and opened the lid.

"Your hero, huh?"

Sam smiled and moved up beside her. "Yes. You've saved my life on more than one occasion. There was the incident in the gas well and the tunnel."

Tori laughed. "You wanted me to shoot that poor nutria rat."

"You made me jump into a muddy creek."

"You tried to drown me," Tori countered.

"And you took a bullet for me. And then up in Angel Fire, you trekked days across the mountains to look for me."

Tori groaned. "Cameron Ross. Talk about arrogant."

Sam's smile faded a little as she remembered that ordeal. Angel Figueroa. She hadn't thought of Angel in a long while. She pushed thoughts of him aside now as she leaned against Tori.

"I still say, Cameron and Andrea would have made a great addition to our little family here."

"And I still say that Cameron would have driven Casey nuts." Tori laughed. "Or vice versa. God, remember Cameron and her pizza?"

Their evening took on a more relaxed tone as Sam refilled their glasses. They chatted while Tori grilled their steaks and they decided to eat outside rather than in. By the time everything was ready, a light rain was falling, and they watched lightning in the northern sky. The breeze flickered the candle that she'd put on the table, casting shadows around them.

Even so, Sam could see that Tori's eyes had taken on a faraway look again. She knew, once more, that she'd been pushed to the back of Tori's mind. Tori was making plans, deciding her next move. Would she confront Thomas Bexley tonight? Would she get her answers? Would her anger—her need for revenge—override everything else?

Or would Tori's love for her, their life together, be more important to her now than avenging her family's murder? Their eyes held in the dancing candlelight, and for a moment, Tori was back, her love shining there for Sam to see. She nodded slightly and Tori did the same.

Yes, Tori was making plans, but she hadn't lost sight of what was real. Sam only hoped that the light was bright enough to dim Tori's rage.

CHAPTER FORTY-EIGHT

Tori parked on the curb beside her uncle's house. The light rain had turned moderate, and she left her windshield wipers on. Sam's parting words had been teasing—*please don't let him shoot you*—but they stuck with her, nonetheless. He could very well simply refuse to see her, refuse to speak to her. After what had happened the last time, she wouldn't blame him.

But she needed some answers. She didn't want to confront Thomas Bexley unless she had all the facts. As she'd told Casey, she was hesitant to go to the others now. But her uncle? If she expected any of them to tell her the truth, she thought it would be him. Of course, she wasn't sure why she thought that. They had no relationship. Never had. Was it just that invisible family bond that she expected? Maybe.

She took a deep breath, then opened the door, jogging up to the front porch and out of the rain. She hesitated only a second before pushing the doorbell. When it opened, Aunt Judith was standing there, and Tori was surprised by the welcoming smile on her face. Apparently, Uncle James hadn't told her what had happened the other night.

"Why, Tori. What are you doing out and about in this weather?"

"Sorry to pop over so late. I was hoping to chat with Uncle James."

Aunt Judith's smile faded, and she shook her head. "Oh, I'm sorry, dear. He just left." Her hands clutched together nervously. "I don't know where he thought he had to go off to in this storm and at this hour, but he left in a rush after his phone call."

"I see. Do you know who he spoke to?"

"No. He wouldn't say. I just hope he's not in some kind of trouble. He's been acting strange for the last week or so. I worry about him."

"Well, I'm sorry to bother you. Perhaps I'll catch him another time."

"I'll let him know you stopped by."

Tori nodded, then hurried back to the truck. Now what? She picked up the burner, calling Simon.

"Yeah, I need a favor. Can you track my uncle's phone?"

"Okay, sure. Give me a second."

"I'm heading to Thomas Bexley's house. I think he must have gone there."

CHAPTER FORTY-NINE

Sam slammed the clip into her gun, then placed it in the holster she'd secured to the waist of her jeans. She'd had no intention of following Tori. None at all. She was going to trust her and hope she came back home to her unscathed. But Tori's words kept running through her mind.

It was personal. The killings had been personal. *"What was the purpose?"*

Yes, what was the purpose of killing her family? Not to eliminate potential witnesses. No. Because Charles Griffin's confession letter stated that he'd been instructed to leave one alive *as* a witness. Therefore, Tori's question was valid. And so was her assumption that it had been personal. It was a view she herself had not thought of before.

She'd been cleaning up the dishes from dinner when Casey had called. Casey couldn't reach Tori—she wasn't answering her phone. That's when her mild worry turned into more. Casey was on her way over. They were going after Tori. Because if it *was* personal, that meant only one thing—her uncle had to be more involved than he let on. He was the only one on the list who had any kind of a personal relationship with Tori's father. Tori had been right. If Bexley was the one who called the shots, there's no way his order would have been to take out an entire family, minus one witness. As Tori had said, what would have been the purpose of that?

She'd relayed her thoughts to Casey and they'd both been worked into near hysteria by the time they'd hung up. Casey's prediction—*Tori's going to fucking snap*—was still rattling around in her mind.

She pulled on a light jacket over her sweatshirt, then grabbed one of Tori's baseball caps and put it on. She went outside to wait on the front porch, out of the rain. Maybe they were way off base. Maybe they were overreacting. Was she? She blew out her breath. Probably. But something in her gut told her that she needed to find Tori. She was going to heed that feeling.

As soon as Casey pulled into the driveway, Sam ran out into the rain, jerking open the door and nearly falling inside as lightning seemed to erupt all around them. She was a little surprised that Leslie wasn't with her. Casey backed out onto the street and pulled away with a squeal of tires.

"I guess those thunderstorms are upon us," she said as she wiped at the rain on her face.

"Yeah, and people are driving like idiots."

"Les?"

"Oh, yeah, she wanted to come, but I told her at least one of us needed to stay behind in case we need to be bailed out of jail or something."

Sam smiled at that. "Good idea. Do you remember where Tori's uncle lives?"

"Doesn't matter. I'm not looking for Tori. I'm looking for my truck."

Sam glanced at her. "What do you mean?"

Casey grinned. "Remember a couple of years ago when Les's car got stolen?"

"Yes. And it was never found."

"Right. So when I bought this truck, I got a GPS tracker put on it." Casey handed over her cell. "Check the app."

"Oh my god. This is awesome." Sam watched the red dot on the app. "Tori's going to kill us, by the way."

Casey laughed. "I ain't scared of her."

Sam frowned. "She's heading west. She just got on the interstate."

"Like heading to Fort Worth?"

"Yes."

"She's not going to her uncle's house then." Casey sped up even though her wipers were making little headway with the downpour. "I thought she'd go find Bexley, but he lives over in Belmont."

"You think I should call her?"

"Yeah. Good luck getting her to answer."

Sam took out her phone, listening to it ring. When it went to voice mail, she disconnected. "She's pissing me off," she muttered.

"Don't worry. We'll follow her."

"Maybe she already went to Bexley's house," Sam said.

"Or maybe she went to her uncle's house," Casey countered. "That was her plan, right?"

"Then why the hell is she on I-30 heading to Fort Worth?" Sam's eyes widened. "She's not going to Fort Worth. She's going *past* Fort Worth."

Casey glanced at her. "What do you mean? Like to the lake?"

Sam's breath caught. "Oh my god. You don't think she abducted him or something, do you?"

"*What?* Abducted him? Which one?"

"Either."

"And is planning what? Like kill him and toss his body in the lake?" Casey slammed her hand on the steering wheel. "God, I *knew* she was going to snap."

Sam felt her heart pound nervously in her chest. "Oh my god. Don't say that. She wouldn't go off the deep end like that." Or at least she hoped not. "I'm going to call her again."

* * *

Tori glanced at her phone, making sure she was still connected to Simon. The rain was fierce enough to cause her to slow to a near crawl, as were the other drivers around her.

"Okay, it looks like he's turned to the north. Boat Club Road. You know where that is?"

"Yeah. It's the road we take going out to our marina." She drummed her fingers on the wheel. "How long would it take you to find Bexley's phone?"

"Which one? Thomas or Vance?"

"Thomas."

"Just a couple of minutes. Why?"

"I'm wondering if maybe they're together. My aunt said that he'd gotten a call and then had left."

"Okay. Give me a second."

Tori saw the notice that she had another call coming in. Sam again. She declined it once more, not wanting to take a chance on losing Simon. As the rain lessened, she increased her speed. Sam was most likely just checking on her. She didn't know what she'd tell her anyway. What was she doing? Heading to the lake? Heading to their boat? Surely to god Bexley wasn't going to attempt another murder on her boat.

"Tori, they're not together, but close."

"My uncle is heading toward Eagle Mountain Lake. Are you saying Bexley is already there?"

"Bexley's phone is stationary. I'm not familiar with this area so I can only go by the map."

"The lake is where I keep my boat. It's where he killed Cunningham. It's a smaller marina. There's only one security camera and it's right at the gate. Easy to slip past on foot if you know it's there."

"Okay, then looking at the map, it looks like he went past where most of the marinas are. There's a road to the right—Bonds Ranch Road. He just went past that."

"He's going to the park," she murmured.

"What park?"

"There's a large park out there. Day use only. It's greenspace. Lots of hiking trails. Woods. But they close up after dark."

"Okay, I see that now. But Bexley—or at least his phone—is about, oh, guessing here but a hundred or so yards before the parking lot."

"It's gated. Locked at night. He wouldn't be able to park there."

She passed the cutoff to the marina and kept going. The rain had picked up again and she slowed her speed on the winding road. She hadn't met another vehicle since she'd gotten off the highway.

"You think something's going down?"

Tori gripped the steering wheel tighter. "Just a gut feeling. They're up to something, right? You think Bexley plans to kill my uncle? That would be a safe place. Especially in this rainstorm. Definitely won't be any people about."

"Looks like he's stopped now. His phone shows up very close to Bexley's."

Tori slowed even more, not knowing how far behind him she was. "I appreciate you helping me out, Simon."

"No problem. I'll be here if you need me."

Tori wasn't familiar with the road. They rarely went past the marina. She was familiar with the park, though. Well, at least from the lake side. They cruised past it often when out fishing. They'd even stopped a few times and docked at the pier. She slowed to a near crawl, trying to see past the windshield wipers.

Through the foggy rain, the truck's lights flashed off the rear bumper of a car. She stopped and killed the lights. A bolt of lightning illuminated the sky enough for her to see that there were two cars parked on the side of the road, one behind the other.

Bexley and her uncle, she assumed. Why the hell would her uncle come out here? Was he that scared of him? Had Bexley threatened Aunt Judith? His whole family?

Christ, should she be doing this on her own? Of course not. Too late now, she thought. She reached into the back seat and pulled Casey's duffel bag up front with her. She hurriedly unzipped it, shoving aside shorts and T-shirts, finally finding a sweatshirt. At the bottom of the bag was a squished ball cap.

She took it out too and shaped the bill, then put it on. It would at least provide a little protection from the rain. She then opened Casey's console, knowing it was where she kept her small flashlight. She grabbed it and turned it on, making sure it worked.

Out of habit, she double-checked her holster, making sure her gun was still secured. She then opened the door and stepped out of the truck and into the storm. For as quiet as it had seemed inside, outside was in direct contrast. Beyond the sound of the pouring rain, thunder rumbled in the darkness. She looked up, squinting into the downpour as lightning sizzled overhead. The sky looked—and sounded—very angry.

She moved along the two cars, shining her flashlight inside. Both were empty. She turned toward the woods, hoping to find a trail that they may have taken. She found it about twenty yards from the first vehicle. She paused, listening, but all she could hear was the raging storm.

She pushed through the branches, the cold rain soaking her, running down her neck and under her clothes. The flashlight did little to cut the darkness and she smacked into the branch of a tree. She lifted it up and away, bending down as she passed. The path she was on—probably nothing more than a deer trail—seemed to close in around her. She turned in a circle, trying to find an opening in the thick woods.

She found no opening, no, but she spotted a faint light beyond her circle of trees. She killed her flashlight, watching as the other light moved deeper into the woods. She fought through branches, jumping as lightning and the immediate roar of thunder made the earth shake beneath her.

"Shit, that was close."

CHAPTER FIFTY

"We should probably call Malone," Sam said for the second time.

"We're out of our jurisdiction. There's nothing he can do to help us out here," Casey said again. "Besides, we don't even know what's going on."

"Why do you think she's going to the boat?" Sam held her hand up. "I know you don't know. I'm sorry. I'm just worried."

Casey nearly jumped out of her seat as a lightning bolt flashed, hitting something in the woods. The loud boom of thunder was deafening.

"Shit, that was close."

Sam held the phone up. "Look. She's past the marina. She didn't go to the boat. What the hell do you think she's doing?"

"We'll find out soon enough."

They drove on in silence and she could tell that Sam was anxious. One hand gripped her cell phone and the other the dash. The rain seemed to be coming down harder now and her wipers struggled to keep up. Yeah, just what in the hell was Tori doing out in this weather?

"We're close," Sam said.

"Is she still stopped?"

"Yes."

Casey slowed even more, the torrential rain making it hard to see. She gave a sigh of relief when she saw her truck parked up ahead. There were two cars in front of it. She pulled up behind her truck and stopped.

"You think they're out in this weather?"

Casey looked at her and shook her head. "Out doing what? We're in the middle of a freakin' storm."

She'd no sooner said the words when not one, but two bolts of lightning lit up the sky. Loud thunder followed, the rumble nearly shaking the car.

"Well, if they're not here, where the hell are they?"

"Maybe they met someone here and left with them," she suggested.

"Yeah? And Tori went with them?"

Casey nearly threw up her hands in frustration. "I don't know, Sam. Where do *you* think they are?"

Sam looked past her, staring into the thick woods. "I think they're in there."

"It's pouring down rain. Lightning is right on top of us. Why would they be out there?"

"I don't know. But that's where they are."

"Gut feeling?"

"Yeah."

She sighed. "Okay then. Let's take a look." She paused. "You got a flashlight?"

Sam shook her head. "No."

"There's one in my truck. Stay here."

Without much thought, she ran out into the storm. As expected, her truck was unlocked. She made a mental note to admonish Tori for that later. She got inside, unmindful of her wet clothes on her leather seats. She noticed her duffel bag on the passenger seat and opened it, searching for her cap. It wasn't there. Neither was her sweatshirt. *Damn.* She opened up her console, but her flashlight was missing too. Then she leaned across the seats and popped open the glovebox. She kept a much larger Maglite there.

"Thank you very much," she murmured as she grabbed it.

She opened her door again, then ducked back inside as lightning popped in the woods, a nearly simultaneous explosion of thunder making her breath catch. They had no business being out in this storm. No, but out they would go.

She got out and turned the light on, motioning for Sam. How the hell would they find Tori? Where would they even start?

As the rain pelted them, they walked along the edge of the woods. Sam spotted the muddy footprint first.

"There."

Casey wasn't sure she would even call it a trail, but she took it, feeling Sam right on her heels.

CHAPTER FIFTY-ONE

Tori literally fell to the ground, not knowing if it was the lightning that made her duck or the blast of thunder that seemed to blow past her. As she got back up she heard rustling behind her. She turned, surprised to find her uncle there.

"Right on time, Tori."

Another sound to her right made her jerk around, but it was too late. A baseball bat cracked across her arm as she reached for her weapon, knocking it out of her hands. She lunged at him, this man she assumed to be Thomas Bexley. She was grabbed from behind by another man, one younger.

"Hold her!"

"I got her!"

Her arms were jerked behind her, and she kicked out, hitting Thomas squarely in the groin. He fell to his knees and she kicked behind her, catching the young man—Vance Bexley?—in his shin. His arms wrapped fully around her then and he swung her to the ground, face first. She closed her eyes against the wet, muddy leaves. A firm knee to her back held her down and she felt her hands being cuffed.

Then she was jerked up and held face-to-face with her uncle. Before he could say anything, Thomas stepped between them, striking her across her cheek and knocking her cap off her head.

"Goddamn bitch," he spat.

She shook her head, clearing it. "You must be Thomas. And Vance. Nephew, is it?"

"How do you know that?"

"Because you're a stupid son of a bitch."

Another blow to her face and she tasted blood this time.

"That's enough," her uncle said. "Let's get to the boat."

Thomas fought through the woods, leading them, and she was shoved roughly from behind. She looked back at Vance, who was now holding a gun. "I'm going to need your insurance information. You know, for the damage to my car and all."

He laughed. "Damn. All this and you've still got a sense of humor."

She smiled. "I'm also going to kill you. All of you."

He shook his head. "Don't think so, lady."

"Lady? Yeah, count on it…son. You're not getting out of here alive."

"Shut up," her uncle said from behind them. "Let's go."

The hand on her arm tightened as lightning flashed and she felt Vance jump at the ensuing thunder that rattled around them. Oh, she was in some kind of predicament now, wasn't she? Yes, she was. Her weapon lay back on the trail. At least she thought so. She hadn't seen any of them pick it up. But for being ex-cops, they weren't being very thorough. Her backup weapon was in a holster strapped above her ankle.

It all made sense now. Staley wasn't the leader. He never had been. What was clear, though, was that Bexley was the righthand man. He'd probably always done the dirty work. If she had to guess, he was probably in possession of the mysterious .45 that had killed so many. What was it that Pete had told her? Bexley had killed a kid and her uncle had protected him. Was this the payback? Bexley did her uncle's bidding?

She wasn't shocked, though. It was something she'd considered—deep down—to be true, only she didn't want to believe it. Even when she'd had her gun held to his head, when she'd looked into his eyes, a part of her had known he was lying to her. She could have pulled the trigger right then. She *should* have pulled the trigger.

But then she'd be sitting in a jail cell and her life would essentially be over with. And he'd be dead. Of course, with the way the night was turning out, she did see the irony in that.

"Why did you do it?" she asked as she shuffled after Thomas. She turned, glancing at her uncle. It was too dark to see his features, but she imagined his eyes. "Why order them to be killed?"

"Does it matter?"

Did it? Yes, it did. Whatever the reason, she needed to know the *why* of it. Why *all* of them and not her? She didn't answer him at first. Instead, she looked up into the night sky, the rain pelting her face. She blinked her eyes, not knowing if she had tears mixed there as well. Her heart ached and she felt heavy. But...

"It matters," she finally said. "Why? Tell me."

She stopped walking and so did the others. Her uncle wiped at the rain on his face, and she wondered if he would answer her.

"Jason thought he could protect me." He laughed. "The fool came over and said he'd found evidence that I'd covered up a murder that Thomas here had done."

"The kid? The one he killed when he was a rookie?"

Her uncle seemed surprised that she knew that, but he shook his head. "That was nothing." Then he smiled. "But I didn't cover up a murder that Thomas had done. I did it. And I couldn't have Jason digging around in it."

"Then why everyone? Why the family?"

"Because I hated Jason. And Donna? Oh, she always thought she was the perfect mother, the perfect wife. The perfect family," he nearly spat. "I hated her too. I hated them both." He motioned with the flashlight. "Enough. Let's go."

She felt like she'd taken a blow to the chest. "That's the reason? Envy? Jealousy?"

"Shut up. I'm through talking. You had your chance, Tori. You should have pulled the trigger the other night."

Vance pushed her from behind, nearly making her stumble. She glanced back at her uncle. "Yeah, I should have. But the night ain't over yet."

He laughed. "Yes, I'm afraid it's over for you, Tori."

A few moments later they came to a clearing, and she heard the sound of water. Lightning flew sideways across the sky, illuminating the lake before them. At the pier, she saw her boat tied at the far end. She turned to Vance.

"You stole my goddamn boat?"

He laughed. "Yeah. She's pretty sweet."

She turned to her uncle. "You're going to shoot me on my own boat?"

"No. You're going to have an unfortunate accident and fall overboard. Out in the middle of the lake. With luck, they'll find your body tomorrow."

She shook her head. "It's too late. You can't cover this up any longer. We've got—"

"You've got nothing, Tori. You should have just left it alone. You stuck your nose in where it didn't belong."

"Didn't belong? That was my goddamn family!" she yelled.

He gave a slow smile. "You're just like your father, I swear." His smile faded. "You should be dead too. Griffin was supposed to kill everyone. Then I wouldn't be in this mess."

Her eyes widened. Charles Griffin said he was instructed to leave one alive. As a witness. Was that not true? Had he lied in his confession letter?

"Then why didn't he kill me?"

"He didn't have the stomach for it, apparently. He said some nonsense about you looking into his soul. Like he was looking into the eyes of God or something. Damn fool." He motioned toward the boat. "Let's go. It's time."

CHAPTER FIFTY-TWO

Sam ducked under a branch, then grabbed Casey's arm when lightning hit again. "It'll be a miracle if we don't get struck."

As soon as the thunder rolled past them, the rain seemed to come down harder. She pulled her cap lower on her head, feeling sorry for Casey, who looked absolutely drenched.

"She will so owe us for this," Casey muttered as she wiped futilely at the rain on her face.

The flashlight Casey held barely cut through the downpour and Sam suddenly felt claustrophobic. The tree branches, laden with rain, seemed to fold around them and on top of them. She felt like they were walking right through the rainclouds as the fog thickened. The dread that hit her seemed to choke the breath from her and she again grabbed Casey's arm to steady herself.

"What is it?"

Sam squeezed harder. "She's…she's in danger. Like right *now*," she said urgently.

Casey stared at her for a moment, then nodded. "Then let's go."

Only twenty or thirty steps farther, they came to a small clearing. Casey's light flashed on something. She went to it, picking up a cap.

"It's mine. She was here."

Casey knocked the leaves and water off on her jeans, then put it on her head. Sam's eyes caught something else, though.

"Over here."

The light landed on the black object nearly buried in the mud. Tori's gun. *Oh god. They've got her.*

Casey picked it up, her words echoing her own thoughts. "Goddamn. They've got her."

They took off running.

CHAPTER FIFTY-THREE

Tori was roughly shoved onto the pier by Vance Bexley. He jerked her arms up behind her, making her wince in pain. She didn't give him the satisfaction of crying out. Thomas walked ahead of her, carefully making his way on the wet and slick boards. Her uncle was beside Vance, holding the only flashlight. It made little difference on this dark and rainy night. They could only see a few feet in front of them.

The lake was shallow here, she knew. Four feet deep, maybe five right here at the lower pier. But the pier made a T, shooting out into the lake where the boat was. She and Sam had docked there before. It had been dredged out and the long pier was added for fishing. She'd been told it was twelve or fifteen feet deep off the end. The sign there warned fishermen as such: DEEP WATER.

What she was thinking was crazy but hell—she'd been cuffed and thrown in this lake before. What choice did she have? She assumed they were all armed, but Vance was the only one who had his gun out. She slowed her pace—not enough to be noticeable but enough to allow Thomas to get a few steps ahead of them.

When she saw the hulk of her boat, bobbing almost violently in the storm, she knew she had to act. She didn't pause to think it through or to consider the consequences. She turned, bumping Vance with her shoulder, causing him to stumble. Then she lunged at her uncle—and the only light—taking them both into the lake.

She heard gunfire as she sank, then she kicked her legs, propelling her under the pier. She surfaced to suck in air, then sunk under again. She curled her legs, her jeans heavy, but she couldn't clear her feet with her hands. Another burst to the surface for air, then down again. She could hear voices yelling, could hear gunfire as it peppered the pier.

She let herself sink to the bottom, her mind whirling. *Of all the times to wear hiking boots*, she thought. She curled into a tight ball and brought her knees to her chest. Her shoulders ached as she stretched her arms as far as they would go. Her lungs were burning, but she held on, finally feeling the bottom of her boots against her wrists. One more stretch and she cleared her feet, pulling her cuffed hands in front of her. She surfaced at the far end of the pier, clinging to the pylon for a few seconds, catching her breath.

"Where the hell is she?"

"I can't see a goddamn thing!"

"She was cuffed from behind," she heard her uncle say. "She's drowned already. Pull me up. The water's freezing."

"What are we going to do?"

"We're going to find her body and dump her in the middle of the goddamn lake like we'd planned. Then we're getting the hell out of here."

That son of a bitch, she thought. She took another deep breath, then went under the water again. She reached down, pulling out her backup weapon from her ankle holster. She was conscious of the snarl on her face as she surfaced. She was about to send them all to hell.

Where they belonged.

CHAPTER FIFTY-FOUR

"Oh my god!"

Casey and Sam looked at each other, then took off in a run. Six or eight shots, Sam thought. That was good. At least it hadn't been a single shot. She slipped down once, then scrambled to her feet, afraid to let Casey get too far ahead. She couldn't see a thing in the dark woods. Then, it was as if they'd fallen out of a jungle and into a muddy clearing. She could hear water now. The lake.

Voices sounded up ahead and she grabbed Casey. "Kill the light."

They crept to the water's edge, only able to see when lightning flashed. She could make out the pier now and what appeared to be a boat docked there. Simultaneously, she and Casey drew their weapons from their holsters. She heard voices from the pier.

"Where the hell is she?"

"I can't see a goddamn thing!" a man yelled.

"She was cuffed from behind," another one said. "She's drowned already."

Sam's heart leapt into her throat, and she gripped her gun tighter, just barely resisting the urge to run toward the voices.

"Three men," she whispered urgently to Casey.

"My guess is Thomas and Vance Bexley and the uncle."

They were almost to the edge of the pier now. It was black dark so when the spotlight on the boat came on, it jarred her. Casey nearly pushed her down as the light swept their way. Then the light was on the lake, searching around the pier— looking for Tori, no doubt.

"There she is!"

"Shoot her! Shoot her!"

Gunfire followed the order, and Sam jumped up before Casey could stop her. She ran onto the pier, seeing two men there at the end. The other man was in the boat, guiding the light. She stopped, taking aim.

"Police!" she yelled.

They turned in her direction, but before she could fire her weapon, four shots came from the water in quick succession. One man collapsed in a heap, then tumbled off into the water. The other fell to his knees, clutching his shoulder. He raised his hand to shoot, but the man on the boat fired first. Sam swore she heard the bullet as it whizzed by her head.

"Sam! Jump!"

It was Tori's voice, and she simply did as instructed, diving across the pier and into the dark, choppy waters of Eagle Mountain Lake. Tori seemed to rise out of the lake like a water goddess, gun in hand, firing again at the man on the pier. Sam couldn't see, but she heard him collapse, his weight thumping on the boards when he fell. Then the roar of the boat's engine sounded and only then did she realize it was *their* boat.

"Tori?" she called as she treaded water under the pier.

She heard running then and Casey flew past, jumping onto the boat— just like in the movies—as it pulled away from the pier. A moment later, a single gunshot rang out, the sound seeming to hang in the air around them. *Oh dear god.*

"Casey?" she yelled across the water, knowing Casey couldn't hear her over the boat's engine.

"Sam?"

She jerked around, seeing Tori coming toward her. "Oh god, Tori. Are you okay?"

"Yeah. You?"

"I think so."

They heard the boat's engine settle, then waves hit them as the boat crept back to the dock. She assumed Casey was okay. She relaxed only a little as Tori reached her. Tori's hands were cuffed, and Sam held her tightly to the pylon.

She tried to smile at Tori. "Thought it was a good night for a swim, huh?"

"I'm freezing my ass off."

"Let me guess, you were cuffed from behind again?"

"Yeah. Part fish, remember."

The boat bumped roughly against the pier and Sam heard Tori's quick intake of breath. "Shit, she never could drive that thing."

The engine was silenced then, and the only sound was the lapping of water and the distant rumble of thunder. She hadn't noticed, but the brunt of the storm seemed to have moved past them. Then she heard footsteps on the pier, and she looked up.

"Tori? Sam?" Casey called.

"Down here," they said in unison.

Casey fell to her knees, looking over the side at them. "Damn. You look like two drowned rats."

"Are you okay?" she asked Casey.

"Oh, yeah. The one on the boat there, I assume was Vance. Younger fella."

"Thomas and...and my uncle were the other two." Tori held her cuffed hands up. "Got a handcuff key?"

Casey laughed. "You let them cuff you?"

"I had them right where I wanted them."

"Sure you did." Casey stood up. "Why isn't there a ladder or something out here?"

"They don't want people swimming. It's a fishing pier."

"Okay. Swim under the pier to the boat. I'll drop the ladder."

Sam noticed then that she was still holding her gun in one hand and so was Tori. *Cops until the end,* she thought with a smile.

CHAPTER FIFTY-FIVE

Tori wasn't sure how she felt. She wasn't sure how she was *supposed* to feel. Malone was there, running interference. Sam and Casey had called him when they'd first gotten there. Of course, they'd ignored his "Wait for backup" command. Thankfully.

"Can you believe Malone," Casey said as she bumped her shoulder. "He's telling them all kinds of shit about this undercover case we've been working on." She laughed. "And having to apologize for not letting them know we'd be out here, *way* out of our jurisdiction."

"I told you he'd have your back," Sam chimed in from the other side of her. She touched her arm. "You okay?"

The rain was only a steady drizzle now, but the three of them were drenched head to toe, she and Sam more so after their dunk in the lake. One of the county deputies who responded had a blanket in his car and they were bundled in it now. Lights flashed around them from the numerous police vehicles that had responded to the shooting. High beams from emergency lights had the pier and surrounding area glowing as if it was daylight already.

The three bodies had been taken away not ten minutes earlier. Vance Bexley had been on the boat. Thomas Bexley's body had floated out into the lake and the sheriff's department's lake patrol had gone out to retrieve it. Her uncle had still been sprawled on the pier where he'd dropped after she shot him.

She knew Sam's question wasn't concerning her physical health but rather her mental wellbeing. "I guess I'm okay. I still don't quite understand the why of it all. Some cover-up." She turned to glance at Sam. "Apparently, Charles Griffin lied to me."

"What do you mean?"

"He wasn't told to leave someone alive as a witness. He was told to kill everyone."

"Oh my god. Then why?"

"It's been so long, everything is kinda fuzzy. But I remember that night clearly. I was the only one left. And he walked up to me. I remember looking into his eyes, just staring at him and he at me. Then I closed my eyes, waiting for the shot. It never came. When I opened my eyes again, he was still there, but his eyes looked different. Then he turned and left, leaving me."

"What do you mean, they looked different?" Casey asked.

"They were...filled with anguish. Compassion, I think. I didn't remember it that way at the time, but I see that now. Charles Griffin wasn't a killer. What he did that night, well, I don't think he could bring himself to finish the job. So, he left me alive."

At the time—and for years afterward—she'd wished he had pulled the trigger. She had to fight through her grief and her guilt—survivor's guilt. It wasn't until Sam came into her life that she let those feelings go. What she never let go of, though, was her anger. And her need to avenge their deaths.

Had she accomplished that? Her uncle—the leader of the Blue Dragons—had been behind it all. She'd shot him. She didn't get the ending she wanted, however. She'd wanted to look into his eyes. She wanted him to know it was coming, just like her family had to. Most of all, she wanted to know the *why* of it. What evidence of a murder had her father stumbled upon?

There was nothing in the notes she'd found. Had he left that out, thinking he would protect his brother? Had he warned James, just like he'd said? Was that the excuse Uncle James had used to order the murder of his own brother and family? Had envy and jealousy played a part too?

Sam leaned against her, her head rolling onto her shoulder. She heard the whispered words, and they made her smile.

"I love you too," she returned.

Her smiled faded, though, as Malone headed their way.

"Does he look pissed to you?" Casey asked quietly. "Because I think he looks pissed."

"Yeah. He looks pretty pissed."

CHAPTER FIFTY-SIX

The sun was bright, the sky cloudless. The wind was nothing more than a whisper as she docked in one of the small coves on the north side of the lake. Casey—like her—was in nothing but shorts and a sports bra. Her partner had a grin on her face as she pulled out two beers from the ice.

"Can you believe the lieutenant suspended us for *three* weeks, Hunter? *With* pay?" Then she laughed. "God, I love that man."

Yes. So did she. Malone did indeed have her back. Oh, he'd yelled too. And pointed his finger at her. And threatened her. *"If you ever pull this shit again, Hunter, I'll have your ass! You understand me?"* She had nodded appropriately, and his expression had softened. *"I'm sorry that it turned out to be your uncle, Tori. That has to be tough."*

Yeah, it was. Of course, it all made sense now. No wonder he didn't want her living with them. It would have been a constant reminder. And even though she was never close with his family or Aunt Judith, she'd have to face them sooner or later. She'd killed him. They would want answers.

She took the beer that Casey held up. "It'll still be on our record, O'Connor."

"Oh, I know. But do we care? You're already talking about retirement, and I'm just a lowly detective. I have no aspirations to move up the chain. So basically, we have a three-week paid vacation." Casey clicked her beer bottle against hers. "You just can't beat that."

"What can't be beat is this weather," she countered. "And a day—and night—of fishing."

"Yeah. We should do this more often. We kinda got away from it."

Tori leaned against the side, staring at the spot where Darrell Cunningham's body had been dumped. Jimmy had had the boat cleaned up and even waxed. There was no sign that anything had been amiss.

She sighed. "We did get away from it. Everybody's always so busy, you know."

"We need to make time to relax more. Hell, Hunter, you're not getting any younger."

She smiled at her, this woman who was her best friend. "I think...I think I'm going to do it."

"Do what?"

Tori met her gaze. "Retire from the force."

"Really?" Casey shook her head. "No, Tori. I don't want you to. I mean, you know, think on it a while. Don't rush into it."

"Sam wants me to give it some time. A month or so. But yeah, I think I really am. I think I'm spent."

"What are you going to do if you retire?"

"Relax. Fish. Learn to cook." She motioned out to the water. "Going to move the boat to another lake."

"But we love it out here."

Tori laughed. "We do?"

"Move her where?"

"I'm thinking Lake Ray Hubbard. It would be a hell of a lot closer to home, that's for sure."

Casey nodded. "Okay. I'll go for that. That's close enough that we could hop over after work during the summers." She leaned next to her. "Sam said I was supposed to find out if you were *really* okay?"

Tori smiled. "I'm pretty sure you weren't supposed to tell me that."

"So are you?"

Tori shrugged. "I guess."

"Not the closure you expected?"

"No. But it's all out of my hands now."

"You turned over all the notes and everything?"

"Yeah. Not Simon's phone records. Malone was going to pull all of that again and leave Simon out of it."

"You talk to him?"

"Simon? Oh, yeah. I owe him like five bottles of scotch," she said with a laugh. "And an expensive steak dinner. I couldn't have done any of this without him." She took a large swallow of her beer. "Malone is giving everything to CIU first, then it'll go to the DA's office."

"Ironic. Is Sam going to get to work it with her new job?"

"Yes. Ironic. She wasn't supposed to start for another week or so, but she went in this morning. And they'll do it the right way. They'll subpoena everyone. McMillan and the other guys on the list." She paused. "Those who are left, anyway."

"So Pete Dewberry too?"

"Yeah. I've already warned him. And speaking of Pete, I invited him to go fishing with us."

"Oh yeah? When?"

"If the weather stays nice, maybe Friday."

Casey nodded. "You know what, maybe we should invite Steve Alton to join us."

Tori arched an eyebrow. "Charles Griffin's neighbor?"

"Yeah. He's widowed too. Seemed kinda lonely to me. Maybe he and Pete will hit it off."

Tori nodded. "Okay, O'Connor. We'll ask them both." She pushed off the side. "Let's fish. And I'll have another beer."

They were going to relax today. Do some fishing. She had two steaks that she would grill for them later. They had a bottle of scotch, too. They'd fish, eat, and probably drink too much. In the morning she'd complain of a headache, no doubt. And she'd fry bacon and eggs and they might do a little more fishing before heading back to the city.

Sam had told her to get away. Away from the TV. Away from the news. Away from her phone. Malone's suspension was for show, she knew that, although it was definitely warranted. Especially for her. She *had* gone rogue, as Casey called it. But the suspension was mostly for her benefit. *"Take some time, Tori. Get your head straight."*

Yeah. So here they were, out in the warm sunshine, pretending that they hadn't just had a shootout here at this very lake a couple of nights ago.

Pretending that she hadn't killed her uncle. The man who had ordered the murder of her family.

CHAPTER FIFTY-SEVEN

Sam was surprised to find an enticing aroma filling the room when she opened the kitchen door. She knew Tori was home. The rental car was parked in her spot in the garage. Sam had touched the hood as she walked past it. It was cool to the touch, so Tori had been home a while.

"What in the world are you doing?"

Tori was at the stove, a dishtowel slung over one shoulder. The kitchen was a complete mess. Pots and pans lined the countertop, and not one, but two cutting boards were out, both showing the remnants of chopped veggies.

"I'm making dinner." She turned and smiled. "Surprise!"

Sam laughed, then moved closer, kissing her. "I missed you last night."

Tori nodded. "Yeah, me too."

"But you had fun?"

"Fun? We about killed a bottle of scotch."

Sam touched her cheek affectionately. "Did it help to get away?"

"I suppose. I didn't dwell on it too much. We fished. Actually caught a few too." Tori lifted the lid on a pot and absently stirred the contents. "My Aunt Judith called."

"Oh yeah?"

Tori shrugged. "I didn't talk to her. I...I wasn't up to it. But she left a message. She said that McMillan had been over to see her. Said he'd shed some light on it." Tori took a deep breath. "She said after things have settled down, she'd like to meet with me. To talk."

"To talk about your family? Or talk about your uncle?"

"Probably both, I guess. Maybe she wants to understand the why of it all too. When all of this comes out, she might feel like she'd been living with a stranger all this time." Tori closed the lid again. "I'm not sure it matters anymore." She turned, finding her gaze. "I feel at peace, Sam. I feel like this weight's been lifted." Then she smiled. "A weight that I didn't even know was still there until Charles Griffin left me that letter."

"You're ready to leave all of that in the past?"

Tori nodded. "I am. I love my life now. With you. It scares me to think how close I came to throwing all of that away, just for revenge."

"And in the end, you got the revenge anyway. He's dead."

"Yes. There are still so many questions, but I don't guess I need the answers anymore. As he said to me out there in the storm—does it matter?"

Sam pulled her into a tight hug. "Only you can decide if it matters or not." She kissed her lightly before moving away. "We found a .45 at Thomas Bexley's residence. I'm sure it'll match the recent killings of Cunningham and the two hitmen. And probably the cold cases you were telling me about."

"Just because you have the gun doesn't mean Bexley was the shooter."

"No, it doesn't. And frankly, the DA's office isn't likely to press charges against those other guys. It's been over thirty years. There's just not enough evidence."

Tori nodded. "I know. It's why I didn't want to hand over my father's notes in the first place."

"We're still going to subpoena them. Try to get more of the story. Maybe you'll get some answers after all. Maybe one of them will confess or something."

Tori was quiet for a long moment, then she smiled. "I don't guess it matters."

Sam watched her for a moment, seeing a calmness in Tori's eyes that had been missing. And not just this last week, either. It had been missing for months now, it seemed.

"I see you've made a decision."

Tori raised an eyebrow. "About?"

"Retiring."

Tori smiled at her. "Think you can read me like a book, huh?"

Sam nodded. "So? You made up your mind already?"

"I think so. Like I told Casey, I'm tired. I'm spent. And not just because of this." She gave a quick grin. "Hell, I'm old."

Sam moved closer to her. "You're not old. You're certainly not old enough to while away the hours fishing every day."

"You worried I'll get bored?"

"Yes."

Tori nodded. "Well, then maybe I'll become a private eye or something. That might be fun."

She laughed. "Fewer rules to follow?"

"Yes. You know me and rules." Tori motioned her out of the kitchen. "Go get changed. Then you can help me with dinner."

"What are you making anyway? I smell bacon."

"It's a beef merlot thing. And it's got bacon in it." She lifted the lid again. "It doesn't look thick enough. And I don't know if I should serve it over rice or some noodles."

"It smells great." Then she looked at the mess in the kitchen. "Must have been quite an elaborate recipe, huh?"

Tori laughed. "You probably wouldn't think so." She waved her away. "Go change."

Sam was still smiling when she went into the living room. She stopped up short, however. Tori's old boxes were out again. She walked over to the table, seeing the framed photo of Tori's family. For a brief moment, she had a flashback to her own family, years and years ago when she'd been a young girl. They weren't a part of her life anymore and she sometimes wondered if she should try again with them. But no. They'd made their feelings clear. So, she pushed that image away. Instead, she stared at all the faces in the photo, all smiling and staring at the camera. She touched the glass lightly, moving her finger there, landing on Tori.

"I thought maybe we could get a new frame for it and…well, maybe put it out somewhere."

Sam turned, finding Tori standing there, the dishtowel still slung over her shoulder. She went to her, nodding.

"I think that's a wonderful idea."

"Something I should have done years ago, I guess."

Sam linked her fingers with Tori's. "I don't believe you were ready."

Tori slid her gaze from the photo to her. "No. I didn't think I'd ever be ready." Tori gave her a gentle smile. "I think you would have liked them. I know they would have loved you."

Sam felt a misting of tears and saw the same in Tori's eyes. She moved into her arms, nestling against her.

"Yes. I would have loved them too."

Bella Books, Inc.

Women. Books. Even Better Together.

P.O. Box 10543
Tallahassee, FL 32302
Phone: (800) 729-4992
www.BellaBooks.com

More Titles from Bella Books

Mabel and Everything After – Hannah Safren
978-1-64247-390-2 | 274 pgs | paperback: $17.95 | eBook: $9.99
A law student and a wannabe brewery owner find that the path to a
fairy tale happily-ever-after is often the long and scenic route.

To Be With You – TJ O'Shea
978-1-64247-419-0 | 348 pgs | paperback: $19.95 | eBook: $9.99
Sometimes the choice is between loving safely or loving bravely.

I Dare You to Love Me – Lori G. Matthews
978-1-64247-389-6 | 292 pgs | paperback: $18.95 | eBook: $9.99
An enemy-to-lovers romance about daring to follow your heart, even
when it's the hardest thing to do.

The Lady Adventurers Club - Karen Frost
978-1-64247-414-5 | 300 pgs | paperback: $18.95 | eBook: $9.99
Four women. One undiscovered Egyptian tomb. One (maybe) angry
Egyptian goddess. What could possibly go wrong?

Golden Hour - Kat Jackson
978-1-64247-397-1 | 250 pgs | paperback: $17.95 | eBook: $9.99
Life would be so much easier if Lina were afraid of something
basic—like spiders—instead of something significant. Something like
real, true, healthy love.

Schuss – E. J. Noyes
978-1-64247-430-5 | 276 pgs | paperback: $17.95 | eBook: $9.99
They're best friends who both want something more, but what if
admitting it ruins the best friendship either of them have had?

CPSIA information can be obtained
at www.ICGtesting.com
Printed in the USA
JSHW080438230523
42110JS00003B/3